# A Lowcountry Murder

Daniel Bailey

*The Overmountain Press*

JOHNSON CITY, TENNESSEE

ISBN 13: 978-1-57072-318-6
ISBN 10: 1-57072-318-4
Copyright 2007 by Daniel Bailey
Printed in the United States of America

1 2 3 4 5 6 7 8 9 0

*I dedicate this book to the families of our fallen public safety officers and to the families of our soldiers fighting on foreign soil for our freedom. May your sacrifices never be forgotten.*

# ACKNOWLEDGMENTS

Thanks go out to friend and author Cathy Pickens, who read early drafts and took a liking to Jed. Her encouragement was critical to his coming to life on the pages of this book. I also want to acknowledge the support of the Carolina Conspiracy, a talented group of mystery writers who strive to make our promotional appearances unique and entertaining.

I want to acknowledge my family's patience and understanding during the writing process. Without their support—especially from my wife, Sharon—the words would never make it to the paper.

Finally, as always, I want to thank my publisher, Silver Dagger Mysteries, for allowing me to tell my stories my way. A special thank-you goes out to Sherry for her keen eye during the editing process, to Karin for her energies in getting the word out about our books, and, of course, to Beth for keeping us all on course.

# CHAPTER · 1

Jed Bradley parked his boxy, black Volvo beside three marked sheriff's cars and stepped out onto the frozen grounds of what used to be his father's church on Winding Creek Road in Sweetgrass, South Carolina. Above him, the sky bore a somber hue as it nestled close to the sandy soil, blanketing the field before him with gloomy, low-hanging clouds and a curtain of fine crystalline mist. He wiped the salty residue from the Atlantic off of his unshaven face and began his reluctant trek through the overgrown field of broomstraw.

An early morning phone call had lured him here. It had delivered him from the depths of fitful dreams, and had he known for sure what lay ahead, he might have chosen those nightmares to what his caller had hinted awaited him.

Pellets of sleet brushed his face as he squinted at hazy images moving about in the gloam of the twilight. Across the field was the tiny graveyard where his family—mother, father, and brother—all now rested.

A harsh gust of wind whistled in his ear, sending a shudder down the recently retired homicide detective's spine. He pulled his black down-filled jacket tight across his chest and zipped it up to the hollow of his throat.

*Perfect day to discover a murder,* he thought.

Nursing a hangover after consuming nearly a fifth of sour mash whiskey the night before, Jed plopped a faded Atlanta Braves cap onto his brown shaven head. Up ahead, a solemn-faced deputy sheriff stood shivering next to a barricade of yellow crime-scene tape.

The youthful deputy's fur-trimmed cap with fuzzy earflaps and oversized thigh-length coat reminded Jed of Elmer Fudd, the cartoon character famous for "hunting wabbits." The man's inquisitive expression wrinkled as Jed drew closer.

Jed smiled.

The deputy didn't.

A taunting gust of wind slapped Mother Nature's icy palm across Jed's cheeks. Misery hugged him.

He scanned the all-too-familiar grounds. A pile of burnt lumber lay where his father's church once stood. Bile stirred in his stomach.

*Faulty heater blew up,* according to the volunteer fire chief's report. *Flames consumed the building before anyone could respond to extinguish them* had been the official line.

Jed lived in Atlanta when it happened. The church member who called told him his father had taken to sleeping in the office behind the sanctuary after Jed's mother had passed. She said the firemen found him inside, and according to their account, he had just gone to sleep and never awoke.

When Jed came home to bury his father, his request for an autopsy fell on deaf, if not bigoted, ears. The sheriff, a grouse of an old man, barely tolerated Jed's questions.

"Boy, this ain't no big city." He remembered the sheriff's callous tone. "We ain't got no money to be ordering autopsies willy-nilly when what we see is clearly an accident. Your daddy was just in the wrong place at the right time. A real tragedy."

*The wrong place at the right time.* An interesting choice of words, Jed had thought. His father had never missed an opportunity to speak out for civil rights, and his outspokenness had often caused angst for the community's wealthy white landowners, some who had never acknowledged the South's surrender at the end of the Civil War. Because of that history, the sheriff's comment hinted of more than an accident.

Jed gazed past the lone deputy to where other deputies busied themselves near a bedraggled-looking pecan tree standing all alone amid the sea of broomstraw. Beneath the leaf-bare branches sat a pale blue 1955 Studebaker, just like the one his brother, Bobby, had driven to meet Abby on the night they both died. Much of the vintage automobile was concealed by waist-high grass, but he saw enough to realize everything else he had been told by his morning caller might come to pass.

Jed glanced back at the sentry and tried to think of a plausible explanation, other than the truth, for showing up at this otherwise out-of-the-way spot on such a miserable morning. As he mulled over a variety of excuses, he knelt by the pile of charred rubble.

He remembered how his father had delivered the kind of fire-and-brimstone sermons that left his charismatic congregation drained of their earthly energies and filled with the divine presence. Jed had watched his father breathe life into this church, and then he saw it suck the soul right out of the evangelical's body, leaving only a void where his faith had been.

*Daddy lived life to the fullest here,* he thought. *He died here too, and when he did, his church crumbled like one built on sinking sand.*

The words from a hymn Jed's father loved silently breached his lips. The pounding in his head thumped to the new rhythm.

A few feet away, the church's toppled spire stuck up from the rubble. Its singed and shattered remains looked as if the devil himself had swallowed it and then belched it back up in fiery defiance of what it represented. Jed picked up a piece of charcoal, held it, rubbed it between his thumb and finger, then let it tumble back to the ground.

He recalled the day his brother died. That afternoon Bobby had secretly shown him a red pouch, told him how it contained John the Conqueror, a root from a plant named after an African slave prince, used to conjure powerful hoodoo potions. Both boys knew that their father absolutely prohibited the practice of hoodoo or keeping its artifacts in their home, but Bobby relished doing things to shock his younger brother.

Jed thought how the contents of that pouch symbolized everything his father abhorred. "Devil worship," the elder Bradley regularly railed from his pulpit upon learning a parishioner had dared to call on a local root doctor for help.

Many believers in the hoodoo arts claimed that only the misinformed considered the rituals a form of black magic. But as Jed surveyed the church's incinerated remains, he couldn't help wondering if his father's lifelong battle against the practice had been lost in some netherworld last stand.

Across the field he watched the deputies hover around the Studebaker. The time had come to find out why someone had chosen to lure him to a place filled with so much pain. He stood and walked toward the young sentinel. As he did, the man's eyes took on the glare of a junkyard dog's. Apprehension and determination both claimed a portion of the deputy's expression.

Jed couldn't blame the man; he figured his own appearance rivaled that of some evil specter summoned from a nearby swamp. Eyes like road maps. Two days of gray-beard stubble crusting his cheeks. He knew the image all too well, had seen it glaring back from his mirror that very morning. *A demonic visage if ever there had been one,* he mused. He eyed the singed ruins. *How odd to think such a thing on this spot, where Daddy vehemently condemned netherworld thoughts as blasphemy.*

"Never let that evil enter your mind," the elder Bradley regularly declared from his pulpit. "Satan's sittin', just a-waitin'. Sure as you affirm your belief in such to him . . . that's when he'll snatch your soul into the depths."

The deputy's back stiffened as Jed stopped within arm's length. The lawman's jaw locked. His hand shot up. The determined glower reminded Jed of an Atlanta school-crossing guard at rush hour.

"That's far enough," the deputy said in a warbling voice.

"Morning," Jed said. He forced a smile through the cloud of fog formed when his warm breath hit the frigid air. He watched the deputy's forehead furrow, felt the throbbing in his own head intensify. "What y'all got out there?" He pointed toward the activity around the Studebaker.

"Some hunters stumbled onto somethin' we're investigatin'." The deputy's glare held strong.

"Hunters? In this weather?" Jed feigned a chuckle, hoping to ease the tension he saw in the young man's expression. "They must've been real hungry or just plumb crazy to be out in a mess like this."

"Can't rightly say," the deputy said.

The bone-chilling cold seeped through Jed's down-filled jacket. He jostled his shoulders, moved his arms to generate a little heat. "Hellfire, you ought to be able to at least take a gander at what you're guarding." His attempt to disarm the deputy with kindness and understanding seemed feeble. "What say you and I ease a might closer? Sneak a peek at what them hunters found."

The deputy's lip twitched. His less than authoritative voice cracked and quivered in the cold air. "What's out there you want to see?" The scrubbed-faced youth sounded like a seasoned investigator probing for answers. Suspicion shaped his expression.

Jed winked. "Come on, don't you want to know what happened to them?"

The officer's eyebrow arched. Uncertainty replaced the suspicion on his face. "Nope," he said in a firm, terse voice. "The sheriff ain't allowin' no reporters past this spot." He pointed at the yellow tape.

Intentional or not, the deputy's remark stung. No greater insult could have been hurled at Jed than to call him a reporter. It was like calling a Conservative a Liberal, a New York Yankee fan a Red Sox fan. Jed barely suppressed a grin, despite feeling miserable. He wanted—no, needed—to get past Elmer Fudd to confirm what else his caller had told him awaited near the graveyard.

The grizzled ex-detective blew a warm breath into his cupped hands, rubbed them together. The press in Atlanta had played an instrumental part in his forced early retirement—at least in his mind, they had. Their relationship with Jed had been tenuous for years. In the weeks leading up to his final days, competition among the various media carnivores had complicated the efforts of his team of investigators in solving what arguably was the biggest serial murder case in Atlanta history. As a result, his already well-established distrust for the Fourth Estate had soared.

"Son, if you only knew," Jed said, instantly creating an even more resentful scowl on the deputy's face. "I'm 'bout the furthest thing from a reporter you'll ever see."

"Then what—"

"He's all right."

The voice, one akin to a bear's growl, had come from behind Jed. He turned to see a man wearing a heavy leather coat with a fur collar and a brown fedora pulled tight over his head.

"Jedediah, you look like hell." The man chewed on the stub of an unlit cigar as he spoke.

"Thanks, Jake. You oughta see me from *my* vantage point." Jed rubbed his beard stubble, surprised he had not seen or heard the approach of his childhood friend.

A tall and lanky redhead with long muttonchop sideburns framing his horse face, Jake Armistead wore a big smile with big teeth. The gold star on the outside of his coat revealed to all who saw it that he was Sheriff of Indigo County.

"Ain't seen you in . . . what is it now? Ten years?" Jake nodded toward the church ruins. "Best I recall, the last time you were here was for your pappy's funeral. What brings you back to God's country?"

A sharp pain cleaved Jed's sinus cavity. He winced. "Long story." He pointed to the sheriff's star. "See you've done well for yourself."

"I suppose." Jake angled his thumb over his shoulder in the direction of the Studebaker. "Startin' the day out like this suggests otherwise." He stared hard at Jed. "You truly don't look all that great, Jedediah. You sure you're all right?"

"Nothing a little hair of the dog wouldn't cure." Jed flashed a thin smile.

The sheriff caught his deputy's confused expression. "Roland, I want you to meet a gen-u-ine, real-life, big-city homicide detective from good ol' Hotlanta. This here is Jedediah Bradley." Jake's words flowed from his mouth the way thick syrup poured.

"Former detective," Jed said in a low voice.

Roland nodded. Confusion still twisted his features as he glanced back at his sheriff.

"Former detective?" A hint of disappointment, mixed with surprise, slid the length of Jake's face. "How so?"

"That's part of the long story. For now, let's just say I made too many powerful enemies." Jed pointed past Jake. "Can I have a peek?"

The sheriff pursed his lips as he stroked his chin with his thumb and index finger. "What for? If you ain't a cop no more, what's your interest?"

*Fair question,* Jed thought. "Just call it a busman's holiday."

"Gonna have to do better than that." Jake peered up at the pewter sky. "What are you doin' out here in this shitty weather this time of mornin' anyhow?"

Jed had no intention of getting into the call he had received an hour earlier. Its mention would just lead to more questions, questions he didn't feel up to answering yet. "Don't act so damn suspicious, Jake. I didn't kill 'em."

The sheriff scorched his deputy with an angry glare.

Roland shook his head, shrugged his shoulders. "I ain't said nothin' 'bout nothin'. All I told him was a couple of hunters found themselves something we were investigating."

Jake's harsh visage returned. "For someone who ain't been around these parts in a while, you sure seem to know an awful lot about my crime scene. Care to explain?"

Jed felt the cold seeping into his bones. He wasn't up to playing Twenty Questions in this nasty weather, but he understood his old friend's concern. "Tell you what," he said, reminding himself of a streetwise suspect trying to negotiate a plea bargain. "Let me have a look. You'll be with me the whole time, and I won't touch a thing without your okay." An icy blast of wind knifed through his coat. He shivered. "I promise to explain later, when we're somewhere warmer."

Jake's bushy eyebrows lifted. He looked across the field then back at Jed. He took his cigar out before he spoke. "Reckon since none of them boys has ever worked a real whodunit, I could use your expertise. But I've got to tell you, I'm a touch uneasy about it."

Jed nodded. "Fair enough."

Jake held the unlit cigar between two fingers. "We've been friends a long time. I need you to look me in the eye and tell me you ain't got nothing to do with that couple's death over yonder."

Jed noticed Roland sidle close, and he hit the deputy with a stern glare. "Let me just say I think that old Studebaker and your victims might be the tip of a much bigger problem," Jed said. "How I know is complicated, and I prefer to wait to explain."

Jake inserted the cigar stub back into his mouth and pulled a wooden kitchen match from his shirt pocket. He cupped his hands, formed a chimney, and flicked the tip of the match with his thumbnail. Despite the wind, he lit the cigar with little effort and then stared at Jed as he blew out a plume of smoke.

A lengthy silence followed before Jake kicked the toe of his boot into the ground, dislodging a frozen block of soil. "Okay," he said and spun around. "Come on, but stay close." A sly grin creased the sheriff's lips as he turned back to Jed. "And just so you know . . . this ain't Atlanta, and right now you're the closest thing to a suspect I've got."

Despite the faint smile Jed saw on the sheriff's face, he detected a worrisome seriousness in Jake's tone. "Thanks," he said, hurrying to catch up to the taller man's long strides. "I think."

They walked in solemn reflection at first, Jed wondering what Jake was thinking, Jake casting puzzled glances at his old fishing buddy and blowing puffs of smoke that dissipated as soon as they hit the stiff breeze. The morning seemed almost devoid of sound except for the crunching of the frozen ground under their feet.

Halfway through the sea of knee-high broomstraw, Jake stopped and pointed toward the distant tree line. "Coon hunters coming out from over yonder found 'em a few hours ago."

"Those hunters must've been drunk on moonshine to have been out all night in weather like this," Jed said.

"You'd think, but when I saw 'em they were stone sober." Jake spit out loose tobacco. "Can't imagine staying out in this mess to kill something ain't all that good to eat."

"Only kind of animal I'd stay out in this weather to hunt walks on two legs," Jed said, focusing on the activity around the Studebaker. "You know, I never wanted to come back here."

"To Sweetgrass?"

"Not just Sweetgrass, to these five or six godforsaken acres we're walking on right now."

Jake peered at Jed. "'Cause of what happened to your daddy?"

"Partly. Bobby died out here too, remember?"

Jake nodded slowly. "Forgot 'bout that. Reckon I understand why this place wouldn't hold great memories for you." The cigar rolled from one side of his mouth to the other. The fire at the tip had gone out again. Now he just chewed the stub.

Jed said, "You remember Bobby's car?"

Jake raised an eyebrow. "Yeah . . . I think."

Jed nodded toward the car parked under the pecan tree. "His was a Studebaker. That one's a spittin' image."

Jake stopped walking and turned to Jed. "What are you sayin'?"

"From what I was told back then, this one's near about in the same spot too."

Jake shook his head. "You think these murders have something to do with your brother's?"

Jed thought back to his mysterious phone call. The caller wanted him out here, wanted him to see the car, the bodies of the victims. Why?

He looked at Jake, shrugged, and then looked away without answering the man's question. Everything around appeared untended and overgrown. Even the cemetery, just a few feet beyond where the Studebaker sat, looked like nobody had been around it in years.

"Doesn't anybody take care of this place?" Jed asked.

"Hmph. Like who? In recent years the only folks coming out here have been the teenagers late at night. And mostly they've other things on their minds." He pointed to a discarded condom package and a pile of beer cans.

The men stopped a short distance from the car. Both front doors stood open.

Jed saw a body in the driver's seat, head slumped forward. The windshield in front of the driver had been shattered by a bullet. He couldn't see the other body, at least not from where he stood.

He surveyed the entrance to the cemetery. The gate was missing, and the wrought-iron fence leaned at a severe angle. Inside, he guessed, might be forty or so graves, some dating back to when slaves were buried there. His gaze lingered on three more recent ones, those belonging to his family.

Jake's expression turned somber as he approached the car. Jed wondered how many murders his friend had investigated over his career. He guessed not many. Back in Atlanta, his team of investigators probably worked more homicide cases in a single year than all the Indigo County sheriffs combined had worked over the past fifty.

"Ever try crawling inside of the victim's skin?" Jed asked.

Jake stopped short. "What in tarnation are you talking about?"

"Have you ever wondered about the victim's last thoughts? Take these two, for instance." Jed pointed to the black female in the driver's seat.

A heavyset man knelt on the ground beside her. Wearing bibbed overalls and a red-and-black checkered wool jacket, he seemed out of place with the rest of the deputies dressed in khaki and brown uniforms. Jed had seen one of the uniformed deputies bend over and whisper something in the man's ear as he and Jake approached. The kneeling man had shot a glimpse in their direction but never stopped what he was doing.

"Aren't you just a little bit curious about her thoughts at the moment she realized her death was imminent?" Jed thought about Bobby. "What it must have been like for her to stare into her killer's eyes, knowing this would be the last face she would ever see? What goes through a person's mind when they reach that pinnacle of terror?"

He adjusted his collar tighter around his neck as Jake stared with a growing look of amazement. Those thoughts had always haunted Jed, motivated him to solve the crimes he investigated over the years, and he knew that in some macabre way, he had Bobby to thank for that perspective.

"That's what I mean by crawling into the victim's skin," Jed said. "To be able to know what each one knew, to consider from their viewpoint what happened in those last minutes leading up to death."

"I'd like to know if she knew the name of her killer," Jake said. "If knowing her thoughts would tell me who did it. . . ." He shivered, shook his head. "You've turned into one sick bastard. Do you know that? What'd they do to you down in Georgia?"

"You don't even want to know," Jed said with a grimace. "Tell me about your victims."

"One's a black female, twenty-eight. She was shot once in the face, likely through the windshield. A white male, approximately the same age, is on the other side of the car near the passenger door. He took a couple shots to the back."

"Like he was running away?"

"That might be how it went down."

Jed angled his head for a better view of the windshield. "Clean shot. Doesn't appear she had a chance to try to run. Anything else peculiar?"

"See for yourself," Jake said, stepping aside and motioning toward the back of the car. "Then you tell me."

On the ground behind the Studebaker, Jed spotted a rectangular pattern of large rocks with two intersecting rows of smaller rocks inside. "Is that what I think it is?"

Jake paused to relight what remained of his stogie. "Wasn't sure you'd remember," he said. "Symbols like this are fairly common round these parts."

Jed knelt down beside the rectangle he recognized as being used in hoodoo rituals. His father's scowling visage hovered in his mind. "Think it might be connected?"

Wisps of smoke rolled from Jake's mouth. "You're the expert, so I was hoping you could tell me."

Jed raked his finger through the mud inside the rectangle. He lifted his hand to his nose and sniffed. "Shoo! Smells like rotten eggs." He looked back at the mud's yellow tinge, then up at Jake. "Sulfur?"

"I'd say so. You'll find dirt's been sprinkled all over both bodies. I'm told root doctors use that symbol to get rid of hexing powders and such. Supposedly it symbolizes a crossroads, and that's where you're supposed to dump leftover potions to neutralize them. Sulfur's a common powder they use."

Jed nodded. "I remember."

Jake walked over to the second victim, a man dressed in jeans with a thin jacket covering his purple T-shirt. Jed followed as three uniformed deputies glared at their sheriff and the stranger with him.

"There's more," Jake said, pointing to the male victim's muddy corpse.

# CHAPTER · 2

"Check just beneath the boy's stomach," Jake said.

Jed dropped one knee onto the icy ground and bent low for a closer examination. He saw a red pouch barely exposed below the body, one similar to the kind Bobby carried the night he died. "What's inside?"

Someone besides Jake answered, "Figured if anyone would know, you would."

Not recognizing the voice, Jed raised his head to see the man in the bibbed overalls and checkered wool jacket staring down at him. He was as wide as he was tall, and he was chewing on something extending his right cheek.

"Why would you figure that?" Jed said, revealing a glower of his own.

"It's your people that practice that hoodoo horseshit, ain't it?"

"That's enough, Stump," Jake growled. His glare bore into his deputy. "Jedediah Bradley, this is Stump Trumble. Stump's short on manners, but he's a capable investigator. He was the first to arrive after the hunters called."

Stump held an annoyed expression. He gave Jed a quick once-over.

"Me and Jedediah grew up together. He just happens to be a former homicide detective," Jake said. "I invited him to take a close look at everything we have out here." The sheriff's words came slow and deliberate.

*Stump?* Jed thought. *Unusual name.*

"Ain't a good idea having too many folks messin' with the evidence," the deputy said. He regarded his sheriff with a critical squint. "Contaminates the scene."

"I'm willing to take the chance," Jake said in a tone as icy as the weather.

Stump's meaty jaws moved in a circular, cow-chewing-its-cud motion. His chilly scowl lingered for several seconds, then he spit a stream of dark tobacco juice onto the ground. Jed stared down. The liquid projectile had missed his right foot by only inches.

Not one to ignore the redneck equivalent of being slapped in the face with a glove, Jed sprang to his feet, no longer aware of the pain in his knees. He returned the deputy's look of disdain.

A dribble of the amber juice lingered on Stump's lower lip before falling to the ground as both men's gazes remained fixed on one another. Several tense seconds passed before the beefy-cheeked investigator turned and walked toward the trunk of the pecan tree. He swept his arm toward the car. "All yours," he said.

"Names?" Jed asked, kneeling beside the male victim.

"Female's Sadie Dunlap," Jake said through a frown. "Leastwise, that's the name on the Georgia ID we found in her pants pocket."

"And this guy?" Jed asked.

"No ID on the body, but his name is Lamar Lassiter. He's a local kid, a mechanic at Hagerman's Garage. I knew his family, and he seemed like a normal, hard-working kid. His daddy died years back, and his mamma's remarried. She moved to Alabama with her new husband. Beyond that, I have no idea why he would be out here with this girl."

Jed wondered if Jake meant he didn't have any idea why this white guy would be dating a black girl. He studied the facedown body, saw two areas of blood on the back of the jacket. "This one was shot at least twice," he said. "You say the girl was shot once?"

"Yep, square in the forehead. But you need to see for yourself."

Stepping to the driver's side door of the Studebaker, Jed saw Stump nestled into a squat beneath the pecan tree. The men exchanged scowls momentarily before Jed turned his attention to the thin and gangly corpse seated inside the car. When he bent down for a closer inspection, he saw a featureless ebony face. A single blackened hole with dried blood caked around it was visible just above her right eyebrow.

During his career, Jed had seen more than his share of junkies with the same malnourished appearance and emaciated body as this woman. She exhibited all the outward physical signs of a chronic drug user. "Any idea if the car belonged to her?"

"None," Jake said. "Tag's been removed, visible serial numbers either gone or filed down. My guess is it's stolen, although it could've come from a junkyard."

"Could belong to the boy," Jed said. "What did you say his name is?"

"Lassiter. Lamar Lassiter. If it's his, I ain't ever seen him in it."

Jed stood and peered across the trunk at the male victim's body. He seemed to have been well fed, well groomed, and healthy. The condition of the woman's body, on the other hand, looked as if she'd lived on the streets for the better part of her young life. She appeared a lot older than twenty-eight.

"What do you think?" Jed asked. "Prostitute and john? Drug dealer and junkie?"

Jake shrugged. "Pick one. Nothing surprises me anymore. Who knows what kids are into these days."

Jed glanced over at the cemetery to three graves with three familiar headstones. And not that many feet away from where his brother rested was a car like his with two young people shot dead. Just like Bobby and Abby.

Despite the similarities, Jed did note an obvious difference. Bobby had been black, Abby white. Today's male was white and the female black. Why would the killer stage a copycat and not stay true to details like race and gender?

Jed's experience told him the variation was somehow significant. He pulled two latex gloves from his coat pocket, wiggled his fingers inside.

"You always come prepared?" A hint of suspicion hung on Jake's words.

"Boy Scouts," Jed said with a wink. He snapped the rubber-ringed ends over his wrists.

From his vantage point, Stump had remained quiet. The heavyset man still knelt next to the tree's trunk, still worked the tobacco in his jaw. His expression revealed his continued disapproval of Jed's interference.

Jake pointed out more beer cans and several empty condom wrappers near the front of the car. "Reckon it could have been some wild-assed party that got out of hand," he said. "They might even have tried to practice their own version of hoodoo."

"Don't know about hoodoo," Jed said, ready to break the tension, "but it does seem they knew enough to practice safe sex."

An almost indiscernible smile cracked Jake's lips. "I guess we can be thankful for that."

With Stump and the others watching in stone silence, Jed leaned inside the car next to Sadie Dunlap. The words from his morning phone call echoed in his head. The caller, speaking in a Creole-like dialect much like that spoken by local Sea Islanders, had warned about generations of children being punished for sins committed by their fathers. Jed had not fully understood everything said, but the last words of the caller had been seared on the inside of his skull: "The first retribution be done. They be found with your brudder's car near where your brudder rests."

Once again, Jed tried to reason why his caller had chosen to reenact the crime scene from when Bobby died. How did the killer know about a crime committed almost forty years earlier? Even Jed hadn't known where the bodies had been found in relationship to Bobby's car. Did this killer know? Did he position these victims to mimic the way Bobby and his girlfriend were back then?

Bobby and Abby had been found with his car. Had Abby been driving instead of Bobby, or was this another variation like that of the race and gender? The inconsistencies gnawed at the former detective.

The girl's short-cropped hair, close to the scalp and uneven, appeared as if she had hacked it off herself. She wore tattered, green-striped Capri pants and a bloodied tank-top shirt that exposed the sides of small breasts.

Jed looked around the inside of the car but didn't see a coat. Her feet were bare, scratched, and cut. He rocked back to where he could see the other victim. The male wore work boots. *Wonder why the girl was barefoot in this weather?*

The boy was left facedown, but the girl was sitting in the car, her eyes wide open in a terrorized stare. Jed also noted her arms had been crossed over in her lap, an unnatural resting place for someone shot through the head.

He felt a knot forming in his stomach. *She's been positioned*, he thought. Modus operandi traits like that were consistent with a murder committed by a serial killer, and that was not a comforting realization.

His thoughts flew to a playground in Atlanta, where a monster had left each of his tiny victims in a sandbox, arms spread over their heads, legs splayed apart, and the image of a snow angel in the sand. The pounding in Jed's head, all but forgotten these past few moments, returned with fervor.

He motioned for Jake to kneel down beside him. When the tall lanky man did, Jed said, "You realize what this positioning could mean, don't you?"

Jake nodded. "Read about it. Don't want to think about it."

Jed pulled a pad and pen from his coat pocket, jotted down his observations of the body's condition. Underneath, he wrote, "girl's body positioned by killer" and underscored each word twice.

Jake would need to contact area sheriffs to see if they had investigated any cases where a body had been left in or near a graveyard, specifically positioned and not just dumped. Most serial killers were very organized, often compulsive about their victims. If this killer had struck before, Jake needed to find out before the next victim turned up.

Next Jed rubbed a fingertip through the powdery residue coating Sadie's body. Just as Jake had said earlier, the coating was of the same yellowish-tinged dirt he had seen in the rock rectangle, only hers hadn't turned to mud inside the car. The mist had created a muddy sheen on the boy, but there was no mistaking what it was.

"It didn't start misting until last night, right?" Jed asked.

"Late, like after midnight," Jake said.

Jed eased to his feet. "That accounts for the dirt on her being dry and his muddy but not washed away. Be right back."

Under the scrutiny of several pairs of probing eyes, he walked the twenty or so feet to the entrance to the cemetery. He stopped, looked toward Bobby's grave, and saw what he had feared.

*Damn him!* The knot in Jed's abdomen tightened.

He returned to the victim and told Jake, "Bastard dug the dirt from Bobby's grave."

The explanation didn't erase the perplexity masking Jake's face.

Jed rubbed his gloved finger across crusty dried blood on Sadie's lips. "What the hell?" Wiping away a layer of dirt and blood, he felt a roughness he knew shouldn't be there.

Jake leaned close.

Jed knelt down out of the sheriff's line of sight. "You see this?"

The sheriff nodded. "What do you think?"

What, at first, appeared to be deep scratches on swollen, bloodied lips were in fact tiny X-shaped stitches sewn with a thin dark filament. "Her mouth's been sewn shut," Jed said, stating the obvious.

"That's a cracker-jack observation." The not-so-under-his-breath comment came from Stump, who had walked back up and now hovered over Jed and the sheriff.

Jed scowled up at the deputy. "I suppose you have an explanation."

"Reckon they wanted to keep her from screaming once—"

"What do you make of it, Jedediah?" Jake said, cutting off his deputy in mid-sentence.

Stump's expression harbored a quiet fury as Jed reached up and closed the girl's eyelids. "My guess is it's a warning."

Jake's forehead wrinkled. "Such as what—keep your mouth shut?"

"Exactly," Jed said. "We had a case where a police informant's tongue was cut out by a motorcycle gang member. When we caught the suspect, he admitted to the killing and claimed he cut the man's tongue out to send a warning to other would-be informants to keep their mouths shut."

"Far as I know, she ain't one of our informants," Jake said. "When I get back to the office, I'll check with the state and feds to see if anyone owns up to using her."

"Sheriff, you want me to bag this pouch?" The question came from a young uniformed deputy relegated to conducting a search of the surrounding area.

Having seen as much of this victim as he felt necessary, Jed climbed to a semi-crouch. Sharp pain knifed through his aging knees. He groaned. "Damn, I hate getting old."

Jake looked down at Sadie Dunlap. "Considering the alternative, old ain't so bad." He extended his hand and pulled Jed the rest of the way to his feet.

The two men walked around the back of the Studebaker toward the young deputy. "After you bag it," Jake said, "let's have another look at that pouch."

The deputy stood proud in his starched and pressed khaki and brown uniform. "Yes, sir."

"Jedediah, this is Deputy Cory Layton. He's new, fresh out of the Marines. He was an MP."

The former Marine thrust his hand out in Jed's direction. He flashed a big smile, the exact opposite of the greeting Jed had received from Stump.

Jed nodded but held up his mud-smeared, gloved hands. "Better forgo the handshake."

"Bag it," Jake said. "Then we'll take a closer look."

The deputy knelt down, unzipped his cruiser jacket, and pulled a silver ball-point pen from his shirt pocket. Sliding the pen underneath the red pouch, he flipped it out from under the victim and into a plastic bag he held.

"This could be significant," Jed said. "It isn't grimy enough to have been out here all that long, and it could've been dropped by our victim."

"Or the killer," Layton interjected.

Jed nodded and grinned. "Or the killer."

Jake took the plastic bag when the deputy stood, gave the contents a close examination, and shook his head. "Definitely more hoodoo," he said. "I don't like the direction this case is taking."

Jed squeezed the bag, felt objects inside the pouch. "I'd be real interested to know the contents," he said, wondering if it too contained John the Conqueror.

"Any number of things could be in there," Stump said. "Hair, plant roots, chicken bones, even bones from rats or mice, even some old cat. Coloreds will put just about anything in these things, talk some mumbo jumbo, and claim they've conjured up magical powers." He rolled his tongue inside his cheek, and then spit tobacco remnants onto the ground. "Nothin' more than a con job, you ask me."

The hairs on the back of Jed's neck bristled. He had been called all sorts of things as a cop, *nigger* more times than he cared to count. Tolerating slurs uttered by folks he was arresting came with the territory. They were expected, and he knew in the end he would have the last laugh. But hearing the intolerance come from another cop had never set well, and now was no different.

As his fists clenched, an inner voice broke through the anger. *You let folks rile you, and they control you.* He heard his mamma's words as sure as if she had walked up beside him. *Don't let it bother you, and you control you.*

Jed had never quite mastered the latter part of her sage advice, but over the years he had learned how to not let what bothered him show so much. "I suppose you can tell us their significance?" he said.

Stump brandished a sinister grin. "Guess you'll have to tell me."

Again, Jed's thoughts were of his mother. He wanted to do to the heavyset deputy what his mamma used to do to the backyard chicken she planned to cook for dinner—wring his neck.

Jake's face turned the color of a ripe tomato, and after he and Jed exchanged glances, Jed realized Stump had crossed a line he would hear more about when the rest were not around. He tossed Jake the bag.

The sheriff examined the pouch sealed inside the plastic bag. "Maybe this symbol stitched on the side will help us learn who owned it."

Jed looked at the pouch. "Maybe, but if it belonged to the victim, I can't say it offered much protection." Bobby had claimed his pouch filled with hoodoo magic would protect him, too, but it didn't.

"I'll take that and put it with the other evidence," Stump said as he grabbed the bag and started back across the field.

"See me when y'all are finished out here. We got us some talkin' to do." The irritation in Jake's tone was unmistakable.

Stump, muttering as he walked away, didn't turn around. He stomped off toward the parked patrol cars.

"You know of any practicing root doctors around here?" Jed asked Jake.

"Not right offhand." His attention seemed to be on Stump wading through the broomstraw. "Ain't as many as when we were young'uns. These days, most are elderly women who still cling to the old ways."

"An elderly woman didn't kill those two." Jed motioned toward the Studebaker. "For that matter, unless members of the spirit world have taken to using firearms, neither did anything else from that realm."

Once Stump had reached the patrol cars and was out of earshot, Jake turned to Jed. "I appreciate the way you handled Stump's remarks."

Jed shrugged. "Actually, I put a silent hex on him. His hair and teeth will fall out by morning."

Jake forced a smile.

The deputies had dispersed. Some, like the young former marine, had returned to their evidence-gathering duties around the Studebaker. The rest had followed Stump back across the field, leaving Jake and Jed alone.

"Got a phone call this morning," Jed said. "A man who spoke with something of a Gullah accent told me I'd find Bobby's old car out here, just like it was found the night he died."

Jake's reaction was surprisingly neutral. "Uh-huh. What else did he say?"

"He claimed a spirit demanded the death of those two kids. He didn't say anything about a ritual, but he did say they died to avenge some long ago injustice."

Jake's eyebrow lifted. "He say what kind of spirit?"

"How many kinds are there?"

"If you're a believer, there's enough. Some are said to be more dangerous than others."

"Are you messin' with me?" Jed asked.

"You've been gone from these parts a long time, but I'm telling you, over the years I've seen things attributed to the supernatural I can't explain otherwise. There are all kinds of stories."

Jed looked past the Studebaker to the cemetery. If the old man had heard what Jake had just said, he would be rolling over in his grave. "Yeah, I remember hearing all those tall tales growing up, but that's what they were then, and that's all they are now—tall tales."

Jake grimaced, shook his head. "I'm not so sure. Tell me about this long ago injustice your caller mentioned."

"Nothing to tell. My caller just said they died to avenge a long ago injustice."

Jake pulled his hat down tight over his head. He glanced around the field. "Let's get out of this weather. Let the younger folks take care of the crime scene and body removal." He started walking toward the cars. "Follow me to my office."

The two men passed Stump on his way back toward the Studebaker and bodies. The detective hit Jed with a callous scowl but said nothing.

Jake said, "I'll be having an attitude adjustment with him once he gets back." Jed didn't comment.

Barely keeping the sheriff's taillights in view as they sped along the narrow blacktop heading back into town, Jed mused at his friend's seeming preoccupation with hoodoo root doctors and what evil might have been conjured up to kill the two out in the field.

The spirit world might be disturbed, he thought, and its specters could be flying around seeking retribution, but whoever sewed that poor girl's lips together bore more of a resemblance to the living, breathing evildoers he had come to know in Atlanta than to the supernatural ones. Practicing hoodoo or simply believing was fine with him if that was what folks wanted to do. Personally, he considered it a crutch, like a placebo a doctor might give a hypochondriac to cure some make-believe illness. He disliked the idea of blaming the supernatural for events not easily explained. Men, not evil spirits, kill other men. Of that fact he was certain.

# C H A P T E R · 3

Jake and Jed parked in front of the Indigo County Courthouse, a two-story granite structure that had survived both man-made and natural holocaust. Legend held that General William Tecumseh Sherman set it on fire near the end of the Civil War, and numerous hurricanes had pummeled it with hundred-mile-per-hour-plus wind gusts over the years, yet it stood strong and sturdy, representative of the character of the lowcountry and all who resided there.

As he exited his car, Jed looked up at the smooth columns and massive oak doors beyond the portico. He had been told General Robert E. Lee once met with his staff inside those walls to plan their defense of Charleston's port. How much truth the story held was a matter of debate between historians, who concerned themselves with documentation of fact, and locals, who hoped to lure tourists to tiny Sweetgrass. If true, Jed couldn't help wondering how much good that strategy session helped the South, given the eventual outcome of the war.

Jake's office occupied one corner of the structure's basement, a humble location, Jed thought, to shuffle off the chief law enforcer for the county. As a boy, Jed had viewed the Sheriff of Indigo County as someone to be both feared and cautiously respected, although most members of his father's church feared Southern lawmen much more than they respected them.

Growing up black in the '60s South, Jed had learned to steer clear of the sheriff and his deputies. Back then, little good came from such contact.

He followed Jake's steady, easy strides down the worn steps into a subterranean corridor of stone walls. The chilly air and musty scent of mildew lingering there reminded him of a recent funeral in Atlanta and the mausoleum where the entombment took place.

At that funeral Jed had joined the mother and father of a little girl whose nude body had been found in a playground sand pile, displayed like three others before her. A few days earlier he had delivered the news no parents ever want to hear, waited with them at their home while they regained their composure, and then he drove them to the morgue where they identified their eleven-year-old daughter. He was not a family friend. He had not attended the funeral because he wanted to or because either parent had asked him to be there. In truth, he believed the mother regarded him with much of the same contempt she held for her daughter's killer.

He recalled how she had approached him after the service, how she bitterly regarded him with cold eyes. She asked why he hadn't caught the sadistic pedophile before her baby was murdered. Jed didn't have an answer for her that afternoon, just like he didn't have an answer for the mayor in the throes of a tough reelection bid when the avaricious, uptight politician asked the same question a few days later.

Jed attended the funeral with other detectives, hoping the killer would follow a pattern sometimes displayed by serial murderers who came to witness the fruits of their labor. This one didn't follow the pattern, didn't show up as they had hoped, much as he had defied every other effort employed to stop his rampage.

Jed was still haunted by the bold black headline of the *Atlanta Journal-Constitution* on the day he drove his Volvo out of town for the last time: ANOTHER PARK ANGEL MURDER BAFFLES POLICE. That one made number five.

The corners of a faded gold star curled on the opaque glass window of a door at the end of the stone corridor. Jed paused, blew a warm breath of air into his hands.

"It'll be warmer in the office," Jake said as he turned the knob.

Inside, Jed didn't notice much difference. He could still see his breath, and the cold nipped at his nose.

Jake bent over a small round heater in the corner of the room. He pushed a red button at its base, adjusted a round black knob until an orange flame appeared through a tempered-glass window. After several chilly seconds, the faint scent of kerosene drifted across the room.

"That'll warm things in no time," Jake said. He pointed to a gray, mottled enamel coffeepot, one like Jed's grandmother always had kept full on top of her wood-burning stove. "Coffee?"

A sharp pain sliced through the former detective's right eye just as Jake made his much appreciated offer. Jed muttered, "Make mine a double."

Jake chortled. "Figured we'd both need something warm to thaw out our pipes, so I called ahead and had my dispatcher cook some up. I'll warn you, though. She makes it stout."

"The stronger the better," Jed said, thinking a super dose of caffeine might be just what the doctor ordered.

While Jake busied himself with the coffee, Jed glanced around the grim office. A few yellowed certificates hung in cheap frames on walls badly in need of paint. Water marks dotted ceiling tiles, and the gray metal furnishings looked to be army surplus. On a shelf behind the sheriff's desk, a tarnished silver picture frame displayed an old photo of Jake dressed out in a Confederate officer's uniform. In one hand he held a saber; in the other he cradled a gray hat with a large feather plume stuck in the band. A big-toothed grin filled his face.

"You still doing reenactments?" Jed asked.

"Nah. No time. Besides I kinda got tired of losing. Now, if we could do one where the South wins. . . ." He laughed his horse laugh as he pulled two cups from his desk drawer.

Not surprisingly, the two men had always viewed the Civil War from different perspectives. Even though Jed's family had moved to the lowcountry from Virginia when he was less than a year old, many members of his father's church descended from slaves, called Gullahs, brought to the Sea Islands of South Carolina and Georgia from Africa's Gold Coast. Jed had grown up listening to their stories about the hardships endured by those sold like livestock in Charleston and Savannah. Jake's ancestors, on the other hand, had owned some of those slaves, and his father had even been rumored to hold a position of authority in the local Ku Klux Klan, notorious for its rhetoric and occasional violence against blacks in Indigo County.

Jed learned what he knew of hoodoo from those Gullah descendants. Although most lowcountry whites, like Stump, wrongly thought all blacks knew the inner secrets of the ancient art, Jed didn't understand its hold on folks. What he did understand, however, was that many Gullahs held strong beliefs in the mystical practice and believed the local root doctor could heal them or hex them, inflicting great pain and suffering, even death.

"You can use my special cup," Jake said as he poured coffee into an oversized brown and white mug. "It has little fornicating bunnies all over the side."

Jed started. "Did you say forn—"

Jake laughed. "You heard right. Happy little fornicators." He continued to laugh as he handed Jed the mug.

"Cream? Sugar?" he asked in a perfectly level voice.

Jed held the hot mug with both hands and examined the sides. "Black's fine," he said, preoccupied with what he saw.

In what looked like abstract art, busy little white rabbits, hundreds of them, assumed assorted provocative positions all around the cup. Despite Jed's aching head, he couldn't help laughing along with Jake. "Where'd you get this?"

"Kat. She said it fit my personality."

"Your sister has true insight, not to mention a great sense of humor. How is she, anyway?"

Growing up, Katherine Armistead resembled her older brother in a number of not so appealing ways. By the age of thirteen, her gangly thin frame stretched to almost six feet. She possessed nearly as many freckles as Jake, and she wore her orange-red hair cut unevenly around her long narrow face. She didn't date much, and up until Jed left home for good, he never knew her to have had any close girlfriends. Mostly she hung out with the guys, working on cars, doing things guys did. Jed couldn't remember ever seeing her in a dress, either, just jeans and T-shirts and scuffed, brogan boots.

"She's fine," Jake said. "Divorced now, but she has two boys. One's at the university in Columbia, the other works on the docks in Charleston." He chuckled. "We get along a whole heap better now that we're grown and not living under the same roof."

Jed thought back to how he and Jake used to chunk crab apples at the lonely girl to keep her from following them to their favorite fishing hole. They would pelt her with the small fruit until she would turn back, then they would run away and hide until they were sure she had given up looking for them and had gone back home.

Jed thought of how running away seemed to be a special trait of his. He sipped his coffee, noted it tasted better than expected, but it wasn't the elixir he had hoped for. "You got any aspirin?"

"I can do better than that." Jake pulled open his desk drawer.

A second later he flipped Jed a small packet of waxy paper filled with white powder. "If that don't do the trick, nothing will." He set a bottle of water on the edge of the desk. "You don't want to try taking that with hot coffee, though. You'll scorch your throat."

Jed looked at the packet, remembered how his father used to always keep a couple in his suit pocket for those times when congregational duties overwhelmed him. The old man had never taken a cure for any physical aches in pill form as far as Jed knew. In fact, his mamma had relied on two primary cure-alls: the headache powders he was about to take, and castor oil, the latter of which Jed believed had been brewed by disciples of the devil. At any rate, neither medication proved to be for sissies.

Staring at the waxy envelope, Jed's mouth began filling with the anticipatory saliva that preceded unpleasant assaults on his taste buds. He had not used the powders since leaving home, having converted to the more citified pill form of aspirin soon after arriving in Atlanta.

He opened the packet, squeezed both sides to form a trough, and dumped the powder onto the back of his tongue. In an instant, his cheeks drew tight and his mouth puckered as the bitter granules bit into his taste buds. He grabbed the bottle of water and gulped.

Jake chortled and said, "Powders are to aspirin what liquor is to beer."

Jed thought the analogy particularly appropriate, especially considering the source of his morning's pain and agony. He breathed a deep breath and chased the water with a sip of coffee. Soon, the liquids began to dilute what bitter remnants remained.

"Let's discuss this caller of yours," Jake said, leaning back in his chair, propping his boots on top of his desk.

"Not much to tell, really. He spoke with that lilting accent you hear round these parts."

"That's consistent with the hoodoo symbols we found. Might be one of the Sea Islanders."

"I don't think so," Jed said.

"Why not? There's still a fair number who speak in Gullah, and when they talk in English, the accent bleeds over."

"I don't think my caller was black."

"Hmmm. Now that's odd. You sure?"

Jed winked. "If there's one thing I know, it's how *my people* speak." Jed hadn't been able to resist the inference to Stump's earlier comment out at the church grounds.

Jake's face pruned. "Guess that's likely, although a lot of whites who've grown up around the Gullahs have taken on that way of talking . . . some intentionally so." His tone sounded disapproving. "What'd he tell you about the victims?"

"He rattled off a verse or two out of the Bible and then called them his first retribution."

"First? What was the quote?"

"It had to do with the sins of the fathers passing down through the generations," Jed replied.

"What the hell does that mean?"

"If I recall my Sunday school lessons, God told the Israelites that if they hated him, their children would be punished to the third and fourth generation."

"The golden calf thing?" Jake asked.

Jed disclosed a reticent smile. "I think that's part of it. My caller told me I'd find his first retribution near where my brother rested."

"I don't much like the way he said 'first retribution,'" Jake said. "It implies a second, even a third or more."

"Yep!"

Jake's left eyelid began to twitch. Jed remembered his friend having the nervous tic since childhood. Anytime he grew concerned or overly anxious, the eyelid revealed his feelings.

"We ain't had a real whodunit murder around here in years," Jake said. "We've had our share of drunks shooting other drunks and, of course, a few domestics that wound up in a killing, but this one ain't like those, is it?"

"Nope. You're not getting off that easy this time." Jed set his coffee cup on the desk and realized that for the first time all morning his head didn't hurt. "That combo of coffee and headache powder did the trick. My head feels better. Thanks."

"Glad to be of service," Jake said, wearing a solemn expression.

"Have you got someone checking with neighboring counties to see if they've had anybody killed in the same manner as those two this morning?" Jed asked. "If so, did they leave any unusual calling cards, like the stitching on that girl's mouth?"

"Ain't been any I've heard," Jake said. "But I did tell Stump to call around and make sure." He leaned forward and pointed to Jed's empty cup. "More?"

Jed held up his hand. "I'll pass. That coffee's more like an illegal narcotic. I think it gave me a buzz."

Jake gave an almost indiscernible nod. "This whole spirit world connection boogers me," he said. "I ain't necessarily all that superstitious, you understand, but like I told you before, I've seen some mighty peculiar goings-on in my day, things you just can't explain."

He massaged his eyelids with his finger and thumb. "Years back, a sheriff a couple of counties over was rumored to not only believe, but folks claimed him to be a full-fledged conjurer, a root doctor."

"A Gullah sheriff?" Jed said, finding it hard to believe that a black, especially a Gullah, could ever get elected to any office in the lowcountry he used to know.

"Don't look so surprised. There's several black sheriffs in South Carolina now. We're making progress. Some say we've even joined the twentieth century." His last comment dripped with sarcasm.

"We're now in the twenty-first century," Jed said deadpan.

"Don't rush us. We'll get there."

"So there *was* a Gullah sheriff?" Jed said.

"Actually, he was white, but folks swore he owned the power. Some say he even claimed to be bulletproof. Whatever he did or was, serious crime in his county became almost nonexistent."

Jed chuckled, shook his head. "Maybe you ought to look into this hoodoo stuff more seriously."

"Funny. You ever have a case involving the supernatural back in Atlanta?"

"Nope. You know any root doctors you can ask about what we found this morning?"

Jake stroked his chin with his long bony fingers. "Not really. We've had a few come through charged by the state with practicing medicine without a license. For that very reason I don't know of any willing to even admit to dabblin' in the stuff."

"It'd be real helpful if we could talk to someone familiar with what's done to conjure up these spirits," Jed said. "Especially the angry, vengeful ones."

"Only angry spirit I ever encountered was my ex-mother-in-law. Now, there was a woman with a true evil eye."

Jed grinned. "The killer sprinkled dirt from Bobby's grave over the bodies. Any idea what it means?"

"Sure do. Remember when the high schools consolidated and you and I ended up in the same algebra class our junior year?"

"Yeah, I remember," Jed said, wondering where the conversation was headed. "Not my favorite year . . . or subject."

Consolidating the all-black Carver High School with the all-white Stonewall Jackson High had been especially difficult for Jed and his classmates from Carver. They held little faith that the authorities would intervene if trouble started, but as it turned out, the kids got along much better than their adult counterparts. Jed and Jake, having lived close to each other for years in the otherwise sparsely populated rural community, had developed a friendship that preceded the forced consolidation. They had fished together, hunted too, since they were young boys, and although they suffered through some tense moments those first few weeks of the school year, their friendship helped to defuse what could have become an explosive time for them all.

"Well, remember how we went out looking for goofer dust to sprinkle under our desks for luck?" Jake asked.

"Goofer dust?"

"Yeah, you remember. Goofer dust. Dirt dug from a grave and mixed with special ingredients. Sulfur for instance. It's used in hoodoo rituals."

"Okay."

"We went out and got us some dirt from the grave of some old woman we'd been told had been a conjurer," Jake said in an insistent tone. "We sprinkled it under our desks, because we had been told her dirt, in particular, would bring us good luck."

"All I recall is that I damn near flunked that algebra course, so whatever we supposedly did didn't work." Jed said. "But I think I see your point."

"My point is, the dirt was dug from Bobby's grave for a reason and must've had some importance to whatever ritual went on out there. So what is the connection to your brother? Any ideas?"

Jed stared at nothing in particular. "I don't know," he said after a prolonged silence. "The Studebaker, two victims—one black, one white—although he got the genders wrong, and both of this morning's victims were a good ten years older than Bobby and Abby. It has to be a copycat, but then there are so many inconsistencies, glaring ones."

"Other than the race and gender reversal and the age thing, what else was inconsistent?"

"The girl behind the wheel, for one. Bobby and Abby were in Bobby's car the night they were killed. He would have been driving."

"Maybe he let her drive."

"Maybe, but Bobby was awful proud of that old jalopy he had rebuilt. What did the hunters tell you?" Jed asked. "How is it they stumbled across the car and bodies, so far away from the woods?"

"According to their story, about the time they got back of the old church, both of their dogs started baying and carrying on, just like they always had when they picked up the scent of a big coon. The dogs took off in pursuit of their quarry.

"Both men said they followed best they could, but after a while the dogs got way ahead. They heard them barking and howling way off in the distance. Then they quit. The hunters said they searched all through the woods and swamp for their pups but couldn't find 'em.

"About the time they left the tree line and started across the field, the dogs met 'em at a full run and zipped right by them. One of the men said the only other time he'd seen his dog running scared like that was when the mutt got chased by a swarm of angry hornets."

"Maybe this time it was a swarm of angry spirits," Jed said, grinning.

"That ain't funny," Jake said.

Jed recognized his friend's no-nonsense glare. The twitching becoming more prominent, so he backed off of the humor. "Is that when they spotted the body?"

"Nope. They said they tried to stop 'em with whistles and calls, but them dogs were headed for home and nothing was going to stop 'em. Knowing no hornets or the like would be out in the dead of winter, the two men decided to look into what might have spooked their animals.

"When they got near the cemetery, totin' their shotguns in a low ready, they spotted that car out in the middle of the field. As they got closer, one claimed he caught a whiff of some kind of foul odor. He described it as akin to a skunk's fart after he'd eaten rotten hen eggs. Said it almost suffocated him.

"That's when they spotted the bodies. That was all it took. They skedaddled away, just like their dogs."

"Wonder why the sulfur smell was so strong?" Jed said. "I didn't detect it until I got a sniff of the soil on and around the bodies."

Jake nodded. "I know. Those hunters were convinced their dogs had run up on some old hant or hag from the graveyard and that spirit caused the air to foul. When they saw the corpses, I think they figured 'em for apparitions crawling out from the old cemetery. Whatever they thought, they sure didn't hang around to find out if they were going to be next."

"Reckon it's possible the killer didn't want them around those two bodies," Jed said. "He might not have wanted anything disturbed until y'all arrived. He might have tried to frighten them away by throwing some stink bombs out."

"Reckon as to how that might be."

Jed studied his friend's expression. The man's eyelid twitched almost nonstop. "You mind if I contact those two hunters?" Jed asked.

"Guess not," Jake said, shrugging his shoulders after a few seconds of quiet reflection. "Why?"

"Just to hear firsthand what they have to say. No other reason."

"Knock yourself out." He scribbled something on a piece of paper and handed it to Jed. "This is where they live. Neither of 'em has a phone."

"Thanks." Jed took the paper. "You sending the bodies to Charleston?" He asked the question knowing that would be the location of the closest medical examiner to perform an autopsy.

"Yep! What few normal murders we have around here are always sent to the Medical University. Don't see no reason to treat our peculiar ones any different." He pulled a cigar out of his shirt pocket, offered it to Jed.

"No, thanks. My body's polluted enough as it is."

Without comment, the sheriff ripped open the cellophane wrapper, bit the end off the cigar, and spit the plug into a nearby wastebasket. He reached inside his desk drawer, pulled out a kitchen match, and flicked the tip with his thumbnail just as he had done out in the field that morning. A flame shot up, and Jed thought of his father sitting in his easy chair next to the old wood stove in their front room smoking his pipe. Jed's father used kitchen matches the same as Jake.

A plume of gray smoke engulfed Jake's head after several puffs, and when it dissipated he pulled the cigar from his mouth, rolled it between his thumb and index finger. All the while, his probing glare never left his friend.

"Help me understand how you come to be sittin' here this morning," Jake said after several reflective moments. "From what you've told me, you got this call, likely from the killer. This caller knows you, he knows your family is buried out by the old church, and he knows you've moved back into the old homeplace—something I didn't even know, I might add. He tells you where to find a couple of murdered kids and a car resembling the one your brother was driving the night *he* was killed." Jake sucked on the cigar. The tip glowed, and smoke rolled out of the corners of his mouth. "Anything else I should know?"

"That about sums it up."

"Then how do you explain—"

"I can't explain any of it. I don't know why I got the call. I don't know why it involves Bobby or anybody else in my family, for that matter. I just don't know."

"So what do you plan to do from here?"

"I can't just walk away from it, Jake. Not if it has something to do with Bobby's death. I'm like an old dog. I don't know where the bones are buried, but I have to keep digging for them."

"When are you going to get around to telling me about how you come to be an ex-detective?"

Jed stood and stretched his arms toward the ceiling. "Not today," he said as his stomach growled loud enough for both men to hear. "I have to get something inside me before I get sick. Care to join me for breakfast?"

Jake shook his head. "Nope, I need to check to make sure my folks are doing what they should. None of 'em have ever been involved in a case like this one." He raked his hands through his gray-speckled rust hair. "For what it's worth, neither have I."

Jake's eye continued to twitch as he stood and stepped from behind his desk. "I can't stop you from following your instincts. In fact, I'm pretty sure I don't want to. God knows we need the help, but you need to be careful. This ain't Atlanta, and your snoopin' around might not be welcome. Get my drift?"

Jed thought about Stump's reaction earlier in the morning. "I've noticed. I'll keep you informed."

"Of everything," Jake said as Jed opened the door leading out of the office and into the corridor. "Everything, understood?"

Jed waved his hand and pulled the door shut behind him. He knew Jake's twitching eye revealed his uneasiness with all that was going on, including his showing up at the crime scene that morning. Still, Jed knew Jake was sincere in wanting help with the case. As his father used to say, Jake was hooked square on the horns of a dilemma.

A good cop should be suspicious, Jed told himself, and he believed Jake was a good cop. Besides, he knew he would be suspicious too if the situation had been reversed.

# CHAPTER · 4

Jed stepped out of the chilly subterranean depths of the Indigo County Courthouse into a welcoming bath of radiant sunshine. Gone were the low-hanging clouds and the stiff breeze laden with a frozen mist. With his hangover reduced to little more than an unpleasant memory and the outside temperature now approaching tolerable, he began to feel renewed. He glanced back at weathered stone steps angling up the front to big oak doors hidden in the shadows behind four towering columns. A flood of memories washed over him.

He thought about Bobby, how the brothers used to beg rides over to the marketplace in Beaufort, how they fished off of the bridges, hoping to catch some whiting or spot to bring home for dinner. He remembered crabbing in the backwater and the occasional mud fights the two had at low tide. His thoughts drifted back to that last afternoon and the carefree nature Bobby exhibited as he drove off to meet Abby and the evil awaiting them both. Jed remembered the good times, and then he recalled the bad.

Like a scene from his worst nightmare, the events surrounding that awful night flickered in his memory. The headlights from the sheriff's car had first caught his attention. They lit up the living room at the front of the house, drawing Jed to the window to see who had come to visit. He saw Sheriff Cletus Renfrow climb from his patrol car, and he saw the tall lawman start across the lawn toward the porch.

No doubt sensing trouble, given nothing good ever came from a visit from the sheriff, his father stepped outside and pulled the door closed behind him. Before it shut, Jed heard Renfrow say, "Preacher, I've got some bad news to share." The sheriff's tone had been as solemn as a funeral dirge.

Jed's mamma remained inside, frozen with trepidation beside the closed door. When her husband came back in, he shooed Jed to the back of the house. The stalwart man's eyes were wet, the rims red, as he looked at his wife and waited for his youngest son to obey. Jed didn't question. He did as his father commanded and disappeared into the bedroom he shared with his brother.

Jed remembered closing the door, too afraid to hear what he already knew in his heart. Seconds that seemed as long as years passed, and then he heard his mamma's wails roll through the tiny home.

He prayed that night, maybe for the first time in his life without being expected too. He fell to his knees beside his narrow bed, right where his mamma had him kneel every night for his bedtime meditation, and he appealed to God. He prayed hard, begging for Bobby to be okay, that the brothers would be able to fish and crab and even fight again in the morning.

Later that night, when his father came into his room to deliver the dreaded news, his faith took a hit. He hated God for not accepting his prayer, for not making it come true. It took a while for that resentment to subside, years in fact, but eventually, for the most part, it had—until this morning, out by the graves of his family. Doubt spawned by his early morning caller fueled its return. Now determination drove him to learn the truth about that night long ago.

Jed had not been allowed into the courtroom during the trial of his brother's killers. His father claimed a fifteen-year-old boy should not be subjected to the sordid details heard inside those mighty oak doors. At the time, Jed didn't bother arguing, didn't question why. He obeyed, because after Bobby's murder, reasoning with his father about anything having to do with his brother's death became impossible.

The elder Bradley grew more reticent with each passing day. He refused to talk about the night Sheriff Renfrow came by the house to deliver the news. He spent more and more time by himself at the church, and Jed's mother withdrew from everyone, never emerging from the debilitating shroud of her son's murder.

During the three-day trial, Jed had listened to recaps of the previous day's events from those who had been inside the courthouse, and he eagerly tried to eavesdrop on predictions of what would happen to the men on trial.

Jed looked up at the overhead canopy of bare limbs cloaked in gray spongy moss. Under these trees he had first heard the whispers of how Bobby had brought it all on himself by dating a white girl. The words had stung his young ears back then. They infuriated him now.

Pangs of hunger rumbled deep inside his stomach. When had he last eaten? He couldn't recall, but he could smell the invitation to breakfast drifting out of the mom-and-pop restaurant near the courthouse. As aromas of sausage and fried bacon teased his senses, he spotted Stump and another man across the courthouse lawn. Stump appeared angry, flailing his arms, pacing back and forth in front of the man. Heavy and broad-shouldered with a flabby face and pear-shaped body, the stranger appeared out of season in his ill-fitted seersucker suit. His stringy blond hair hung limp against his shoulders, and something, a hint of familiarity perhaps, caused Jed's gaze to linger.

Stump stopped his tirade when he saw Jed looking. He pointed, not trying to hide the fact. The other man stared across the lawn, but Jed turned and walked away without bothering to look back.

The cinder-block restaurant owned by Joe and Dot Cramer sat in the shadow of the Indigo County Courthouse. Between the morning hours of six and ten o'clock, it served as the social and business center for much of South Carolina's lowcountry. In this unassuming setting, with its whitewashed exterior and greasy plate-glass window, court cases were negotiated and multimillion-dollar land development decisions for nearby resort communities were consummated. The eclectic gathering of lowcountry citizenry came every day. Lawyers and executives drove up from Savannah and over from Beaufort and Hilton Head in a Mercedes or Lexus or Jaguar, and they parked next to rattletrap old pickups and big-tired tractors. Inside, dressed in their thousand-dollar suits, they sat at tables or on stools next to farmers wearing dusty bibbed overalls and mechanics in grease-stained work clothes. They all came to discuss their business and sometimes just the weather over paper platters filled with biscuits the size of pancakes and generous portions of fried eggs, sausage, and bacon.

By the time Jed arrived, all of the stools at the counter had been taken. He glanced across the crowd, spotted a vacant table, and hurried to it before someone else could.

As he settled into the wobbly, ladder-back wooden chair that creaked with his every move, an attractive brunette with creamy white skin and pink cheeks appeared. She smiled through braces.

"Coffee?" she asked with a soft drawl. Without waiting for a reply, she placed a white mug on the red-checkered vinyl table cloth beside plastic flatware wrapped in a paper napkin.

"Please," Jed said, trying not to be obvious as he inspected her tight jeans and well-filled baby-blue cotton T-shirt. A red and white, candy-striped lighthouse with HILTON HEAD ISLAND written in white script beneath it adorned her chest.

She poured the steaming dark liquid into his mug and pointed to the packets of sugar and assorted artificial sweeteners in a container next to a small pitcher of cream. "Know what you want, hon?"

Jed smiled as he looked up into the woman's silvery blue eyes. He thought about how his father had been arrested in the early '60s for trying to eat in a restaurant just like this one. Now this very attractive, very white waitress had just called him "hon." Progress.

"Two eggs over-easy, fried liver mush, and grits with redeye gravy," Jed said.

"Toast or biscuits?" she asked with a voice akin to a songbird's.

"Biscuits please."

Jed's grandmother, who always heralded breakfast as the most important meal of the day, would have been proud of his order, but not what he was thinking about the young waitress half his age. As he watched her walk away, a voice dissolved his fantasy.

"Mind if I join you?"

Jed looked up but didn't recognize the man standing beside his table.

"All the others are taken," the stranger said. "Do you mind?"

Jed did, but he didn't say so as he glanced around as if to verify the truth of the man's statement. He studied the bedraggled white face and the disheveled brown hair. He stared at the frayed sleeve of the man's gray-and-black herringbone sport coat and then toward the empty chair across the table from where he sat.

In Atlanta the homeless sometimes came into restaurants to bum a free meal off of the patrons. Jed had not expected it in Sweetgrass.

From deep inside, he heard his mamma's soft voice whispering another Bible verse. *What you do for the least of them, you do for me.* He sighed, wishing he hadn't remembered.

He shook his head, forced the words from his mouth. "Go ahead." He motioned toward the empty chair.

"Thanks," the rumpled stranger said. He extended his hand. "Name's Hap Gentry."

Jed visualized the hand foraging through grimy entrails inside a Dumpster and kept his arms by his side. "Jedediah Bradley," he said.

Wrinkles covered the collarless tan shirt, some of which were visible through a raggedy hole beneath the man's coat pocket. Jed braced for the inevitable pitch for money.

The pretty waitress again appeared next to the table. "Morning, Hap. Having your usual?" Her sing-song drawl sounded more syrupy than before.

"Morning, Sue. Same as usual. You know I'm a creature of habit."

Sue handed the man a mug, filled it with coffee, and then hit Jed with a cautionary wink. "Watch what you say, hon, if you don't want everybody round these parts knowin' your business." Before she turned to leave she said, "Yours'll be up anytime now."

Jed watched her stride away again, before turning and narrowing his stare into a pinpoint aimed across the table. "What did she mean by that?"

"Sue's a cynic," Gentry said, lifting his cup to his lips, sipping the coffee without looking away from the swaying backside of the young waitress.

"So am I, and I'm taking her advice for now." For the first time since the stranger's arrival, Jed realized Hap Gentry's appearance at his table was no coincidence. "What do you want?"

Gentry pulled a business card from his shirt pocket and slid it across the table. "Heard you've been getting some mighty interesting phone calls," he said.

Jed gave the card a slow appraising gaze. He didn't pick it up.

"Hap Gentry, *Savannah Courier News,*" the man said as if reading the card for Jed.

Jed groaned. In retrospect, he preferred the man to be homeless. He pinched the bridge of his nose with his thumb and forefinger. "I should have guessed."

"You act as though you don't care for us journalist types." Gentry's voice feigned hurt feelings.

Jed clasped his hands and intertwined the fingers as he leaned across the table. "A long time ago, a veteran sergeant pulled a rookie cop aside after the sergeant overheard him talking too freely with a reporter about an investigation. He told him a story about a shipwrecked sailor and a snake ending up on the same raft. You heard the story?"

"No, but I think I'm about to." Gentry cradled his coffee cup in both hands and leaned back in his chair.

"At first the sailor feared the snake," Jed said. "He feared it so much, he started to kick it off the raft into the ocean, but the snake pleaded with the sailor to spare him. The snake claimed they could coexist, even become friends."

Gentry sat quietly with an expectant smile across his face. He continued to sip his coffee.

"They floated for days," Jed said. "Finally they drifted into shallow water close to a small island. The sailor jumped off the raft and started toward shore. The snake pleaded, 'don't leave me. I can't swim.'

"After some soul-searching, the sailor waded back to the raft and picked up the snake. He carried it high out of the water, but as the sailor stepped onto dry land the snake bit him and slithered off. The sailor, injured and dying, called after the snake and asked why it bit him after he had helped it. The snake replied, 'You knew what I was when you picked me up.'"

Gentry chuckled, sat down his coffee mug. "Yeah, I hear the press in Atlanta can be brutal. That why you packed it in and moved home?"

The muscles in Jed's back grew tense. "Listen—"

"One order of eggs, liver mush, and grits," the syrupy voice said.

Jed leaned back just as Sue set his platter in front of him. "Thanks," he said, maintaining a harsh glare on his tablemate.

"And a biscuit smothered in sausage gravy," she said, placing Gentry's breakfast in front of him. "More coffee?" she asked.

"Just enough to warm it up." Gentry slid his mug near the edge of the table.

"I'm fine," Jed said in a curt tone he instantly regretted. He softened his voice and smiled up at the girl. "Thanks."

By the time Sue left, Gentry had already cut into the large, white-gravy-soaked biscuit.

"What do you know about me, and what is it you want?" Jed asked. Using his fork, he cut a chunk off one corner of the liver mush and swirled it through the egg yolk.

Gentry chewed slowly, swallowed, and again began cutting the biscuit with the side of his fork. Without looking up he said, "I know you've spent most of your career in Atlanta, that you came up through the ranks of the PD to become chief of detectives, and that all hell broke loose when some pervert started killing little girls and littering the city's parks with their bodies. I believe your friends in the media dubbed it the Park Angel Murders and accused you and your men of not doing enough to stop the killer."

By the time Gentry finished his recitation of Jed's career high and low points, the former detective had placed his fork beside his plate and leaned back in his chair. "The mayor needed a scapegoat," he said. "I was the logical choice."

"The Bulldog got sent to the kennels."

Jed stared incredulously. The only people who had ever called him Bulldog were other investigators in the tiny Atlanta squad room. They all had nicknames, like Gravedigger, who earned his unusual moniker after discovering shallow graves behind an antebellum boarding house near downtown. The matronly woman who owned the home had been systematically poisoning the single men who came to live there. All, it turned out, were from up north. They moved in, and a few months later they just disappeared. Gravedigger discovered that several of the men's credit cards were still being used, and he traced them back to the woman and her boarding house. In all, he solved six murders. Obviously mentally ill, the woman had claimed she was only doing her part to rid the South of carpetbaggers.

"How do you know all this?" Jed asked. "I can't believe crimes in Atlanta carry that much interest this far away."

"You're being too modest, Chief. Even out here in the boonies, we hear about the big-city legendary cases and even some not so legendary."

Jed shook his head as he listened to the line the reporter was feeding him. He didn't exactly consider the Park Angel case legendary, and he didn't think the reporter really did either. Jed studied the rather odd looking man, wondering what it was he was after.

Jed's nickname had grown out of his reputation for being tenacious, like a bulldog. Rumor had it that some claimed the facial resemblance was close also, but no one dared tell him about their observation.

"You seem to know an awful lot about me," Jed said. "How is that? And how do you know about my phone calls?"

"Oh, word gets around in a small town like Sweetgrass. Think the killer's the one who called?"

"I have no idea," Jed replied, growing weary of the reporter's questions, considering some of his own. "Jake got a leak?"

Gentry's gaze wavered, an almost imperceptible movement. Jed knew he had hit a nerve.

"Mostly I just keep my ears open and listen," Gentry said. "Besides, round these parts, finding out what cops are up to isn't all that difficult."

*That annoying fact seems to be a universal problem,* Jed thought. "Maybe so, but even Jake didn't know I was back in town until this morning."

"Somebody knew. I got a call too. Several days ago. But it wasn't about a couple of dead kids, just an interesting former detective who'd moved back home."

Jed's forehead furrowed. "'Interesting'? How so?"

"For one thing, he said your friendship with the sheriff goes way back. That true?"

Jed nodded and scooped a spoonful of grits. He held it in front of his face. "What's that got to do with anything?"

"Sure would like to do a public-interest piece on the two of you. You know . . . childhood friends with different perspectives on the South . . . both grew up to be cops . . . that sort of stuff."

Jed lowered the spoon and its contents down to his plate. He glared at the reporter. "One white, one black; one a Confederate soldier in Civil War reenactments, one the son of a preacher who marched for civil rights?"

Gentry's eyes brightened. "Yeah, that's it."

"Forget it."

The reporter didn't appear surprised or disappointed. "Did the sheriff ask for your help solving the murders?" he asked.

"No." This time the grits made it to Jed's mouth, but they had become cooled to the point that they had lost their flavor.

"What about the rumors of hoodoo being involved. Any truth there?"

Jed grimaced. "Do you think some evil spirit swooped down to do the dirty deed?"

"Never underestimate the power of the root," Gentry said.

Jed's eyes widened. "That's an interesting perspective coming from a reporter." He wiped his mouth with his napkin. "I thought you folks stuck with facts—verifiable facts. Are you saying *you* believe in this 'power of the root' stuff?"

Gentry smiled. "I'm not sayin' I believe or don't believe. I'm keeping my options open, but I've seen enough unexplained happenings over the years to make a body wonder."

That was the second time over the past few hours Jed had heard a similar statement to avoid taking a position on the supernatural. He tossed his napkin on top of his now too-cold-to-eat breakfast and stood up. "I believe the flesh-and-blood beings who walk this earth are a whole sight more dangerous than some so-called conjured-up spirit—even an especially evil one." He flipped a couple of one-dollar bills on the table for Sue and grabbed his check. "Interesting talking to you, Mr. Gentry."

At the cash register, Jed handed a ten-dollar bill to a woman with snowy white hair. While she fished his change from the cash register's money drawer, Jed cast a furtive glance back at Gentry. Learning more about the inquisitive journalist would be added to his to-do list.

*Maybe the next time we play Twenty Questions,* Jed thought, confident there would be a next time, *I'll be able to level the playing field. After all, a newspaper reporter just might be the type of person to have access to old files about Bobby's death and to be able to stage a near-perfect reenactment of the original crime scene if he had mind to.*

Despite the early morning hour, Attorney Parker Granville filled his tumbler with bourbon once again, dropped in a couple of ice cubes, then staggered over to his desk. Through bloodshot eyes he squinted at the dial pad on the phone and punched in the number for Senator Bain Granville's office in Columbia, the state capital of South Carolina. With the receiver pinned between his flaccid jowl and shoulder, Parker collapsed into his chair and slugged down a quarter of his drink in one big gulp.

"Senator Granville's office." The woman's voice oozed with the sweetness of refined honey.

Parker's curt words slurred. "Need to speak to Bain."

A lengthy pause preceded the woman's response. "Pardon?"

"This here's Parker. I need to talk to my cousin—right now." He turned up the tumbler and gulped more bourbon.

An audible sigh could be heard. "Just a moment."

Soft music filled Parker's ears. He rolled his eyes and drummed his fingers on the desktop.

Senator Bain Granville's voice roared into the phone. "What is it, Parker? I've got a roll call in fifteen minutes."

"They found that Lassiter kid and Willie Sims's granddaughter out by the old colored church on Winding Creek Road this morning. They both'd been shot."

"So?"

"So, don't you find it weird?" Parker asked.

"The only thing I find peculiar is why Trent Lassiter's boy was out with some negra whore. He into drugs?"

"Shit, Bain. That ain't the point. The point is, they were killed out by that old burned-out church and Elijah Bradley's son showed up at the scene."

"So? What's he got to do with anything?"

"He moved away a few years after that miscreant brother of his got dispatched to hell, remember?"

"Yeah, I remember." The senator's voice betrayed his annoyance of the recollection. He grew silent and then asked, "You drinkin' already?"

Parker didn't answer. Instead, he downed the last of the bourbon in his glass, dribbling part of it down his chin as he stood and pulled the decanter from the credenza behind him.

"You're gonna pickle that liver of yours—if you ain't already. If that's all you wanted, I gotta go, Parker."

"He's been a homicide cop down in Atlanta."

"Who?"

"The Bradley boy. Stump was out front this morning, briefing me on what they found out at the killings. 'Bout that time, Bradley came out from the basement of the courthouse, where he must've been talking to Jake. Stump says the sheriff all but turned the investigation over to Bradley out there. He told me Jake treated that boy like the second coming."

"You're gettin' yourself all worked up over nothin'. I'll be back in Sweetgrass tonight, and we can drop by our good sheriff's office tomorrow morning for a chat. Those two being killed ain't no big deal, neither. Sounds like a drug deal gone bad, you ask me."

"There's one more thing," Parker said, slurring his words.

"What is it?" the senator asked, not hiding his exasperation. "Hurry up, boy, I gotta go vote."

"They found 'em around an old Studebaker. Just like—"

"That's enough said on this phone." The senator's tone became conciliatory. "I'll get to the bottom of what's going on. Ain't nothing I can't handle. I'll have some state boys contact Atlanta, too, check out Bradley. As for you, you need to do less drinking and more lawyering, or you'll find yourself worse off than those two did this morning."

# CHAPTER · 5

Buckra Geechee watched the two men in dark coveralls muscle the black body bags into the back of the blue panel van and slam the doors shut. Minutes earlier the wrecker from Turner's Body Shop had hoisted the Studebaker up onto its flatbed and driven away.

*Won't be long,* he thought. *Soon everyone will be gone from out here. All that will be left will be the rumors of what happened and speculation spreading through Sweetgrass like kudzu.* He smiled. *Just like Granny planned.*

The van's engine roared and backfired, dislodging a flock of white herons from their perches in the surrounding treetops. Buckra Geechee watched the frenzied flight and listened to the fluttering thunder as he mused about how some back in town would react when they learned of the carnage discovered near the ruins of the old church. They were the ones who knew the truth, and once they heard, they would begin to ask questions. Soon they would understand that he had come for them too.

The terror would follow. Fear would suffocate them, and finally retribution would be his. Granny Leech would be proud. She had waited so long for this day. He had too, patiently preparing to fulfill his destiny.

Still, he longed to return home, to take the johnboat out into the swamp among the cypress, to be near the creatures he understood. Order existed amid the brackish, muddy shallows and mangroves and teeming life-forms, some unchanged since prehistoric times. Back home, survival hinged on strength and cunning and respect. Betrayal did not exist in the world he loved.

Life in the truest sense began for Buckra Geechee just before he turned five. He did not remember the day his mother brought him to the swamp and left him at the shake cedar shanty with Granny Leech. All he knew was his mother never returned. Now, after all the years spent chasing deer and boar, watching the hawks and osprey and owls, communing with the lizards and snakes and gnarly old crocs, he knew he was better for being abandoned and didn't regret what had happened to him in the slightest.

The old woman with leathery, mahogany skin had nurtured him and given him his new name—Buckra Geechee—which, translated from Gullah speak, means *White Gullah*. She taught him to love and trust the animals and to respect the power of nature. She schooled him in the practice of hoodoo and instilled an everlasting belief in the power of the root. She warned him of the evils lurking outside their world and how, of all of God's creatures, man was the one not to be trusted. For Buckra, those living outside of the swamp came to be regarded as vile, far crueler than the most vindictive hag or plat-eye and far more dangerous than any creature he would encounter in the forest or wetlands.

So when she awoke him before dayclean—a term the old woman used to refer to the sunrise of a fresh new morning—and glared down on him with her sightless, milky-blue eyes, he knew the time had come to fulfill his destiny. He had been trained for this day since his rebirth in his new home, and he felt eager to take on his challenge. He had gathered the amulets and potions conjured for him by his foster mother, waited as she summoned the spirits who would protect him, and then he had set out to exact justice on those who for so long had avoided it.

He would give those who knew the truth time to learn of his presence, time to feed their fear—but not too much time. His next victim would further awaken their dread and signal their days on earth were coming to an end.

# C H A P T E R · 6

After Jed left home at eighteen, guilt rode his back like those ornery old hags he had heard stories about. He had set no goals, made no plans. Early on, an inner voice had pleaded with him to return home, but he joined the Army instead. He drank a lot during those years. He volunteered for posts in Texas, a long way from Sweetgrass, and served a short stint in Germany, even farther away. After four years he left the Army and joined the Atlanta police force, where he became immersed in his work. He stopped drinking and focused all of his energy on his job. He came to realize his investigative skills as intuitive, and he developed the dogged determination necessary for tracking down society's vermin. Instead of becoming an alcoholic, he became a workaholic. He never was sure which was worse.

In retrospect, he considered himself the antithesis of the Bible's prodigal son. He left home to seek his way in the world, but when he realized his mistake, he never returned to be welcomed back by his father. There had been no fatted calf, no feast. He stayed away wallowing in self-pity and did not return home until too late.

These thoughts cluttered Jed's mind as he turned onto his driveway after having spent the afternoon visiting the small community just outside Savannah, Georgia, where Sadie Dunlap once lived. Along the way, he had seen firsthand the power hoodoo held over the region.

Before making the short drive to Savannah, he had tried to locate the hunters who had stumbled onto the grisly scene near the cemetery. They weren't anywhere to be found. One's wife told him they had taken off in her husband's pickup truck toward Charleston, hoping to find potions to ward off the spirit they had angered when they stumbled across the two bodies. The woman, visibly shaken, clutched a wooden cross the entire time of Jed's visit. Clearly, her husband's trepidation over the morning's events had left her trembling and fearful of what evil curse might befall her household and family.

Later, in conversation with Sadie Dunlap's uncle, Jed had detected much the same reaction in the elderly man's expression when the mystical practice was mentioned. At first the uncle had remained aloof, not indicating much interest or sympathy in the fate of his niece. Jed took note of the girl's lack of family support, even though he knew that sort of thing was more common than not for drug addicts and prostitutes who had lived a life of homelessness.

"Choices," her uncle had told Jed. "She be the victim of bad choices. Some hers, some belonging to others."

According to the uncle, Sadie had been on her own since running away from an abusive father at age fourteen. She lived on the street, rarely coming around family except when she needed money. She'd show up, beg or steal what she needed, and then be gone again. The man told Jed he hadn't seen his niece in over a year.

"Her sister fared better," the old man had said.

"Where can I find her?" Jed asked. He hoped that if Sadie would have confided in anyone, it would have been her sister.

"Can't," he said, dipping his finger into a can of snuff and scooping a mound of the finely ground tobacco in between his lower lip and gum.

"Why not?"

"Cuz she be dead. Hung herself in her pappy's chicken coop when she was twelve. Sadie be who fount her hangin' there. That's when the girl set off on her own."

Jed had remained silent when he heard about the sister, not the least bit surprised. He had investigated the same outcome in Atlanta too many times in the past.

"Reckon she tired of her daddy comin' home drunk, climbin' in bed wit' her. That and the regular beatin' both girls took from him. You ask me, Sadie blamed herself for what happened to her sister."

Jed nodded. He didn't need to ask why. He knew the old man was probably right.

The man's eyes narrowed. "My brudder got hisself stabbed to death about a month later. Reckon God took care of what others wouldn't or couldn't. That's God's bidness, you know."

*God's business, indeed,* Jed thought to himself, recalling the old man's words as he pushed his Volvo's gearshift into park and stared out the windshield toward the house where he had grown up feeling safe. He looked around the yard, spotted a frayed rope hanging from a hickory tree beside his nearly dilapidated smokehouse. Once upon a time, those knotted hemp strands led up to the best tree house two boys could ever have wanted.

The now rotting platform sat perched between two broad limbs about eight feet off the ground. The four walls were gone, but not the memories forged there. More than just pieces of crudely nailed lumber, the simple structure had been a fortress for the brothers, a place to hide from chores, a refuge for transporting them anywhere their imaginations would take them.

Yearning for those days of innocence, Jed stepped from the car. Long gray shadows, the product of a sun sinking behind nearby loblolly pines, crept across the front lawn toward him. They reminded him of a scene from a movie where shadowy demons came growling to drag away the damned, and they seemed to be waiting for him, a prospect he didn't find altogether surprising.

He watched his breath race ahead as he lumbered across the sparse plugs of grass growing from sandy soil. His knees had stiffened from his travels, causing him to limp up onto the cinder-block steps leading to the front porch.

A crunching sound beneath his feet stopped him. When he looked down, he saw shards of glass. The faint odor of rotten eggs wafted past his nose.

Jed wheeled around, peered into the shadows, but saw no one. Upon closer inspection, he saw the yellowish powder coating the steps and realized what had happened. His home had been hexed.

He considered returning to his car to retrieve the gun he kept locked in the glove compartment, but instead he eased up onto the porch and jiggled the doorknob. The house was secure, just like he had left it.

He unlocked the door, stepped into the cold darkness of the front room, and flipped on the light switch just inside the doorway. The dim glow from a corner lamp revealed the roomful of furniture arranged just as it had been when his parents resided there.

Jed drew a breath, detected the scent of his father's pipe tobacco seeping from the walls and furnishings. The yellow and green afghan his mother had crocheted as she mourned for Bobby still draped the back of the sofa, and his father's Bible lay open to Psalm 11 beside the preacher's favorite chair, a black Naugahyde recliner. Jed remembered how his father had read that passage over and over again in the days following Bobby's death. Jed had read it too, that first night after moving back home.

Memories roamed this home like ghosts in a castle. He imagined being ten again, coming in through this very door to see his father look up from his reading to inquire as to whether or not he and Bobby had completed their chores. Jed thought about how the entire family would gather around the kitchen table for dinner; how he and Bobby returned there after helping their mother clean the dishes to listen to his father read Scripture. Following the nightly devotional, they all would join hands in prayer, then the two boys would be sent off to complete their homework before retiring to their room for the night.

Elijah Bradley believed in going to bed early and rising early, neither of which particularly suited Bobby or Jed, especially as they grew older. With a sigh, Jed longed for a whiff of his mother's perfume, the fragrant halo surrounding her as she leaned down to peck his cheek after tucking him in for the night. He wished he could tell them all how much he loved them, how much he missed them.

*Guilt makes for a lousy roommate,* he thought.

The chill in the house equaled the one in his soul. The furnace was still broken, and at last check none of the repairmen he had called more than a week earlier would be able to get to him for a couple more days.

With darkness blanketing the outdoors and a heavy weariness shrouding his tired body, Jed decided his father's idea of turning in early just might have some merit after all. As he undressed, he thought back to his visit with Sadie Dunlap's uncle, how the old man had reacted when asked about the signs of hoodoo found near her corpse.

The man's disregard for the fate of his niece left, along with his bravado, when Jed mentioned the red pouch. Fear replaced both in the uncle's demeanor as Jed described the rectangle of rocks and the dirt dug from Bobby's grave sprinkled over the bodies.

"Don't be talkin' 'bout none of that stuff," the old man had said. His lowered head shook back and forth to avoid making eye contact with Jed. "No, no, no. Don't need no hag ridin' me, and you best be careful she don't latch on to you neither." As he spoke, he retreated to his front door. "You keep talking 'bout it, she will. You'll see."

He didn't say anything else. Jed tried to ask him more questions, change the subject back to Sadie's acquaintances, but the old man had made it plain he was through with talking about hoodoo or anything else. Once the uncle had backed his way near the home's threshold, he whirled around and hurried into the small, tar-papered building, slamming the door shut behind him.

*Conversation over,* Jed remembered thinking. The power of the root, if there was such a thing, seemed to have cast a spell on his investigation.

On the drive home, he had encountered a similar reaction to questions about hoodoo when he stopped at a roadside general store for a MoonPie and an RC Cola, neither of which he had enjoyed for over thirty years. Inside the one-room store, the warm air reeked of stale vegetables. The three elderly black men sitting on makeshift stools of crates and barrels around a blackened potbelly stove had seemed friendly enough at first, but when Jed asked if they could help him locate a local root doctor, their hospitality chilled.

Only the sound of sizzling wood sap inside the old stove could be heard amid the silence. Everyone stared at him as if they had just encountered a leper.

"You better be goin'," the store clerk said after slapping Jed's change for his purchase onto the counter.

"I just—"

"I said you best be goin'." The second time he told Jed to leave, the man reached under the counter as if to seize a bat or gun or something even more threatening to punctuate his directive.

Jed didn't wait to see what it might be. He grabbed his change, the MoonPie, and RC Cola and hurried out the door, but before he got outside, one of the men hollered to the others.

"He liable to wake up wit' an old hag draped o'er him one night, her nasty skank skin be hangin' on his bedpost."

"That's so," another said. "Yes, sir, that be so."

"And she smother the life right out o' his body too."

Believer or not, as he readied for bed, the image of some old hag's skin hanging from his bedpost lingered. Jed flipped the bathroom light out after brushing his teeth, then he crawled under the covers and cut off the bedside lamp. He lay there with his eyes shut, feeling like a small child afraid the boogeyman might jump out of the closet.

At some point sleep came. His fitful dreams dredged up grotesque images of witches and goblins and apparitions drifting in the air. Police sirens wailed as squad cars raced to another park, to another tiny victim.

He awoke with a start. His phone's annoying peal shattered the quiet of the night.

Jed closed his eyes tight. He tried to ignore the shrill intrusion to his slumber, but the ringing continued until he slapped his hand on the receiver and snatched it from the cradle.

"Retribution for the sins of the father comes for the souls of the damned," said a weird voice he had heard before.

Jed's eyes popped open as he sat bolt upright in bed. "Where?" he asked.

"Plat-eye take her to join her kin," said the voice. "Their remorse brings justice, not retribution."

Somehow through his sleepy fog, Jed remembered Jake had told him that the plat-eye were the most vengeful of all the spirits. But what did that mean?

"Where is she?" he asked. Maybe this time, if they could find her in time, they might be able to save her.

"Those who find the first lead the way. Follow their path, and you find her too."

"Is she alive?"

The line went dead.

Jed threw back the covers, jumped from his bed, and grabbed his pants and shirt off the footboard. As he reached for his boots, he stopped with a start. Out of the corner of his eye he spotted a shadowy shape hanging from his bedpost.

He gasped.

His heart pounded in his throat as he eased his hand along the wall to the light switch, his eyes never leaving his discovery. He drew a deep breath to steady his trembling fingers and flipped the switch.

Much to his relief, the soft glow of the dresser lamp unfurled the mystery. Draped over the bedpost was his rumpled coat. He had flung it there as he undressed for bed.

Jed's heartbeat slowed, but his feeling of stupidity had hit an all-time high. *Damn hoodoo mumbo jumbo.*

At least no one else knew, or ever would, for that matter, he thought as he snatched the coat off of the bedpost. He pulled on his pants, knelt to tie his shoes, and finished dressing on the way to the car.

Thick gray fog engulfed the highway, reducing visibility to only a few feet in front of the Volvo as he sped out of the driveway and onto the blacktop, where he could at least use the reflective center line of the roadway as a guide. He decided to head into town, try to find Jake at his home. If the victim was still alive, he knew time was of the essence.

"Those who find the first lead the way." Jed repeated the caller's words, hoping he could better understand the riddle or message.

He punched Jake's home number into his cell phone. When he didn't hear it ringing, he looked at the display. A blinking symbol indicated his battery was drained. "Damn it," he said and tossed the phone onto the seat beside him.

*Think. What did the caller say? He did say "she," didn't he?* "Yes, I'm sure," Jed said aloud, pressing the accelerator.

"Those who find the first lead the way." Again, he repeated the words.

He remembered the caller had said something about following their path.

"Those . . . who . . . find . . . the . . . first." He spoke the words one by one.

*Could the caller be referring to the hunters? He had to be. Nothing else makes sense.*

Jed wheeled the car onto Winding Creek Road. *He has to be talking about the church grounds. Damn him. He's dumped his third victim there too.*

"Damn him!"

As Jed raced toward the ruins of his father's church, the fog lifted, as if preordained, to reveal a crystal clear sky. A full moon shone down to light the final miles.

Minutes later, Jed saw blue lights flashing on the horizon. *They know too. But how did they find out?*

# CHAPTER · 7

Lit by the Volvo's headlamps, Jake's brow furrowed when he turned and saw Jed's car pull in next to his. Behind him, the moon lit the field and cemetery like a spotlight shining on Act II of a deadly play.

"Another call?" the sheriff asked in a sour voice.

"Uh-huh," Jed said as he slammed his car door shut. "He said the victim was a girl, but you must've gotten a call too."

"Nope, a note. One of my deputies rode up on an abandoned car a mile or so down the road. Inside he found a note stuck to the windshield."

"What did it say?"

"Basically what your call did, I suspect. That we'd find another victim near the first two."

"Is she in the graveyard?" Jed asked, looking in that direction. He saw flashlight beams crisscrossing the field.

"Nope, ain't found her yet."

Jed reached back into his car and grabbed the small Stinger flashlight he had bought in Atlanta. "The caller said to follow the path of those who found the first." He zipped his jacket and pulled on gloves.

"What the hell's that supposed to mean?"

The beams from flashlights belonging to the deputies searching the field looked like glowing spirits rising from the nearby graves.

"I took it to mean the hunters," Jed said. "Mind if I join in on the search?"

"Might as well. You're here." Jake's invitation lacked enthusiasm.

Jed had to admit his showing up at the second crime scene in two days did look a bit suspicious.

"I'm still not clear on the connection to those hunters," Jake said as he started through the broomstraw toward the others.

Jed pointed to the dark tree line on the other side of the field. "If we don't find something near the cemetery, I suggest looking around the woods."

Jake shook his head. "You hit swamp less than a hundred feet or so in there.

It's thick with bramble and scrub trees. If she's there, we likely won't find her till dawn."

"That'll be too late."

Jake stopped, shone his light in Jed's face. "You sayin' she's still alive?"

"Don't know." Jed squinted. "I got the sense the killer had just left her when he called. If that's so, she might still be alive."

Jake's flashlight beam fell to the ground. He grunted, pulled a half-smoked cigar from his pocket, and lit it. After a few puffs he said, "I'm damn tired of finding bodies around your pappy's old church." Smoke rolled from his mouth as he spoke.

"I'm not thrilled about it either," Jed said. "By the way, you know a reporter named Hap Gentry?"

"Gentry?" Jake gave a look of uneasy puzzlement. "What about him?"

"What's he like?"

"An old opossum."

"Meaning?"

"He's very deceptive in appearance . . . and intelligence," the sheriff said.

"I never heard opossums were intelligent."

"Nope, but don't underestimate them."

"He sure is nosy . . . and well-informed. From what he told me, you would've thought he'd been out here yesterday morning when y'all found Sadie Dunlap. In my opinion, he knew a lot more than he should've."

Jake frowned. "Yeah, he has a way of finding out things you'd rather keep under wraps."

"It has to be a deputy," Jed said. "Who else knew?"

"The coroner, folks from the funeral home who carried off the body, maybe even them hunters. They all were out here at one time or another."

"I don't know," Jed said. His pulse raced. Keeping up with Jake's long strides had him at a near jog. "He knew about the mojo we found. The coroner wasn't out here when that was found. The hunters were already gone, too."

"Our coroner don't hang around murder scenes longer than he has too," Jake deadpanned. "Claims they make him nauseous."

Jed laughed. "A squeamish coroner. Go figure."

"He runs the tire recapping shop in town," Jake said. "He got elected coroner by default, didn't even want to run, but nobody else would. His daddy used to be coroner until he dropped dead of a heart attack, so I reckon he considered it a family tradition."

"A tire recapper? What the hell does he know about dead folks?"

"Nothing, and he's the first to admit it. Makes his obligatory appearance, takes a look at the corpse, declares it dead, and then leaves. That's about it, other than presiding over an inquest when one's needed, which don't happen often and don't require much when it does. The solicitor and I handle the rest."

"A tire recapper for coroner." Jed continued to chuckle at the thought. "Now, that's a curiosity." The two men walked on in silence before Jed asked, "Is Gentry from around here?"

"Yep, from over near Edisto. His daddy was a sharecropper, but Hap never took to working the dirt. He was the first in his family to graduate college—Charleston, I think."

"He knew about the hoodoo connection," Jed said. "And he didn't exactly dismiss his belief in the practice. I found his reaction interesting for a reporter."

"Not surprising. An aunt somewhere on a limb of his family tree is rumored to dabble in the root."

"Yeah? Now that *is* interesting."

"Supposedly she once put a hex on a landowner after he cheated Hap's pappy out of his wages. Next thing folks knew, the man takes a sudden turn to illness. Locals claim she put a hag to ridin' the poor schmuck near to death."

"And you believe the story?"

Jake shrugged. "Accordin' to what's told, the desperate man promised to make good on the wages, plus more, if the woman would lift the spell and drive the hag away. She agreed, and almost overnight he got better. The landowner was so grateful—and scared—he gave Hap's pappy a section of acreage for his own. Supposedly that's where the money came from to send Hap off to college."

"His aunt was . . . white?" Jed asked. "A white conjurer, like that sheriff?"

"Black," Jake said matter of fact. "Hap's not purebred." In typical lowcountry fashion, Jake's remark made blending the races sound like a discussion about breeding cows or maybe hunting dogs.

Jed thought back to his breakfast with the reporter at Joe and Dot's. "Can't tell by looking at him."

Jake stopped, looked into his friend's eyes. "That's the word round these parts. Won't swear to it, but I ain't got no reason to not believe it. Once somebody's tagged a conjurer, nobody dares to question them for fear they really might be."

Jed shook his head. "You're not jerking my chain are you, old friend?"

Jake grinned. "Now, would I do that?"

"I believe you would. Truly, I do believe you would."

Jake snorted, and then Stump walked up.

The stout deputy ignored Jed altogether. "No sign of anyone, Sheriff. That note might've been somebody's idea of a sick joke."

Jake looked around the field. "You run the registration to get a fix on the owner?"

"Car's registered to a Columbia address. We've contacted the PD there to verify ownership."

*Columbia*, Jed thought. "From what my caller said, I'd guess she's young. Maybe she's a college student."

Stump scowled. "Another call? Now ain't that just too damn convenient."

Jed glared at the deputy. "Anybody bother to check the woods?"

Stump looked toward the shadowy line of trees, shook his head. He turned his attention back to his sheriff. "Crocker's on the way to process the car. I told him we'd call if we found anything out here. We ain't."

Jake pulled the cigar stub from his mouth. "What about the woods? Anybody check there?"

Stump sighed. A look of exasperation colored his features. "Sheriff, you know as well as I do, that place ain't nothin' but swamp and bog. That and a healthy growth of grabby ol' briars." He glared at Jed. "Assumin' our victim's even in there, we ain't gonna find her tonight. Shit, you wouldn't be able to see your hand in front of your face."

Jake puffed on his cigar, stared intently toward the trees. "Jed, here, thinks she might still be alive. If that's so, we gotta go in to see."

"But—"

"Get all of the cars over there with their high beams on. We're gonna have us a look."

Stump groaned. "Son-of-a-bitchin', wild-ass goose chase if you ask me."

"Way I figure it," Jake said, cutting off his deputy's protest, "if the killer went to the trouble of leaving a note and callin' Jed, then he wants us to find her. I'm bettin' she ain't far inside that tree line."

"I'm with you," Jed said.

Stump muttered as he walked away toward the others.

Jake continued staring at the forest. "Come on," he said to Jed. "By the time the others drive over, we'll be there."

Four sheriff's patrol cars parked side by side along a path leading from the field into the woods. Their high beams and spotlights lit the area.

Deputies in a straight line, ten feet apart, stretched out on either side and marched toward the forest. Just as the searchers reached the edge and were about to step into the black morass, a harrowing howl froze everyone in their tracks.

Jed's narrowed gaze probed the darkness just beyond the trees. "What the hell?"

"Plat-eye's cry," said a black deputy to his left. The man's voice trembled. "They be warning us to stay out."

Jed looked toward the deputy, a giant of a man with biceps as big as melons.

His huge right hand clutched the grip of the revolver holstered on his side; fear flickered in his wide-eyed glare.

"You believe in spirits?" Jed asked.

Shock and incredulity sculpted the deputy's expression. "Don't you?"

Trying not to sound judgmental, Jed replied, "It's probably just a wild dog. Besides, it sounded pretty far off."

Jed's words had no sooner left his mouth when another heart-stopping howl bellowed. This one sounded closer.

"Coyote," Stump said. "He's just bayin' at the moon, warning the others we're here. At any rate, he's likely more scared of us than us of him."

"Ain't so sure 'bout that," the black deputy said, his words barely rising above a whisper.

"Coyotes in South Carolina?" Jed said to anybody listening.

"A while back we had some real intelligent folks decide coyotes would help control the deer population." Sarcasm rode Jake's words. "What they didn't count on was the coyote being damn near as prolific as the deer. Now instead of crops being eaten by deer, livestock and pets are being killed by the coyotes."

He took one last draw from his cigar, dropped it on the ground in front of him, and crushed it under his boot. "Come on, let's see if that girl's in there."

He stepped into the shadows, almost disappearing from sight. Jed and the others followed the sheriff into a world so dark, even their flashlight beams failed to illuminate much beyond ten feet or so. A short distance into the woods, Jed saw black water in front of him shimmering in the glow of his flashlight. "I've got swamp here," he said to the others.

"Me too," a deputy said.

"Same over here," another officer hollered.

"Over here!" a third deputy's voice raised an octave. "It's her."

Jed hurried to the lawman. Jake and the others joined him.

Sitting in the misty glow of the deputy's flashlight beam, a girl looked as if she might be asleep, sitting at the base of a spindly cypress tree. Her long brown hair draped her shoulders.

Jed knelt down and shined his light on the girl. She sat on a small island no more than five feet into the swamp. Her skin held a blue-gray tint, and he thought he could see a trickle of dried blood streaking her cheek from her temple. Her hands were positioned in her lap, and all of her clothes were in place. She even wore a heavy coat.

Jed looked over at Jake. "She's dead. I'll go over and confirm if you want. We'll need somebody to take pictures before we do much more, though."

"Trophies?" Stump's sarcastic remark came from the darkness behind Jake.

"Just get Crocker," the sheriff said in an irritated tone. He turned around to confront his deputy. "And call the state. See if they have anybody close by to help him collect evidence."

Jake walked up beside Jed. His flashlight swept across the inky swamp.

"If you'd rather one of your folks check her, that's fine," Jed said.

The sheriff's light stopped on a jut of ground that extended out into the water. "You might be able to step there and then over to her without getting wet," Jake said.

Jed nodded, stuck his slender flashlight in his back pocket. He planted his right foot on the soggy piece of soil, stepped onto a cypress stump sticking up from the black bog, and leaped to the tiny island, landing on a spongy patch of moss next to the girl. He moved his arms back and forth to steady his balance, and then turned to Jake and gave a thumbs-up.

A smoky mist rose from the water all around Jed. Behind the girl thick darkness lingered, and he couldn't help wondering what might be out there watching his every move. *Too late now,* he thought.

On the ground around the body, he looked for signs of anything the killer might have left. Seeing nothing, he knelt down and checked the girl's pulse. Her skin was cool to the touch but didn't feel as though the body temperature had dropped to that of the air. Jed detected no heartbeat. Her facial muscles felt taut, telling him she had been dead long enough for rigor mortis to begin setting in. He checked her fingers. The rigor hadn't reached them yet.

Experience told him rigor began sometime around two hours after death under normal conditions. But these weren't normal conditions. With the temperature hovering around freezing, the beginning of rigor mortis would take longer, and given the fact the stiffness hadn't reached her hands, he guessed she had been dead somewhere around four hours.

He thought about his phone call, how he had been led to believe she might still be alive if he hurried to find her. She was already dead. The bastard was playing him like an old fiddle, and Jed didn't like it a damn bit.

He pulled latex gloves from his pocket and traced the dried blood trickle he had seen earlier on the right side of her head. He shined his flashlight along the scalp line, parted her hair slightly, and spotted a gunshot wound in her temple. The entry wound was small with heavy charring surrounding it. In cases he had seen with charring this significant, the ripped skin left a star-shaped pattern, meaning the gun barrel would have been very close to the girl's head, if not completely against it, when it fired. Once the wound was cleaned, they would know for sure, but Jed had seen enough to recognize what in most cases turned out to be a suicide.

He checked the ground beside the girl, felt behind her and between her body and the tree. He checked under her coat and hands. No gun. He couldn't imagine how it could have fallen from her hand in a way that it would have bounced five or six feet into the swamp.

If this girl didn't choose to end her life out in this putrid smelling muck, someone else made that choice for her. But why stage it to look like a suicide and not leave the gun? In some unexplainable way, the killer wanted it to look like a suicide when anyone could see it wasn't.

Jed stared at the corpse. *Why?*

As with past investigations, Jed's thoughts drifted to the victim's last seconds. She must have been terrified beyond comprehension. Did she find peace or sheer terror, knowing death would likely come fast? For her sake, Jed hoped peace won out, but he wasn't so sure. Then another much more macabre thought came over him.

Her hands were folded on top of one another in her lap, just like Sadie Dunlap's in the Studebaker. Without running a residue test, he couldn't tell just by looking if the killer had made her hold the gun against her own head or if he had held it there himself. No doubt he would have controlled it even if she had held it, but did he make her pull the trigger? Let her—*make her*—choose the time? Jed let the sick scenario roll around inside his head. *What a bastard!*

He called back to Jake, who stood no more than fifteen feet away across the bog. "Single gunshot to the head."

"Suicide?" a deputy asked.

"No chance," Jed said. "Gun's gone. Besides, if that's what she had in mind, why leave her car a mile or so away and walk in this cold weather to a swamp to do it. That and the fact women rarely shoot themselves in the head. . . ."

As he stood, he noticed a ring of yellowish powder and knew instantly what it was. He touched one spot of the arc with his finger and brought it to his nose. "Dammit," he said as the stench invaded his nostrils.

"What is it?" Jake asked.

"Sulfur. A ring of it circles the body."

Jed took one last long glance around the girl, then maneuvered his way back across the stumps and submerged logs to drier ground. Somehow, he managed to navigate the obstacles without landing facedown in the smelly muck.

"What now?" Jake asked.

"Wait on your photographer and crime-scene guy, I guess." Jed looked back over at the girl. "Damn shame. From the looks of her, she was a beauty. I'd guess her to be twenty to twenty-two."

"According to a book bag found in her car, her name is Kristin Clay," Jake said. "And it looks like you were right about her being a local college student. We found several textbooks in her bag. Did you locate any other signs of hoodoo other than the sulfur?"

"Nope, so now I guess the $64,000 question is, why her and why make her death look like a suicide when it clearly wasn't?"

The sun was above the treetops in a cloudless sky by the time Jed walked out of the forest. He started toward the fallen steeple and piles of charred rubble, where every Sunday and most Wednesday nights of his childhood he came to hear his father supercharge the small congregation. Jed caught himself humming the hymn "This Is My Father's World" as he passed the cemetery where his family was buried.

He stopped momentarily beside the tilted fence and reflected on his last year at home. Everything he did and said back then had caused conflict. His father had been the powder keg and he the short fuse. Jed's mamma ignored both of them, self-exiled in her room away from the world that had robbed her of a son.

When he climbed into his Volvo and started toward the highway, Jed adjusted the knob on the radio, desperate to find just one jazz station among the plethora of rowdy rock and twangy country music offerings. He wanted to forget about the girl in the woods. He wanted to forget about Sadie Dunlap too. Back in Atlanta he had discovered that listening to the mellow tone of a saucy sax or soothing trumpet provided an escape when a case became too much a part of his psyche. He needed that escape now.

He found no jazz, and instead of forgetting, he remembered. He recalled every vivid detail of the past couple of mornings. Question after question marched through his mind like members of a precision drill team high-stepping down Main Street. Sharp, crisp, and succinct, they formed one after the other, and they demanded to be answered.

Why would a killer go to such elaborate means to stage a suicide, when a rank amateur could see the girl didn't kill herself? Why sprinkle sulfur powder around her body if you want everyone to believe she killed herself? Why not leave the gun, for heaven's sake? A person can't shoot themselves, alone, and the gun not be there.

Answers to none of those questions materialized on the drive back home, and as he slowed the car while passing Luther Rainey's farm—the last before the driveway leading to his house—he began to feel the heavy weight of fatigue and depression slumping over him.

But then, as he turned onto his drive, he saw a miracle in the form of a white van with JACK'S HEATING AND AIR CONDITIONING painted in red letters on the side. His prayers for warmth had been answered. *Hallelujah!* A man stood between the open doors at the rear of the van, gathering his tools.

Jed's pulse raced with excitement. He wanted to jump from his car and grab the man in a big bear hug, but he thought better of the idea. He calmed his exuberance so as not to appear completely idiotic, but the ear-to-ear grin displayed when he stepped from his car would not go away.

"You Jack?" Jed asked, bouncing around to the back of the van, his arm extended to give a welcoming handshake.

"Yep," the man said without turning around.

Jed dropped his hand and stepped closer. Left staring at the back of the stoop-shouldered guy in gray coveralls, he said, "Sure am glad to see you. Can I help you with anything?"

The man slung a hose with what looked like a pressure gauge over his shoulder and turned to face Jed. "Nope. Been backed up, what with the cold snap and all." He revealed a smile full of tobacco-stained teeth. The name JACK was scripted in the white oval over his right breast.

Jack wore an oil-stained, faded orange Clemson University baseball cap over his yellow-gray hair. He looked to be in his early sixties, and when he picked up his toolbox, a grimace appeared on his face.

Jed reached for the metal box to help. "Let me carry that—"

"I'm fine," Jack said in a hoarse voice as he swung the box back away from Jed's outreached hand. "Just show me your furnace."

A soothing breeze whisked against Jed's cheeks as he rocked on the front porch and listened to Jack clatter away under his house. The temperature had climbed steadily all morning. The forecast was for it to reach the mid-sixties, a welcome change from just a day or so earlier.

A lone squirrel skittered across the yard, carrying an oversized acorn wedged in its mouth. Jed watched, thinking about the games he had played with Bobby and others here. The squirrel showed little alarm at his presence as it arrived at the base of a nearby tall oak, where it paused to paw at the acorn before scurrying up the side.

Jed's mind drifted back to Atlanta and the phone call he had received delivering the news of his father's untimely passing. He thought about the old sheriff's refusal to do anything more with the investigation and how Jake, a deputy back then, had promised to call if anything turned up indicating the fire had started from means other than accidental. Jake never called, not that Jed really expected him to.

After Bobby died, Jed's father refused to talk about his older son's death. He attended the trial, but after the two men were convicted, he rarely spoke of Bobby or how he died again. At first Jed believed his father closed out the circumstances because his mamma grieved so openly for Bobby. But Jed wanted—needed—to talk about Bobby, to try to understand all that had happened. His father had refused, and the elder Bradley's silence, his seeming disregard for Bobby's memory, festered into anger for Jed. As a result, Jed and his father grew farther and farther apart, until they didn't speak at all. Then, after graduating from high school, Jed left home.

Over the years, with his own maturity, Jed came to realize that his father had coped with a son's death and the loss of a wife the best way he knew how. And now Jed regretted never trying to patch things up.

"She's working again."

The repairman's voice pulled Jed from his remorseful recollection, back to the present. He turned to see Jack walk around the corner of the house.

"You're gonna need to replace her before long, but I've patched her up for now. She's pretty old, you know."

Jed rocked to his feet and glanced at his watch. Several hours of daylight remained, and he felt the need to get away from the source of his melancholy memories.

"How much do I owe you?" he asked, walking down the steps to meet Jack.

"We'll bill you," the man said. "Wife handles that. I just do the repairs." Jack held out a clipboard with a receipt clipped to the surface. "Just your John Hancock showing I was here is all I need for now."

Jed signed the receipt and watched as Jack returned his tools to the van. "Thanks for coming out," he said. "I'll finally be able to walk around without wearing a coat."

Jack nodded as he slammed the doors to the van. "You look right haggard, pal. Were I you, I'd get in there and enjoy myself a nap."

"Might just do that," Jed said, although he knew sleep would have to wait.

As he watched the van drive out onto the highway, his thoughts returned to the girl found overnight in the woods. A nap would be nice, but learning more about why that poor thing ended up dead in a smelly old swamp would be better. He reasoned that if she had been a college student like Jake said, then she likely attended the only one nearby, the Sweetgrass campus of the University of South Carolina.

# C H A P T E R · 8

Palmettos, the state tree of South Carolina, stood like sentries along the road leading past brick columns onto the Sweetgrass campus of the University of South Carolina. A bevy of students, both men and women, played touch football on a grassy meadow near the roadway. Dozens of concrete benches, most empty, stood under the dipping and twisting broad limbs of moss-laden live oaks. A green hue, the beginning of new growth, shaded the smaller branches. Jed spotted a baseball field in the distance, a soccer field, and a few windows open on nearby red brick buildings. He remembered how his mamma used to freshen their home on those warm, late winter days by raising all of the windows.

Spring wouldn't be far away, he thought as he parked his Volvo in front of a sign that read REGISTRAR'S OFFICE. Having recharged his phone's battery while Jack repaired his furnace, he had tried calling Jake on his way to the school, but there had been no answer. He had no way of knowing whether Stump or the others had located friends or even family of Kristin Clay.

He glanced at his watch just before stepping out onto the sidewalk. He felt energized, despite his lack of sleep. Maybe it was the weather or just the feeling of knowing he could be the one to stop some maniacal killer. A break in a case rarely came out of the blue; it occurred because of good police work, interviewing witnesses, and asking the right questions. They were due for a break—he was due for a break—and maybe this would be the place to begin developing that all-important lead. He whistled as he walked to the door, pulled it open, and stepped inside.

A heavyset black woman stood behind a counter. She wore an African-style wrap with a matching headpiece of bright oranges, greens, and reds. Two large hoops, with half moons dangling inside, hung from her ears. A necklace of thin shells shaped like tiny bones hung around her neck. A few of the shells disappeared into a deep crevice of cleavage between massive breasts. She resembled what Jed imagined a modern-day, upscale hoodoo conjurer might look like.

The woman's smile was big, her eyes happy. Jed felt confident he could charm her as he swaggered up to the counter, his head high, chest puffed out, to explain why he had come to visit.

The woman winked and smiled even bigger than before. "May I help you?" she said in a lilting tone that sounded like the beginning of a love song.

Jed grinned. He tilted his head slightly and summoned his very best throaty, Barry White voice. "Yes, I think you can."

But when he told her what he wanted, her reply came with a crisp staccato flare. Her broad smile held. "Already gave that information to the sheriff's deputy earlier this morning," she said.

Jed coughed a Barry White cough and cleared his throat. He returned her luminescent cheeriness as he leaned across the counter on folded arms and stared into her big brown eyes. He even fluttered his lashes. "Can't you show it to me too," he said, continuing to use the deep, throaty voice.

Her round happy eyes locked on Jed's. She didn't blink, didn't look away, and her voice grew as stern as her smile was big. "You a deputy?"

Jed straightened, felt as if a trapdoor had opened in his stomach. "Uh . . . no, but—"

"Can't give it to you," she said in a firm voice with no hint of contrition. She picked up a stack of papers and tapped their edges firmly on the counter. The gesture affixed an exclamation point to the finality of her denial.

Through it all, the woman's now-demonic smile never faded. Jed locked onto the full-moon eyes. He would have bet good money that behind her congenial expression, she was having a knee-slapping good time at his expense.

She reminded him of Annie, a tomboy who had lived the next farm over from his grandfather. Whenever they played together, Annie could always run faster, climb higher, and hit a ball harder than Jed. She even made better grades in school, which was not all that great of an accomplishment. But the thing that bugged him the most about Annie was *the look,* the way it always appeared after she bested him in some endeavor.

The registrar staring at Jed from the other side of that counter wore *the look,* just like Annie. She made him angry, which meant she controlled him, and he hated her for it.

Without another word, he spun around and started for the door. That's when she hit him with the unexpected. "The deputy this mornin' told me not to give out any information about Kristin Clay to anyone except a deputy sheriff with proper identification."

Jed suspected the woman contributed that little tidbit to rub salt into the wound she had carved into his ego. The muscles in his face tightened.

*Stump, you asshole.*

Jed yanked open the door leading outside and stepped into a welcome pool of sunshine. So far this investigation was going no better than the one he had left behind in Atlanta. He squinted across the campus as he pondered his next move.

"Hi," a perky voice said.

The pleasant greeting from a young girl approaching the steps to the administration building with two other students grabbed his attention. He returned the greeting, thinking the presence of this friendly trio in this place at this particular time could only be providential.

"Say, do either of you know Kristin Clay?" Jed asked.

The girl who initially spoke shook her head. "I don't think so." She looked at the boy accompanying her, then at the other girl.

The boy asked, "Is she the one I heard about? The one they found dead this morning?"

Hope reclaimed Jed's psyche. "That's her," he said, mildly surprised word had traveled so fast. "Do you know her?"

"I knew her from class," the second girl said in a quiet, mournful voice. "I didn't know she'd been found dead, though." She looked at the boy. "Geez, that sucks."

"Do you know where she lived?" Jed asked.

The girl glanced at the boy as if uncertain she should answer.

He returned her concerned look with a shrug and said, "I didn't know her that well."

"I don't think I know her at all," the first girl said.

The second girl nodded. "Yes, you do. She's . . . she *was* Ginger's roommate."

All three looked at one another. The first girl squinted as she glanced back at Jed. "Oh . . . my . . . gosh!" she said. "That totally sucks."

"Then you do know her?" Jed asked hopefully.

"Absolutely. Well, I don't really know her. Not like I know that much about her. I know Ginger."

"Do you know where she lived? And Ginger, is that her roommate's name?"

"I can't believe that's who you're talking about." She stared straight at Jed, shock masking her face. "She was quiet; didn't hang out much. They live . . . she lived in the Marsh View Apartments, just down the road. And yes, Ginger's her . . . was her roommate."

"What's Ginger's last name?" Jed pulled his notepad from his shirt pocket.

"Lane, Ginger Lane," the girl said, shaking her head. "Do you know what happened to her roommate?"

"Not exactly," Jed said. "We're working on it." He stuffed the pad back inside his pocket, thanked the trio for their help, and hurried down the short flight of steps.

*Finally something productive,* he thought. He knew so soon after the murder of her roommate, Ginger Lane would be distraught. Even if that asshole, Stump, hadn't gotten to her first like he had the registrar, she still might not be very willing to talk. Interviewing those left behind after a violent death of a friend or loved one was often difficult. He knew he would have to proceed slowly with his questions. On the other hand, with a little luck, she might be angry enough to postpone her mourning and want to talk about anything and everything that might help catch her friend's killer. Jed usually encountered one of two extremes when trying to interview friends and family of victims so soon after a crime had been committed—either stone silence brought on by the shock of what had occurred or effervescent talkativeness fueled by anger and the urge to avenge the loved one's death. Either way, he hoped Ginger knew something that might lead him a step closer to finding out who had turned his life upside down and why they chose to include his brother in their chaos.

"Sure, I know both of them," a helpful blond-haired guy washing his car said after Jed inquired about the roommates and displayed his Atlanta Police ID with RETIRED stamped in red letters across the front. "They live in the next building, the apartment with a red door."

"Have you seen Ginger today?"

"Not today, man." The boy's somber expression told Jed the news about the death of one of his neighbors had already reached him. "Kristin was a real cool girl, you know. Heard someone may have killed her, and that really blows. Hope they catch the bastard."

"How well did you know her?" Jed asked, fishing for any information he could.

Wearing a pair of jeans with ragged cuffs and a black Grateful Dead T-shirt with a purple picture of Jerry Garcia on the front, the boy shrugged his shoulders. "I knew her. . . . We chilled some with others as a group, but we didn't date or nothin' like that, if that's what you mean. She was straight, man, straight as an arrow."

"She have any boyfriends?"

The boy tossed a sponge into a bucket of soapy water. "Don't think so," he said after giving the question some thought. "Not from around here, at any rate."

Jed turned to leave but stopped after thinking about the boy's responses. "What do you mean when you say she was straight?"

"You know," he said, motioning his hands in circles. I never knew her to do any drugs, that sort of thing. She didn't really go in for the party scene, either. She was just straight up, a good person."

"When was the last time you saw her?"

"Couple of days ago, I guess. We crossed paths on campus and spoke. Kind of creeps you out to know that was the last time you saw somebody you knew alive and everything seemed okay. Then boom, they're dead. You know what I'm sayin'?"

"Yeah," Jed said, "I do."

He thanked the helpful student and walked across the parking lot to the door the boy had pointed out. The lack of cars parked out front hinted no one would be at home. He knocked anyway. No one answered.

Jed visited several nearby apartments, all with little to no results. One girl eyed him through a crack in her partially opened door, but she told him she didn't know anything about Kristin Clay. She knew about Kristin's death, though. Jed could see it in the terrified way she acted when she first peeped out and saw a stranger standing at her front door. He figured the news of Kristin's death had spread through the campus community like a highly contagious disease. Fear and concern masked the face of nearly everyone, so he chose not to push the scared girl for answers.

By the time he decided to leave, the sky looked like a painter's canvas. The sinking sun shot streaks of pink, red, and blue across the treetops. A yawn leaked from his mouth, reminding him that he couldn't go like he used to. Fatigue from activities the previous nights had sapped his energy. He could feel the strain in his back and shoulders and knew he had to get some rest before continuing.

Thoughts of the murders continued to swirl inside his head as he drove home. He couldn't figure the link between a homeless drug addict, a mechanic, who by all accounts didn't do drugs or pick up prostitutes, and a well-liked college student, a straight one, as she had been described. No drugs, little partying—the two girls were polar opposites—and the Lassiter kid did not fit any victim profile.

Other than the phone calls he had received before each was found, nothing connected the two crimes except the gunshot wounds. He tried Jake's cell phone. No answer.

A brilliant orange glow lit up the sky beyond Luther Rainey's farm. Jed's fingers squeezed the steering wheel. He saw a plume of smoke coming from where his driveway connected to the two-lane blacktop. A sickening wave of nausea flooded his gut.

When the dirt drive came into view, so did fire trucks and sheriff's cars and flames licking the tops of nearby loblolly pines. Where his childhood home had stood just hours earlier, he now saw only smoldering rubble. Even his mailbox post was snapped into two charred halves. Pieces of smoking lumber lay alongside the highway, and blackened bricks from his chimney were scattered along the roadside ditch. Jed stopped his Volvo, pushed the gearshift into park, and sat staring in disbelief.

# CHAPTER · 9

Jake met Jed halfway up his driveway. Black smudges covered the tall man's solemn face as he wrapped his long arm around his old friend's back and clasped his shoulder in his hand.

"Jedediah, I'm as sorry as I can be." His voice was a lifeless monotone.

Jed heard him, but the words didn't register. He stared straight ahead, blinded by spotlights, the red and blue strobes flashing from the trucks and cars parked all over his front yard. The front steps, the cinder blocks cemented together, led to nowhere now. He spotted the old wood stove that once stood beside his father's chair. It looked like a charred and crumpled beer can, tossed on its side in front of what used to be the fireplace. The smell of wet charcoal filled the air as ghostly wisps of smoke curled up out of the blackened ruins. He saw dark lumps where chairs and sofas once sat and blackened remnants of picture frames and lamps. Nothing was left.

Jed stared at the simmering shell of his homeplace. "What the hell happened?" he asked.

Jake didn't sugarcoat his theory. "No thinkin' about it," he said. "Somebody blew up your house."

The words bounced off Jed like rubber balls hitting a hard surface. "I never lit the stove in the kitchen. The furnace—" The repairman's ruddy, wrinkled face, the yellowed teeth of Jack's grin suddenly appeared sinister in Jed's mind's eye. "Son of a bitch." The whispered expletive went unheard by Jake.

"This weren't no accident, Jedediah. Somebody blew up your house."

Jed thought back to how he had sat passively on his front porch, rocking, reminiscing, as the gray-haired bastard went about planting a bomb in his home's narrow crawl space. The repairman's last words echoed in Jed's head: *Were I you, I'd get in there and enjoy myself a nap.*

"You know a furnace repairman named Jack?" Jed asked.

Jake's forehead furrowed. "Jack? No, can't say as how I do." He eyed Jed suspiciously. "Why?"

"'Cause some bastard driving a van marked with Jack's Heating and Air Conditioning showed up this morning to fix my furnace."

The sheriff's Adam's apple bobbed up and down. His eye began to twitch. "Describe him."

"White, sixtyish, weathered looking. He walked stoop-shouldered and seemed friendly enough." Jed shook his head, chuckled. "I should've known somethin' was up when he wouldn't let me help him carry his toolbox."

Jake slid his boot back and forth on the loose gravel in the driveway. "Reckon you oughta know. A call came in sometime midafternoon, said, 'Tell that nigger cop to mind his own business or he'll become a good nigger.'"

Acid bubbled in the pit of Jed's stomach. "Now ain't that shit. Those calls taped?"

"Yep. I had 'em pull a copy, but I ain't had time to listen to it yet."

Jed wandered back down the drive and looked out across the highway at the dark and barren field beyond. Tobacco once grew there, tobacco so tall and thick a person could hardly walk between the stalks. His grandfather had lived on the other side of that field, and Jed recalled a late-night visit from his grandpa when he was seven.

His grandfather's pounding on their front door had awakened him, and when he came out from his bedroom, he saw his father standing in the open doorway talking to his grandfather. The old man was more animated that night than Jed had ever seen him. Rivulets of sweat rolled down his weathered, acorn-colored face. His big hands trembled, and for the first time in Jed's young life, he saw fear in his grandfather's eyes.

He talked of trouble at a friend's house, and as Jed crept close, he heard how Klansmen wearing robes and riding horses had set the home of his grandfather's friend on fire. "Just because they claimed he stole a chicken to feed his family," his grandfather had said.

The elderly man's voice shook as he recounted how the Klan shot the man's mule and tied the suspected chicken thief behind one of their horses. He told how the night riders had dragged the farmer off into the woods, where his wife found him beaten near to death a short time later. She had come to Jed's grandfather for help.

After listening by the door for several minutes, Jed boldly walked out onto the porch and saw the glow in the distant sky. Mesmerized by what he saw and heard, he feared his father would strike out against the Klansmen, but he watched with surprise as the two men dropped to their knees in prayer.

Jed recalled that prayer and the lessons he had learned from those two men of peace. Then he kicked a smoldering piece of wood across his driveway.

*That was then and this is now,* he thought. And what he wanted most right now was five minutes with the son of a bitch who blew up his house. Forgiveness wasn't even close to what he contemplated.

"Dammit, Jake. This ain't the '50s. What's this all about?"

"We're working on it," Jake said. "I've called in the state arson boys. They'll be here in the morning." The bleary-eyed sheriff rubbed his rusty-red beard stubble. "You've made enemies over the years."

"Not from around here, I ain't." Jed's teeth ground together when he saw Stump sifting through the rubble. "What the hell is that bastard doin' here?" He stepped around Jake, planning to extricate the oversized deputy from his property.

Jake's hand clamped Jed's shoulder. "Hold on, now. I know you're upset, but he's just doin' his job."

Stump glanced over his shoulder, sneered as if he heard the exchange.

Jed glowered back. "I wouldn't put something like this past him and his bigoted friends," he said.

Jake pulled a handkerchief from his back pocket, wiped the soot off his hands. His eye twitched harder. "Come on over to the car. I want you to write down everything you remember about this Jack fellow."

Opening the door to his car, Jake said, "You're welcome to stay at my place until you find something else." He paused and both men knew why. "That is, if you want to."

Jed didn't respond.

Jake handed Jed a legal pad and pen and then walked away toward the county fire marshal. Volunteer firemen sprayed streams of water onto the last of the hot spots.

In all their years fishing and hunting and just hanging out doing what boys did to wile away the time, Jed had visited Jake's house only once. Both were around sixteen or seventeen at the time, and Bobby had already been killed.

Over his entire lifetime, the only person Jed considered more of a friend than Jake was Bobby. And yet, that one visit to Jake's modest home very nearly unraveled the bond the two had developed.

Before they arrived that afternoon, Jake had tried to talk Jed into going on ahead to the fishing hole they were planning on trying out for the first time. Jed had insisted they go to Jake's house first. He had heard the rumors that Jake's father belonged to the local Klan, and knowing Jake, he found the association hard to believe. Still, if the rumors were true, Jed found the prospect of coming face-to-face with Jake's father in the Klansman's own house an idealistic opportunity. He planned on winning over the elder Armistead. *After all,* he recalled thinking at the time, *what could happen?*

As it turned out, no one had been home when they arrived, and the relief on

Jake's face was evident. The house was about the same size as Jed's, and looking at it from the outside, one could see a lot of similarities. Both were modest in size and whitewashed. Both had small porches and postage-sized yards. An old smokehouse even sat behind Jake's home, just like the one in back of Jed's. Once inside, however, the similarities ended with a diverse cultural abruptness.

Jake's great-great grandfather, Confederate General Eustace Armistead, had fought in the Civil War, and inside Jake's house memorabilia from that conflict held prominent status. Pictures of Robert E. Lee and Stonewall Jackson hung on either side of General Armistead in the living room, and as the teenage Jed walked through, he felt as if their eyes followed his every move. Old pistols were displayed on the fireplace mantel, and an officer's saber hung over a doorway. Uniform buttons and patches representing various detachments of the Confederate States Army were displayed under a glass-covered table. And of course there were the pictures of Jake and his father, donned in the regalia of their reenactment uniforms. The home reminded Jed of a museum he had visited with his parents on a day trip to Savannah.

Those artifacts and photos were out for everyone to see, but others, ones meant only for the eyes of close friends, proved to be the most disturbing for Jed. While waiting on Jake to change clothes and grab his fishing gear on that long ago afternoon, Jed opened an album he mistook for a photo collection of Jake's family. The scrapbook had nothing to do with kinfolk, at least not Jake's. To his shock and surprise, Jed found himself flipping through page after page of faded and cracked photos of black men being whipped and of them hanging from thick live oak branches, their necks stretched unnaturally. The young teen gawked at pictures of slave auctions, of black men and women, even children, being herded past well-dressed white men who had come to purchase them like livestock.

When Jake came back into the room that afternoon and saw what Jed had discovered, the future sheriff's face flushed. Visibly shaken and embarrassed, he snatched the book from Jed's hands, slammed it shut, and slid it into a drawer. He didn't offer an apology or explanation other than "Somebody must have left the book out by mistake."

After Jake had closed the drawer, the two youths left the house together, but they didn't go fishing as planned. Jed went home, and, at the time, he had cared little where his longtime friend departed to.

Several days passed before Jake stopped him in the school hallway. "Just to chew the fat," the lanky redhead had said. His greeting came with a hint of shame instead of the customary toothy grin.

Their friendship resumed, but neither ever spoke of the album again, and Jed never returned to Jake's home.

Jed knew he couldn't this night, either.

"Jedediah," Jake hollered, breaking the spell the past held on Jed's thoughts. "Take a look at this."

Jed walked over to the sheriff and fire marshal, who both stared down at the cinder block steps leading nowhere.

Jake asked, "What do you make of this?"

Jed glanced at the shards of glass. "I saw it before, after I came home from your office. There was a hint of sulfur at the time, and I figured someone decided to toss a hoodoo spell in my direction. I planned on cleaning it up, just never did."

"Might explain the fire," the fire marshal said.

Jed looked at Jake.

"Might have some connection," the sheriff said.

Jed looked down at the wet glass glistening in the glow of the fire marshal's flashlight, then back up at the two men. "Evil spirits didn't burn down this house, just like they didn't kill that boy and those two girls."

"I'm not suggesting they did," Jake said with an edge to his tone. "I'm just saying there might be a connection. Whoever busted this glass on your steps may have killed them kids, and he might have even hedged his hexing with an incendiary device."

Jed shook his head, felt grief growing like cancer. "I'll be staying in town tonight. I appreciate your offer, Jake, but I need some time to myself."

Jake nodded. His eyes held a wounded look, and he smiled apologetically as Jed turned and walked away. Jed knew his old friend understood the reason. That was why he hadn't questioned the decision.

Jed found new living quarters in an efficiency apartment at the Wayfarer Motor Lodge located only a couple of blocks from the Indigo County Courthouse. Small and cramped, the room with a kitchenette reeked of disinfectant cleanser, so he left the door open in hopes the cool night air would cut the pungent aroma before bedtime.

Not overly fond of motels, and always weary of sleeping where someone else may have slept the night before, Jed pulled back the covers to inspect the sheets and pillowcases. They looked fresh. He checked the kitchenette and then grabbed his toothbrush and toothpaste, both purchased on the way at a convenience store near the interstate. The sign in the store's window read OPEN 24 HOURS A DAY. An invitation to be robbed, Jed had thought as he browsed the shelves in search of his hygiene products.

The smell of the disinfectant hung heavier in the bathroom than it did in the front room, but Jed considered this a good sign. While brushing his teeth, he pulled back the curtain that concealed the combination tub and shower. The floor of the tub appeared clean enough to stand on, and that was all that mattered. He finished brushing, rinsed his mouth out with a plastic cup on the sink, and began unbuttoning his shirt as he walked back into the room.

Only three steps out of the bathroom, Jed stopped short. He sighed. An unwelcome figure stood in the doorway.

# CHAPTER · 10

"Stopped by what's left of your homeplace," Hap Gentry said. Wearing a wrinkled jacket over a stained white shirt, the slovenly attired man leaned against the doorframe with his hands wedged into the back pockets of his faded jeans. "Some of the folks at the sheriff's office said I'd find you here. What they're sayin' suggests somebody don't care much for you. A couple even thought it might be in your best interest to go back to Atlanta."

"That was real nice of them. It's comforting to hear they're so concerned. Now let me guess who *they* might have been."

"You think you've been a victim of a hate crime? We haven't had one of those around these parts in years."

Jed chose not to answer, yawning instead, hoping the reporter would take the hint. He didn't.

"I asked the sheriff about that possibility, but he wouldn't comment," Gentry said.

"And I won't either. Suffice it to say that if the fire was intentionally set, then whoever did it didn't exactly love me."

Gentry stepped into the room, glanced around. "Nice place. Clean looking." He sniffed the air. "Even smells clean."

"Yeah, it's a real gem." Jed looked at his watch. "Now, if you don't have anything else, I've had a long day and need some sleep."

Gentry walked to the bedside table. He slid open the drawer. "Wouldn't you love to be the owner of the company printing all of these Bibles for motels? Talk about a niche market." He turned and stared. "Do you think there's a chance that girl last night committed suicide?"

"Ask your source inside the sheriff's office." Jed yawned again for emphasis.

"Did that already. They say she was murdered."

"Then why ask me?"

"They seem suspicious of your coincidental calls, the ones telling you where to find the bodies."

"Do *they* now."

"I get the impression the sheriff doesn't share their suspicions," Gentry said. "Not yet, at any rate."

"That's good to hear." Instead of insisting he leave, which Jed realized was a mistake, he joined in the reporter's game of Twenty Questions. "What about you? Do you share their suspicions?"

Gentry gave a sly grin. "I think the calls are curious, but at this point I'm not jumping to any conclusions."

"Objective reporting?" Jed motioned toward the open door. "It really is late."

This time Gentry started out, but he stopped in the doorway. "The girl's roommate is due back tomorrow, but I hear she won't be around long. Her parents don't want her staying by herself, especially if a murderer is loose."

"How do you know this?"

Gentry shrugged. "I just listen when people talk. If you keep your ears open and listen, you hear all sorts of things." He stepped outside and turned just before Jed closed the door. "One other thing," he said.

"And that is?"

"Sadie Dunlap's grandfather works over at Rifkin's Grocery. You might want to pay him a visit."

"Yeah, how come?" Jed said. "An uncle already filled me in on her past."

"You'll understand when you get there," the reporter said, throwing his hand up. A sly smile appeared. "See you around, I'm sure."

"I'm sure," Jed said just before slamming the door.

Sometime after midnight, restless sleep conquered Jed's sudden onslaught of insomnia. In his dream the Studebaker chased him around the cemetery, and then he was chasing the killer but couldn't catch up to him. The demon, dressed in a Ku Klux Klan robe and speaking nonsensically in the Gullah dialect, led him past Bobby's grave, through the swamp where they had found the second girl, and back to the courthouse lawn. Jake was there, watching the pursuit, but didn't offer to help.

Then the killer stopped. He whirled around to face Jed, and the face Jed saw was his own. Hap Gentry appeared, laughing, walking toward Jed with handcuffs. Then, just as Gentry reached to grab him, a car horn blew. Jed awoke with a start.

He lay in the bed with his eyes closed, unsure if he was really awake or not and afraid if he opened them he would see Gentry slap the handcuffs on his wrists. He felt his thoughts drift, his senses numb. Once again, a welcome cocoon of silence began to wrap around him, but before he could drift into the restful slumber he craved, someone called his name.

"Hey, Jed!"

Jed's eyes popped open. He picked at objects in the darkness and for the briefest of moments didn't know where he was.

"Jed."

The second call caused him to sit bolt upright in bed. He was sure he had heard someone call his name. Slivers of light slipped past the edges of the thick curtain drawn across his window and crept across the foot of his bed.

*Did someone call me?* He doubted his hearing. The voice had sounded distant, almost surreal.

Jed pushed the covers off and slid his feet onto the floor. Leaning forward, he parted the curtain and looked out. A single vapor lamp on a pole out near the street combined with moonlight to cast a soft glow over the parking lot.

His black Volvo sat all alone in front of the door leading into his room. His sleepy gaze roamed the remainder of the empty asphalt. *Someone called.* He was almost positive he had not been dreaming. Almost.

He squinted into the eerie night. Just before giving in to his fatigue, he spotted a light brown dog sitting under a red and green neon arrow at the entrance to the motel. Jed stared in disbelief. The dog looked just like the one he and Bobby had rescued from a sandbar at low tide years earlier. He recalled how they had taken that malnourished mutt home and fed him. Afterward, the dog must have realized he was on to a good thing, because he stayed. He took up residence on their back porch, and Bobby named him Rascal.

*That was almost forty years ago,* Jed thought. *No way could this dog be Rascal. No . . . way.*

Bobby loved that dog. He named him after the "Little Rascals" television show, and he never went anywhere without Rascal . . . except. . . .

After Sheriff Renfrow had left their house the night he delivered the news about Bobby's death, Rascal began to howl. Jed had never heard a more mournful sound from an animal, not before Bobby died, not since then either. That pup didn't stop until Jed went out onto the back porch and slept curled up beside him. The fact that Rascal actually knew Bobby would not be coming home to play fetch or go on long hikes in the woods still puzzled Jed. *How do animals know these things?*

Jed opened the door and stepped out into the flickering glow of the vapor lamp. The dog was gone.

He walked to the edge of the motel and back. He even knelt down and peeked under his car. No dog.

Jed whistled the way Bobby had taught him, with the tips of two fingers positioned under his tongue. Rascal always came when Bobby whistled, so maybe this dog would come too.

Jed trained his eyes on the void just beyond the light, looked for any signs of movement, but saw none. He whistled again and listened for the dog to respond, but he didn't see any sign of him.

Perplexed at the dog's presence and then its sudden disappearance, Jed sighed and gave one last sweeping glance across the lot and roadway. Nothing. No sign of the dog or any other living creature, for that matter. Jed rolled his shoulders and returned to his room, closing the door behind him.

Too wired to sleep, he grabbed the television remote and mounded the pillows against the headboard. A mournful baying came just as his head nestled into the soft cradle he had formed. This time it sounded like it was coming from right outside his window. He jumped to his feet, raced to the door, and jerked it open.

The dog sat at the rear of his Volvo, its head cocked sideways. Big, eager eyes looked straight at Jed as if to ask, *What's all the fuss?*

When he saw Jed, the dog tilted its head back, its snout pointed to the heavens, and bayed again. The mournful sound was unmistakable, and this canine was a dead ringer for Rascal. *Impossible,* Jed thought.

The animal's head dropped. It looked back at Jed and barked. Then it loped off toward the roadway. Jed recalled how Rascal had acted the same way when he wanted Bobby or him to follow him to a new discovery.

At the edge of the parking lot, the dog turned back and barked again. Jed remained in the doorway, unsure what to do next.

The dog loped toward Jed, then turned and ran back. It howled one more time and bolted down the side of the highway.

Jed rushed back inside, grabbed his car keys off the dresser, slid into his jeans, and slipped his bare feet into a pair of loafers. By the time he got to his car, the dog was nowhere to be seen.

*I must be crazy,* Jed thought as he slid the key into the ignition. *Why am I following this animal?*

The answer, if there was one, hadn't materialized by the time the Volvo's front wheels rolled onto the two-lane road. He looked for the dog, but it had vanished. Nowhere on either side of the roadway did he see the animal.

He looked up at the starry sky. "I didn't imagine him . . . did I?" Jed asked.

Up ahead he thought he caught a glimpse of a dark shape darting across a ditch. His pulse throbbed in his neck. His foot mashed the gas pedal. He drove faster than he knew he should, catching periodic glimpses of what he thought might be the dog alongside the road ahead of him. Regardless of the car's speed, he couldn't catch the elusive animal. Finally, he eased off of the accelerator.

The car slowed to a stop in the middle of the roadway. Jed saw no sign of the dog, not even an old opossum, a regular nocturnal visitor to lowcountry roadways.

By the time Jed decided to give up on the teasing tricks the night had played on his eyesight, he realized where the phantom dog had lured him. He blew out a deep breath of air and resigned himself to the fact that he needed to play this prelude to madness all the way to the end.

He drove off the asphalt onto the sandy, weed-filled drive and pulled his car next to the ruins of his father's church. After shoving the gearshift into park, he killed the engine and lights and sat staring out across the moonlit field, waiting to see if the dog would materialize once again and beckon him to follow him off into something akin to the Twilight Zone.

Several minutes passed without his seeing anything but wisps of gauzy clouds sidling between the moon and earth. He rolled down his window and whistled. He waited, his eyes trained on the dark field. He saw nothing, heard nothing except the whispering rustle of the broomstraw swaying in a stiff breeze coming straight off the Atlantic Ocean. Not one to give up easily on the unexplainable, even reincarnations of former pets, Jed once again let loose with a shrill whistle and once again listened as only silence surrounded him. If the dog did come this far—that is if Jed had not imagined the creature—it wasn't responding to his call.

The next thing Jed realized, he was climbing from the inside of his car and stepping out to meet whatever unseen force compelled him to this place of memories—both good and bad.

*This is nuts.*

The thought played over and over in his head like a stuck record. Stepping over a discarded strip of yellow crime-scene tape left to slither like a serpent guarding the gates of hell, he headed toward the broken-down fence surrounding the cemetery.

Jed knew he was no hero, and despite having spent most of his life as a cop, he considered himself a pretty big chicken when it came to things that go bump in the night. He even refused to watch horror movies, especially those geared toward having something jump out at the unsuspecting hero or heroine at the most inopportune time. And yet here he was, walking toward a graveyard, through a field lit only by moonlight, hearing nothing except the rustling of the broomstraw. Sure insanity had already overtaken his feeble mind, he half expected to hear the hooting of a nearby owl, Hollywood's telltale sign of impending doom.

Before he could cross the field, the wind kicked up, the temperature dropped, and a thicker, gauzier cloud crossed the moon. Visibility decreased. With only a T-shirt covering his chest, he crossed his arms for warmth and regretted his hurried exit from the motel without giving thought to bringing along a jacket. Of course, he had not planned on going for a walk in some netherworld at the time.

All he had set out to do was to find a dog and to disprove any crazy notion he possessed that the animal could somehow be Rascal reincarnated after all these years.

Approaching the fallen gate to the cemetery, he stopped. *What in the hell do I expect to find?* Clearly the dog was not around. Now he couldn't see more than ten feet ahead, and he was starting to tremble from the cold seeping into his bones. He blew warm air into his hands, realized the effects of the past two days were beginning to work on his mental state in ways that worried him.

Without warning, the wind began to wail. The clouds covering the moon thickened. Jed and the field became enveloped in an even deeper darkness.

In that instant he thought he detected a shape move through the opening leading from the cemetery. He rocked back on his heels, sucked a deep breath of cold air into his desert-dry mouth. His eyelids blinked, narrowed into slits to allow his lenses to grab a sharper focus. Shadows in front of him came to life, dancing and rushing around. Whispered voices rode the wind.

He wanted to turn and run, but he didn't. He wasn't even sure he could. His legs felt rubbery. His feet had become affixed to the ground as if planted there.

The next few minutes were a blur, perhaps because unbridled fear gripped Jed so tightly that he couldn't discern reality from pure fantasy, or perhaps lunacy.

A whistle, just like Bobby's—sharp, shrill, and crystal clear—rode the raucous breeze. He heard his name called again, just as sure and as succinct as he had heard it called back at the motel.

"Jed."

He looked to the graves where his family lay side by side. He stood alone, but at that instant he felt an unseen presence.

His fear and trepidation began to dissipate. The wind stilled. Calm washed over him, and he detected the sensation of having an arm slip across his back. It tightened around his shoulder and felt much as an embrace would feel. The cold left him; so did any lingering apprehension. An incredible warmth spread through him, despite the earlier chill in the air.

The mind distorts reality. He came to know this well-accepted fact interrogating mental patients accused of unspeakable crimes. Yet, as distorted as he knew one's thoughts could become, he believed with absolute certainty that Rascal, Bobby's trusted companion, a canine long departed from this world, had been sent to fetch him to this place at this time. He believed it with every fiber of his being.

Jed believed the call came from the grave, and he knew it had come so he would know he was not alone in his search for the truth. Jed didn't question this revelation. He just accepted it.

* * *

The next morning Jed awoke with the sunrise. What had happened during the night seemed like a dream, but he remembered the drive back to his efficiency, and he remembered falling into bed, exhausted but somehow renewed. Now, as he looked into the mirror at the face covered with shaving cream staring back at him, he didn't even try to understand what had occurred. Last night had been the first time in over thirty-five years he had truly felt his big brother's presence, and he was not about to apply logic or reason in an attempt to discount the experience.

Now, more than ever, Jed felt ready to take on the idiots of the world, like the one who had bombed his homeplace. He owned a new resolve to find his mysterious caller, too. The overnight experience had reinforced his need to learn what had happened the night Bobby died. He now believed that understanding why the two girls and the boy had been murdered would lead him to uncover the secret of what really happened to Bobby, and that alone served to drive him to catch their killer.

Jed's stomach growled. He pulled back the curtains and looked up the road toward Joe and Dot's. Cars and trucks, even a big green tractor, filled the lot in front of the eatery. Breakfast was served.

# CHAPTER · 11

Jed sat inside his car and watched a man with shriveled ebony skin wash the front plate-glass window of Rifkin's Grocery. The man's thin arms hoisted a dripping mop up high, exposing bony elbows and scaly arms. Jed watched the suds dribble down over the red letters painted on the glass and then watched as the man raised a squeegee to rake the water and residue away. A rainbow of colors trailed the squeegee as the morning sunlight refracted in the moist streaks.

The man stopped, leaned the squeegee into the corner of the window, and briefly glanced in Jed's direction. His face featured dark sunken sockets with black marble eyes peering from them. The brown skin, stretched tight over his cheekbones, revealed every contour of his skull. His visage bore a haunting familiarity.

Goose bumps rippled across Jed's arms. He knew this man.

Caffeine from three cups of Joe and Dot's coffee coursed through Jed's veins as he both cursed and thanked Hap Gentry for luring him here with the smug leer he had shown on his way out the door of the Wayfarer Motor Lodge the night before. Jed no longer wondered why the reporter wanted him to find Sadie Dunlap's grandfather.

Jed had seen him only once, long ago, but despite the dulling effect time has on memory, the man's face was not one he could ever forget. The window washer turned his head, revealing the unmistakable profile and a scar, blackened over time, running from the bridge of his nose to the curve of his jaw. Jed's skin prickled.

He opened the car door and stepped onto the pavement in front of the store. The man picked up the mop, dunked it into a bucket at his feet, and then slapped the mophead back onto the window.

Pausing next to the fender, Jed swallowed a mouthful of air and prepared for the first time in his life to come face-to-face with one of the men convicted for killing his brother.

Hap Gentry had known.

"Willie Sims?" Jed asked, stepping up onto the sidewalk behind the man.

"Who's askin'?" The window washer didn't turn around.

Looking into the mirrored reflection of the window, Jed watched the man's eyes watching him. "I want to talk to you about Sadie."

Sims dropped the head of his long-handled mop into the bucket of suds. Again, he pulled it out and swabbed the glass. As soapy ribbons slithered over the letters spelling RIFKIN'S, Jed wanted to ask about another murder, one the man had committed years before, but he chose to postpone that conversation for another time. Learning as much as he could about this man's granddaughter and why she died was more important at the moment.

*For everything, there is a time,* his father often said. *Patience is the virtue of a mature man.*

Giving a look of exasperation at the window, Sims slammed the mophead into the bucket. Foam and water sloshed out onto the cement. He whirled around. "You a cop?"

Jed stood with his thumbs hooked on the front pockets of his jeans and one foot propped up on the curb. "Not exactly."

An almost indiscernible graying eyebrow arched. "Then just who *exactly* are you? She owe you money?"

"You do know your granddaughter is dead, don't you?" Jed regretted the blunt announcement as soon as he said it.

"I heared." His weary eyes swept the ground before looking back up. A hint of sadness lingered in his gaze. Sims leaned the mop handle against the window and grabbed the squeegee. "I ain't got no money for her debts. 'Sides, I ain't seen her in more than a month."

"I'm not here about money," Jed said. "I want to find out why she died, who might have killed her."

Even as Sims turned away to busy himself with his chore of window cleaning, Jed could see the pained expression reflected in the glass. Sims raked suds off of the window with one long pull.

"You ain't no cop, why you care? 'Sides, won't bring her back, and likely she's better off, anyhow."

Jed had heard the same hopeless tone many times before in Atlanta. The ex-con sounded beaten, tired of fighting the world.

Sims said, "Last time I seen her, she was okay—okay as could be, all things considered."

"Considering what?" Jed asked.

Sims glanced at Jed's reflection. "What you think? Drugs, a life of whoring, no chance to climb out of it." He shrugged. "Anyhow, next thing I hear, she be dead. Don't know nothin' 'bout how she got that way or who might've done it. All I know, it's likely a blessin'." The old man turned with a glare. His features hung heavy. "The girl suffered most her life. When she needed me most, I weren't around."

*Strange,* Jed thought. The man's tone held no anger, just contrition. An odd reaction for someone hardened by prison life.

"Did she live with anybody in particular?" Jed asked. "A young man, a white man, was found near her."

The window washer's eyes narrowed. He shook his head. "She stayed where she could, mostly on the street. Her choice."

"The sheriff found signs of hoodoo near her body. She ever mention her interest in the spirit world, seeing a root doctor?"

Sims looked as if a ghost had walked up behind his visitor. "Ain't be knowin' nothin' 'bout no conjurin' ways." His head shook hard. His voice quivered.

"Think somebody put a curse on her?"

His head continued to shake back and forth. "Not so's I know."

Jed pressed harder, despite the fear creeping across the man's face. "What about you? You know any hoodoo conjurers?"

Sims gathered his cleaning supplies and started for the door. "Can't say what my granddaughter been into. As for me, I don't be messin' with no hexin' and such." His eyes narrowed. "You don't neither, you know what be good for you."

"How long you been out of prison?"

Sims held a hard glare. He said, "Don't be botherin' me. I gots work to do."

With his arms full, Sims pushed open the front door to the grocery and disappeared inside. Watching the old man, a strange notion hung over Jed. He realized he actually felt sorry for the man who had killed his brother.

Sims bore the callused features of an ex-con, but his demeanor seemed much gentler. He didn't fit the mold of a murderer, especially one who had served time for ruthlessly killing two teenagers.

Jed left Rifkin's, deciding to stop by Jake's office to ask him about Sims. He wondered if Jake knew the ex-con had moved home, and if he did, why he hadn't mentioned it.

When Jed arrived at the courthouse, he found Jake's office door closed and locked. The lights inside were off. The thought crossed his mind that the sheriff might be inside grabbing a nap after spending a long night with the fire marshal. He knocked on the door glass. The loose frosted pane rattled, as if it would dislodge with the next strike. Jed backed away from the door. The last thing he needed was to be charged with trying to break into the office of the sheriff.

"Jake," he called out in a loud voice.

No answer came from inside. He walked back down the hallway to a solid wooden door with MAINTENANCE printed across the top, tried the knob—locked.

*Jake's dispatcher will be in,* he thought. They always were, twenty-four/seven, and surely someone there would know how to get up with their sheriff.

The Indigo County Sheriff's Dispatch Center, what there was of it, was located in a small room down the hallway from the clerk of court's office on the second floor of the courthouse. As Jed stepped out of the stairwell onto the wooden floor darkened by decades of oil and polish, he noticed the light on in the clerk's office.

He had been meaning to stop by to see if the transcript from the trial for Bobby's killers could be retrieved from the archives. *A long shot at best*, he thought. *But since I'm already here, why not check?*

The clerk's office occupied a more prestigious location in the courthouse than that of the sheriff's. So did nearly all of the offices for other county officials, for that matter, from the solicitor to the tax collector. Only the sheriff and the janitor had been relegated to the basement. Jed considered the irony.

Inside the clerk's office, an elderly woman stood hunched over the front counter, reading one of those gossip newspapers one finds while waiting in line at the grocery checkout. She looked up and over her bifocals, squinted hard, and slid a file folder over the newspaper. Her prune face bore a slight jaundiced tint with a large liver spot on her left cheek.

"You're a Bradley, aren't you?" she said before Jed could introduce himself.

Slightly taken aback by the woman's recognition, not to mention the unwavering confidence in her voice, he nodded. "Yes, ma'am, Jedediah Bradley. But how in the world. . . ?"

She grinned. "I heard that a Bradley boy moved back, and since I know everybody else who comes through that door, I figured he had to be you." She eyed Jed suspiciously. "You wantin' something?" Hints of azure in the woman's pewter-colored hair glistened under the harsh fluorescent lighting.

"I'm trying to locate an old transcript," Jed said.

The woman's nostrils flared with an air of haughtiness. "How old?"

"Thirty-eight years."

"Can't help you." She thumped the file covering the newspaper on the counter. "Any idea how old this is?"

Jed huffed, mildly irritated with the woman's hubris. "Nope."

"Ten years . . . and it's the oldest file in the place." She swept her arm in a big arc as she looked around the room full of shiny steel-gray filing cabinets. "We used to have wooden cabinets for the files. They were here long before I came to be clerk, over forty years ago. Fire got 'em . . . ever' last one."

For the first time, Jed noticed the gleam of the metal cabinets. "Before the fire, how far back did your records go?" he asked.

Suddenly looking forlorn, the woman said, "Some dated back to the war."

"World War II?"

The clerk shook her head, leaned forward with her elbows on the counter. *The* war, sonny. The War Between the States." She sighed. "They're all gone."

On the ceiling in the back of the room, Jed spotted traces of soot missed by the painters. The thin coat of green paint on the walls looked dirty, just as the white paint on the ceiling looked dingy.

"How'd it happen?" he asked.

"Even had a letter signed by President Davis. You know—*the* President Davis."

Jed nodded.

"The old clerk stared off into space. "Bet it'd be worth something now."

"I 'spect so," Jed said, not really caring.

She cleared her throat, emitting a deep guttural rumble that sounded like everything in her lungs would be coughed up in one monstrous wad of phlegm. "What'd you ask?" she said.

"Do you know how the fire started?"

The woman shook her head. "Nope, no idea. Janitor smelled smoke and called the fire department. Most of the office was pretty much gutted by the time they arrived." She exhibited a look of indignation. "I had to work out of the basement for nearly three months."

"That must have been terrible," Jed said more sarcastically than he intended. "And it happened about ten years ago?"

"Ten, that's right."

"You remember the month?"

The skin above the woman's nose scrunched together. "Sure do. January, because the basement was so cold, I liked to caught my death. Why?"

Coincidences kept popping up in Jed's head. His father's church had burned around the same time, but he knew this woman wouldn't understand, or likely care. He ignored the question.

"I'm wanting to read about a murder trial, the one for my brother's killers. You remember it?"

"Course I do," she said. "One of the biggest we've had around these parts, 'specially given them two killed Abby Granville that night."

Jed heard the clerk's message loud and clear, whether the woman meant it to be heard or not. If only a young black man had been killed, then it would have been just another trial. No big deal.

"I don't recall a lot about what went on back then," he said. "Can you tell me what you remember?"

She nodded. "Sheriff had 'em dead to rights, what with the black boy testifying against the white one. Whole thing lasted only a few days." She pursed her lips together and shook her finger in the air to note the importance of the swift verdict.

"So, Sims testified against Nash."

"Don't recall their names exactly," she said. "But the black boy testified against the white."

"Wasn't it a bit unusual for the juries back then to take the word of a black man over a white one?" Jed asked.

She shrugged. "I reckon some of the time, but this case was different. That white feller was as mean as a cornered varmint." Her eyes narrowed to symbolize the way an angry animal might look. "He did the shootin', according to the other one, and should have been electrified for what he did to that poor girl. Would have too, if them liberal-assed judges up in Washington hadn't put a stop to the death penalty."

She chuckled under her breath. "Guess you heard he got his anyhow. Truly the Lord works in mysterious ways. Just when you think you've done gone and got away with something . . . wham!"

The woman slammed her hand on the counter. Jed jumped.

"Clear out of the blue, he'll zap you," the clerk declared with a stern glare.

*The old gal missed her calling,* Jed thought. *She'd fit right in to the evangelical thunder thumping Daddy did so well.* He visualized her in a pulpit, doubted a single parishioner would dare doze once she commenced to sermonizing such as he had just witnessed.

Jed had already heard about how Roy Nash had met his fate. A prison guard had told him the prisoner died in a fight in the prison laundry. The guard suspected the fight was orchestrated to cover up an outright murder. He also suspected that someone on the outside had hired an inmate to kill Nash, but he couldn't prove it. All he knew was that Nash wound up facedown in a laundry tub full of grimy water. Coroner's report ruled his death a drowning.

"Anything else?" Jed asked.

"Weren't much else to it. They did it, got convicted, and went to prison." Her eyes saddened. "It was plumb awful what happened to poor Abby." She looked at Jed as if struck by an afterthought and said, "Bad what happened to your brother, too."

*Bad, but not plumb awful,* Jed thought. "Wonder why nobody tried to kill Sims in prison?"

"Guess he kept his head low and minded his own business," she said with little concern. "I hear he's out and living back around these parts somewhere."

"So I hear," Jed said.

He thanked the elderly clerk for her help and turned to grab the doorknob, but before he could exit the office, she said, "Hear tell you got yourself a phone call telling where to find them dead young'uns." The tone of her voice held more than a hint of suspicion, and what came next sounded downright accusatorial. "How is it you figure you got chosen?"

Jed swallowed the first snappy retort that popped into his head and responded as truthfully as he could. "If I could answer that, I'd probably be able to find the killer."

"Exactly! Listen, young feller, you better own up to any sinful ways before it's too late," she said, sounding like Jed's third-grade Sunday school teacher about to deliver a scolding. "The Almighty knows all and sees all, and once you get tossed into that fiery lake, there ain't no redos.

Jed's cheeks flushed, but he managed to hold his tongue like his mamma always cautioned. "I'll keep that in mind."

He snatched open the door, stepped outside, and slammed it closed. Someone had been offering up their own theories and suspicions about the murders to anyone willing to listen, and he had a pretty good idea who that someone had been.


Jake's dispatcher wore her bleached blonde hair teased high on her head. Bright red lipstick, thick and smeared at the corners of her mouth, covered her thin lips. She was as skinny as a thermometer, and when Jed walked through the door of the dispatch center, ignoring the AUTHORIZED PERSONNEL ONLY sign, her mercury shot all the way to the top, coloring her face a purplish shade of red.

"Can't you read? Civilians ain't allowed." Her high-pitched voice sounded like one of those wiry little terriers yipping instead of barking.

The small, dimly lit room reeked of stale cigarette smoke, and as his eyes adjusted to the low light, Jed spotted the source swirling up from an ashtray next to the woman's right hand. The serpentine coils hung stagnant just above her head, shrouding the peak of her bouffant in a cloud.

"Jake around?" Jed asked.

The woman exaggerated a sigh. She glowered as she chomped on a wad of gum. "Ain't here," she yipped.

Her curled lip resembled a terrier's snarl just before the animal attacked a person's ankles. Jed knew this from an investigation into the death of an eighty-something widow, whose terrier felt it his noble duty to protect the corpse of his late master. Jed's detective had keenly noted the dog's dislocated jaw and chipped teeth in his case notes. A few days later they questioned a suspect, a handyman who did odd jobs for the woman. He walked with a limp, and closer inspection revealed infected bite marks on his shin and leg. A confession soon came, and a tetanus shot was administered by the jail nurse.

"Know when he'll be back?" Jed asked.

"Sheriff don't check in with me," the dispatcher said.

Jed found the woman's snippy bark amusing for some reason and grinned. "What if there's an emergency?"

"Then I'd find him," the woman responded with a scowl. She glared. A bubble made a brief appearance between her lips and then disappeared with a pop. "But you ain't got an emergency . . . do you?"

"Nope, but I still need to see him," Jed said. The joy of the sparring diminished. Irritation began to erase his patience.

The spindly woman spun her chair around and grabbed a pad off the radio console. When she turned back, she tossed it in Jed's direction.

"Leave your number. When I see him, I'll give it to him."

Jed caught the pad between the palms of his hands and, in one motion, tossed it back. "I'll check later."

Turning to leave, he heard the woman mutter under her breath. He couldn't quite make out what she had said, but he was pretty sure the word he heard her use to refer to him didn't reflect well on his race. He hesitated, again remembering his mamma's words about people making him angry, and continued out the door. The last person he wanted in control of him was a woman who reminded him of a rat terrier.

# CHAPTER · 12

Standing at the top of the courthouse steps, Jed watched the time and temperature alternate on the sign hanging in front of the bank building on the corner. Forty-six degrees at 10:01. He inhaled through his nose, filling his nostrils with the familiar brackish scent of salt air that had always reminded him of the lowcountry. So much had been written about returning home—some negative, some positive—and at this point he had not decided exactly where his return belonged in that continuum. What he did know was that savoring the senses of his childhood somehow soothed him, just like his late night visit to the cemetery. He glanced up at a pigeon cooing on the crest of the roof as he pondered his next move.

"Jedediah," a woman's voice called out.

He looked down the steps and across the street, half expecting to see Rascal luring him to follow after him again. This time, though, he saw a woman's silhouette backlit by the bright sun. She waved. Jed squinted and cupped his hand over his brow. That was the moment he saw another vision from his past, one that produced a jumble of mixed emotions. He descended the steps slowly.

She waited until Jed reached the bottom, then she started across the road. They met in the middle, and Jed lost all perspective of his surroundings. Her radiant brown eyes met his.

"Morning, Jedediah. I heard you were back."

He thought her voice sounded as sweet as honeysuckle nectar tastes. He recalled the last time he saw her, felt the pain of that night all over again. He forced a whispered "hi" past the boulder-sized lump in his throat.

"I'm so glad I ran into you," she said.

Jed whispered, "You look great, Jes."

He knew her as Jessie Braddock, and she had been his one and only love in high school. He did not date much back then, not until he worked up the fortitude to ask her out in the fall of their junior year.

He marveled at how she looked after all of the years. She still stood tall and shapely with big round doe eyes and a huge smile that, once upon a time, always managed to reduce him to a puddle of admiration. She wore her straight black hair shorter now but in an elegant way that flattered the soft features of her face. She had aged beautifully.

A hot and muggy July night had marked the end of their relationship. They had parked on a knoll overlooking the Tullifinny River, where they watched the moonlight sparkle off the rippling waters. They were both eighteen, and Jerry Butler's "Only the Strong Survive" floated from the speakers of Jed's '58 Plymouth. Instead of cuddling close, savoring each other's touch as they had so many times before, they remained on opposite sides of the car, each leaning back against their doors. The distance between them seemed endless. Her words ripped open his heart.

"Mamma says we have to quit seeing each other for a while. She wants me to spend the summer getting ready to go off to college."

"Is that what you want?" he asked.

A long, maddening silence followed. Jed didn't remember much after that moment. Not even her reply. He became lost in Jerry Butler's throaty lyrics, allowing them to drown out the rest of Jessie's words. At that time and place, only a few years after Bobby's death, he held only one thought: life as he knew it had come to an end.

He did remember Jessie had blown him a kiss from her porch before disappearing inside her house that night, and in that instant, he realized the time had come for him to leave Sweetgrass. Two days later he did, without telling Jessie or Jake, or even discussing his plans with his father.

Now, standing in the middle of the street in front of the courthouse, Jed looked at Jessie and wondered what might have been if he hadn't left.

He glanced at her left hand. "Is it still Jessie Braddock?" Seeing a ring, but not a wedding band, he couldn't help but ask.

"Green," she said.

Her response stabbed deep into Jed's heart, despite his best effort not to care. He felt his features collapse as if melting wax covered his face.

Jessie no doubt noticed. "My husband died last year." Her tone was somber. "He was a good man, Jedediah. A lot like you."

Jed swallowed hard, felt an urgent need to change the subject. "You really do look terrific."

"All in all, life has been good to me," she said. "How about you?"

He glanced skyward and shrugged. "You know me. I'm a survivor."

"Married?"

"Ah, no." The question caught him off guard. "I was . . . once, a long time ago. Not one of my more notable accomplishments." He flashed a sheepish smile.

"I'm sorry."

"Oh, no, don't be. Being married to a cop isn't the easiest relationship to maintain, and being married to me as a young cop turned out to be impossible for her. She realized it early on, before children complicated the issue, so we managed to remain friends."

Jessie adjusted the white sweater draped over the shoulders of her peacock-blue dress. "I often thought of you, even checked with your dad from time to time. After he died I lost track."

A horn honked up the street, prompting Jed to grab Jessie's hand. The couple scurried to the side of the road.

As the truck passed, Jed continued holding her hand. Her fingers were long, her skin soft and wonderful feeling. He remembered how they had once spent nearly every waking hour together. They had even studied together. She focused on her lessons; Jed focused on her. The grades she made reflected the amount of time she spent on her schoolwork. Unfortunately, his did too.

"You ever get that chance to go to college?" he asked.

A demure smile appeared. "Uh-huh. College of Charleston . . . then the Medical University."

"You're a doctor?"

Her shy gaze swept the roadside. "Psychiatrist."

"Doctor Green." Jed inexplicably felt inept. "Now, ain't that somethin'."

Another bashful smile. "Actually, I kept my maiden name for professional purposes. I didn't marry until ten years ago."

*All those years she had remained unmarried,* Jed thought, realizing his pride had kept him away. Maintaining relationships never had been his strength.

"I heard you'd moved back into your parents' home," Jessie said.

Jed nodded, suddenly aware that she had not tried to free her hand from his. "I did, and I was just getting comfortable when somebody blew it up."

"Yes, I heard that too. I'm glad you're okay, but are you sure it wasn't an accident?"

"About as sure as I can be. I'm just not sure why, and I doubt any suspects will turn up." Stump's fat face appeared in Jed's mind. *Not when one of the best ones works for the sheriff,* he thought.

"I can't imagine someone wanting to do that," Jessie said, "but it seems I'm having a hard time understanding a lot of things going on around here." She raked her teeth across her lower lip. "Are you in a hurry? I'd like to talk to you about the recent murders."

Surprised and noting her look of concern, Jed said, "I've got time." *What could Jessie possibly want to know about the murders?* He pointed to a green metal bench encircling the trunk of a live oak on the courthouse lawn. "We can sit over there."

They sat side by side and Jed turned toward her. "You have my undivided attention."

Jessie moistened her lips then spoke words that stunned Jed. "Kristin Clay was my goddaughter."

Jed clasped his hands in his lap as he leaned forward and looked at her pained expression. Reflected there he saw the gruesome images of the young girl leaning against the tree, the dark bog beside her. He saw the bluish tint of the girl's waxen face. He groped for the right words to express his sorrow.

"Oh, Jes. . . ."

"Kristin's mother, Carol Ann, roomed with me in college," she said. She stared off into another time and place. "When we graduated, we attended medical school together. I was a bridesmaid in her wedding." Jessie paused, looked glum. "In short, she's the best friend I have in the world, and she's devastated."

The battle-weary detective reached out and took her hands in his. He wanted to say something intelligent and comforting, but nothing appropriate came to mind.

A thin smile broke through the helplessness sculpting her expression. "Word got out pretty quick that a big-city homicide detective had begun looking into the murder of those two poor kids out by your daddy's church. I heard that detective was you."

Try as he did, he couldn't suppress a tingling sensation in his chest, a feeling of pride. He nodded.

"Then, yesterday, came the news about Kristin. At first I heard she might have taken her own life. Nobody would say how. I couldn't believe she'd do that. Then I heard you showed up there, too."

She reached out and touched Jed's hands. Her hand felt warm.

"This morning," she said, "I decided to come see you, find out why Jake's deputies weren't tellin' Carol Ann more about her daughter's death. On the way, I heard about the explosion on the radio news and didn't want to impose."

She wiped away moisture from under her eyes. "When I saw you walk out of the courthouse, I was on my way to confront Jake, to force him to tell me the truth. Seeing you standing there was an answer to a prayer."

Jed chuckled softly. "I've been called a lot of things over the years, Jes, but never an answer to a prayer."

Jessie's lip twitched as if she wanted to smile at his ill-fated humor, but her face remained paralyzed with grief.

Jed said, "Jake's not there. He's had a rough few days, and he's likely out beating the bushes for answers as we speak."

"Carol Ann's heartbroken. She needs to know the truth. She deserves that much." Jessie's voice quavered. "I want to know, too, and the way I figure it, you're our best hope."

Jed grimaced. "I'm afraid I don't have much to tell you. Not yet anyway. I *can* tell you Kristin's wounds weren't self-inflicted."

"I never thought otherwise."

"I understand," Jed said softly.

"Why would anyone want to kill her? She's never hurt anyone. She's just a . . . kid—a good kid—trying to get through college."

Tears welled in Jessie's eyes. Jed sat motionless, guarding his emotions.

"Oh, sweet Jesus, this makes no sense at all," she said in a voice muffled by her hands.

Jed slipped into his investigative mode, hoping Jessie could help supply some vital background information. "You feel up to answering a few questions?"

She looked up with tears streaming across her coffee-and-cream-colored cheeks and nodded.

For the next several minutes he asked the usual eliminators about drug usage, boyfriends, and lifestyle choices. As far as Jessie knew, Kristin didn't date much and had no steady boyfriend. A bit shy, she had spent most of her time studying and visiting with her grandmother, who had lived in Sweetgrass until her death.

"If Kristin was guilty of anything," Jessie said, "it was spending too much time looking after family and not enough time enjoying being young and in college."

"No drugs?" Jed asked.

"Heavens, no. Why? Did drugs play a part in her death?"

"Not that I know of, but the Dunlap girl was a known junkie. She lived on the streets and prostituted herself to sustain her habit. Don't guess you ever heard Kristin mention her name?"

Jessie hit Jed with a sidelong glance. "No. I take it you think the murders are connected?"

"To more than just Kristin, I'm afraid. I found out this morning that Sadie Dunlap's granddaddy is Willie Sims."

"Willie Sims?" Jessie's forehead furrowed.

"One of the two men who killed Bobby," he said. "Maybe a coincidence, but it's noteworthy, nevertheless."

Jed had long ago quit believing in coincidences. Given the phone calls he had received, he was not about to change his belief system, but Jessie didn't need to know all the sordid details just yet.

"What about the occult?" he asked. "Did Kristin ever talk about the practice of hoodoo?"

"Hoodoo?!"

"Did she ever wear good-luck charms to keep away evil spirits?"

"What in the world—"

"Signs of hoodoo rituals were found near all of the bodies . . . but keep that information to yourself."

Jessie shook her head. "I know folks still dabble in hoodoo around here. Some are ardent believers, but I can't imagine Kristin being interested unless it had something to do with a course she was taking in school. Anyway, she never mentioned it to me."

Jed shrugged. "It may not be important. I'm just trying to make sense of what we know . . . which isn't a whole lot at this point."

"So what's next?" Jessie asked.

"I was on my way over to visit with Ginger Lane. I hear she's back in town, and I'm hoping she'll shed some light on what Kristin was doing prior to. . . ." He decided not to state the obvious.

Jessie nodded. "Ginger's a sweet kid. She must be devastated . . . and terrified." She stood up, brushed wrinkles from her dress. "I won't keep you." She grabbed Jed's hand and pulled as he stood. "I appreciate you being candid with me about Kristin. I know you didn't have to tell me what you did."

Standing face-to-face, she put her arms around Jed's neck and hugged him. She kissed his cheek, slipped a card into his hand. "Here's my number—home and work. Please call me if I can be of any help whatsoever."

When she let go, Jed looked down at the card and thought again about what might have happened if he had come home before Jessie married. Mamma Braddock's disapproving scowl loomed in his memory.

By the time he thought to ask Jessie about her mamma, the tall woman's long strides had carried her halfway across the courthouse lawn. She stopped next to a silver BMW two-seater, turned, and waved before climbing into the sports car. Jed's feet remained planted until the car turned the corner and drove out of sight.

# CHAPTER · 13

Around the world, especially in the South Carolina lowcountry, the arrival of spring marks a time of renewal. Life is resurrected. Animals emerge from hibernation, and people leave the shelter of their homes to fish, tend their gardens, and bathe in the wonders of God's creation. Refreshing warmth rides the ocean breezes. Leaves appear on the trees, azaleas bloom, and jonquils pop from the soil, transforming the dormant brown landscape into an artist's rainbow palette of colors.

*This is a time of miracles,* Jed thought as he pulled into the parking lot of the Marsh View Apartments, where Kristin Clay had shared a town house with Ginger Lane. A miracle was exactly what he believed he needed to help solve the murders.

He bounced from his car, bounded to the front door of the apartment, and was about to knock when he noticed the two cars parked in front. One was a red Jeep Cherokee, the other a black Mercedes. He had not seen either one on his previous visit.

Seeing Jessie had been a distraction, but the job at hand reclaimed his attention. *The Mercedes must belong to Ginger's parents,* he thought.

Experience had taught Jed that parents can be very protective in times of crisis, and sometimes this instinct makes it difficult for seekers of fact and truth to gather the needed information to solve the crime or allay fears. As he stepped up onto the concrete stoop and grabbed the tarnished brass door knocker, he wondered what reaction awaited him inside. Jed banged two sharp strikes against the red metal door and stepped back to be viewed through the peephole in the middle of the door knocker. He tucked his shirt in tighter, hiked his belt.

The door opened.

A stern scowl from a man with thinning rust-colored hair, a face full of freckles, and pale orange eyebrows greeted him. Wearing a yellow golf shirt and pleated khaki slacks, he looked like he had just arrived home from *the club.*

"Help you?" His chilly tone followed a suspicious scan of Jed's presence, an inspection that crawled slowly up the former detective's body from his shoe tops to his head.

Realizing this was a man who did not want his family bothered and likely one used to getting his way, Jed engaged his most disarming smile. "My name is Jedediah Bradley," he said. "I'd like to speak to Ginger Lane. Is she home?"

The man's eyebrow lifted. His posture showcased his distrust and caution. "About?"

"Her roommate, Kristin Clay," Jed said in an unrelenting voice of authority. "The sheriff asked me to help with the investigation into her death." He gambled the small white lie that Jake had sent him might get him inside the apartment.

The man studied his daughter's visitor quietly before glancing over his shoulder into the room behind him. When he looked back, his eyes narrowed. "Got any identification?"

Jed fished his wallet out of his back pocket and held up the retired Atlanta Police Department ID he carried. The man took the wallet, scrutinized every word.

"Why didn't a deputy come with you?" he asked, handing the wallet back.

Jed admired the man's caution. In fact, he was pretty sure he would have asked the same question if the roles had been reversed.

"The sheriff and I are old friends," Jed said. "His department is small, and he asked if I'd help out. With just a few deputies, he sent us in separate directions."

The man's mouth twisted. Jed could tell he wasn't sure what to do.

"I've retired here after investigating murders in Atlanta for more years than I'd like to admit," the former detective said with a sheepish grin. "I promise this won't take long."

The man looked back inside, then out at Jed with a perplexed expression. Clearly he didn't want his daughter put through any more torment if he could avoid it. On the other hand, Jed believed the man's instinct told him the sooner the killer was caught, the sooner her life, and his, could return to something closer to normal.

He stepped back and opened the door wider. "Okay, but I'm going to be with her."

"That's fine." Jed stepped into the apartment before Ginger's father could change his mind.

Jed always looked for clues in a victim's home. Indications of how they had lived. "A person's habits speak volumes about their lives," he had told newly assigned investigators to his squad back in Atlanta. "Clues to why they might have died often are found in plain view."

A confluence of generations and lifestyles could be seen in the living room of the small apartment. The furnishings and window treatments, mostly new and moderately expensive, attested to the affluence of the parents. Posters of musicians on the walls, a half-eaten bag of potato chips and some empty Coke cans on a wooden coffee table, and opened textbooks littering the floor of the unkempt room reflected the frenzied lifestyle common among college students.

More textbooks were piled on a chair in front of a modular desk, where a computer monitor sat with little yellow sticky notes clinging to its sides. The keyboard in front of the monitor lay buried under pads and folders. A trash can with a miniature basketball goal affixed to it overflowed with discarded balls of paper. A gray sweatshirt partially covered a printer on a printer stand at the opposite side of the desk from the wastebasket. Women's clothing—blouses, jeans, even a pair of lime-green panties and matching bra—hung from the back of a wooden chair in the dining room, just to the right of the front door. A full laundry basket rested at the base of the stairwell leading to the upstairs bedrooms of the town house apartment. Everything looked altogether normal for two college students.

"Ginger." The father called for his daughter as Jed studied the room.

A barefoot girl stepped from the kitchen. Her hair, the same color as the man's, was cut in a pageboy. Her faded jeans bore frayed cuffs, and the sleeves of her green V-necked sweater were pushed midway up her arms. Petite in stature and build, her ivory skin featured an ocean of tiny brown freckles, a trait she inherited from her father.

*No question about the gene pool with these two,* Jed concluded. He looked around but didn't see the girl's mother.

"This man's with the sheriff's department," the dad said. "He'd like to ask you some questions about Kristin."

Jed stepped toward the girl. He extended his hand.

Her emerald eyes flickered concern as she slid her hand onto his, barely allowing it to touch before pulling it back. "What kind of questions?" she asked. Moisture pooled around the red rims of her eyes as she looked at her father. "Do I have to go through this all over again?"

Picking up on the cue that somebody had already interviewed the girl, Jed said, "Sometimes it helps in cases like these if two different detectives interview folks at different times. It is a matter of perspectives and helps to keep from missing something important." He pulled a pad and pen from his pocket. "By the way, do you recall which deputy interviewed you before?"

The girl nuzzled against her father and buried her face as if trying to hide. Her dad stroked her hair softly but didn't dissuade the continuance of questions.

"No," she said. " He was heavy and didn't dress much like a cop."

*Stump.* Jed offered a silent prayer of thanks that the deputy had not left the same instructions he had given the registrar at the university.

"This really won't take long, but something you remember might help us catch Kristin's killer." Jed smiled thoughtfully. "It'll be painless."

Ginger squirmed uncomfortably. "Daddy?" Her expression pleaded for him to make the intruder go away. Her gaze remained fixed on her father for several more seconds, but he didn't relent. Following a long sigh of exasperation, she returned her attention to Jed. "What kind of questions?"

"I'm looking for something out of the ordinary. Something that might have struck you as odd, like seeing a stranger hanging around the area or overhearing an argument between Kristin and someone else."

"Nothing," she said. "I don't remember . . . anything like that." Her words caught briefly in her throat.

"I'll also be asking about the obvious," Jed said. "When you last saw Kristin. Who she dated. Did she have any enemies?"

"I've already answered those," she said.

"I know, but maybe this time you'll recall something you didn't before."

When she realized he wasn't going to be put off, the girl's shoulders slumped into submission.

Jed motioned toward a cushioned chair covered in expensive-looking shiny fabric. "May I?"

Ginger gave her father one last desperate glance. He said, "I'll sit with you on the sofa."

She glared back at Jed and, in an irritated tone, said, "Sit. Let's get this over with."

The news that Stump had already interviewed Kristin's roommate only mildly surprised Jed. More than surprise, he felt he had underestimated the disagreeable investigator's tenacity. Most seasoned detectives knew the first forty-eight to seventy-two hours of an investigation were the most critical. The competent ones worked nonstop those first days, hoping to ferret out that key piece of evidence before the trail grew cold. *Funny,* he thought, *I never figured Stump for competent.*

As father and daughter settled onto a sea-green sofa covered in the same shiny fabric as the chair where Jed sat, the former detective couldn't help wondering why someone would buy such nice stuff for two college students. He thought about the shiny black Mercedes out front, the practically new red Jeep parked beside it. He thought about the differences in the lifestyles of the victims, one homeless, one a blue-collar mechanic, the other the daughter of a doctor. His search for commonality had become more difficult.

As Ginger sat down, she made no pretense about resenting Jed's presence. Even so, he didn't read too much into her reaction. He had seen it before and recognized it as a typical stage of grief. He knew at a later time she would be able to talk with more comfort about her friend and roommate. She would be more willing then—another step in the grieving process—but waiting might allow important facts to fade from her memory. Jed pressed on with his questions.

Ginger's responses were short and measured at first. She described Kristin as the typical student, with typical student relationships, who participated in typical student activities. Nothing out of the ordinary came from the initial questions, so he moved in another direction.

"Tell me about the last time you saw Kristin. Was she happy, sad, angry? How did she act?"

"Happy, I guess. She was going to class and then to the library to study. She has . . . had a test next week." Ginger clinched her hands together in her lap.

"When did you realize something might be wrong?"

"I didn't," she said deadpan. "After she left for class, I went home to see my boyfriend." She paused, staring off into space for a moment. "I didn't know anything until that other deputy came to my house and told us she was . . . dead."

Ginger choked back tears. Her father squeezed her shoulders. Jed waited for her to compose herself.

"I tried to get Kristin to go with me," she said, still sobbing. "Billy Lamb was coming home from Georgia with my brother, and Kristin had dated him before. They liked each other."

"The University of Georgia?" Jed asked.

"Huh?"

"Your brother and his friend. Were they coming in from the University of Georgia?"

"Oh . . . yeah."

"If Kristin liked Billy, why didn't she want to go with you?"

Ginger looked up, brandished a look of exasperation. "I've already told you. She had a big test coming up. She wanted to study."

"Kristin would rather study than go see a boy she liked?" Jed asked, sounding more skeptical than he intended.

"Yeah," Ginger said, revealing her disgust for the question. "Some kids really are here to earn an education, and Kristin is . . . was one of them. You might say she romanced books more than men."

"I understand," Jed said.

"Nothing came before her studies." She paused, angled her jaw, and narrowed her eyelids as if in thought. "Nothing, except maybe her grandmother."

"Her grandmother? Tell me about her family."

"She and her grandmother were real close. Kristin spent a lot of time talking to her and visiting her. She'd call home to talk to her mom maybe once a week, but she talked to her grandmother almost every day. She'd go over to help her get her medicines, that kind of stuff."

"Was her grandmother not able to do for herself?"

"I . . . don't think that was it so much as she just didn't like leaving her house. It was sort of like she was afraid to be out around people. If she needed something, Kristin would go over to help her get it." Ginger swiped her cheek with the heel of her hand. "Kristin was that way."

Jed recalled Jessie's comment that Kristin spent too much time looking after family. "Her grandmother's dead, right?"

Ginger nodded. "Automobile accident a couple of months ago. It really tore Kristin up."

"I can imagine, them being so close and all." Jed glanced at his notes. "But I thought you just said her grandmother didn't go out."

"She didn't, as far as I know. Kristin once told me she'd have to force her grandmother to go to the doctor, and then she'd have to drive her. She even had her groceries delivered, and Kristin would go over and help her put them away. Kristin loved her grandmother, but she'd be the first to admit the old woman was a little wacky."

"Do you know anything about the wreck?"

"No, not really. I think she lost control of her car and drove off a bridge, something like that."

Jed made a note to ask Jessie if she knew what happened to Kristin's grandmother. "Did Kristin ever talk about her grandmother's death? Who she was with or if she was by herself when the wreck happened?"

"No, and that was the odd part. I'm pretty sure no one else was in the car. After her grandmother died, Kristin got real upset if I asked her anything about what happened."

"Why do you think she got upset?" Jed said. "Because her grandmother died so unexpectedly?"

"That and. . . ." She took a breath and then shrugged. "Nothing."

"Ginger." Jed leaned forward and spoke in a soft voice. "Anything you know—even the smallest detail—might help us catch the person who killed Kristin. You want that, don't you?"

Anger flickered in the girl's green eyes. Her body grew rigid. "Of course I want that." She glanced at her father, who had moved his arm from behind her and leaned forward.

"Tell him what you know, honey," he said.

"That's just it, Daddy. I don't know."

"I don't understand," Jed said.

Ginger sighed. "A week or so before her grandmother died, Kristin came back from visiting her. She was real distraught. She said her grandmother told her something awful."

"About what?"

Ginger eyed the ceiling. "That's what I don't know. For the next few days, Kristin was ill at ease about something she had learned from her grandmother. She referred to it as her family's curse. At first I was real curious. I probed and asked questions, but she'd just clam up and get mad. After her grandmother died, I quit asking."

Jed scratched his head, felt as if he had missed something. "Ask what?"

Ginger glared. Through clenched teeth she said, "I . . . don't . . . know!"

"That first time she came home, when she said her grandmother told her something awful, did she elaborate at all then?" Jed asked.

"No." Ginger squirmed on the sofa. She released a deep breath. Her discomfort betrayed her.

"There's something you're not telling me. It might be important."

Her dad said, "Ginger, do you know something you're not telling us about Kristin?"

"I promised her I wouldn't say anything." Ginger began crying as she spoke.

"Honey, she's dead," the father said. "She's been murdered. If you can help the sheriff catch the killer, you need to tell this man what you know."

Ginger choked back tears. "The only time she talked about it was right after her grandmother's funeral. Kristin was pretty bummed out that night. For some reason, she didn't want to be around her family, so we both came back here and got slammed."

"Slammed?" Jed said. "Do you mean y'all got drunk?"

"Uh-huh. We stayed up all night drinking and talking. She never told me exactly, but she did say God punished her grandmother for a dark family secret. She was scared he'd punish her next."

"She didn't even hint at what the secret was?" Jed asked.

"No. She told me she was afraid if I knew, God would punish me too."

"God didn't punish or kill Kristin, Ginger. He didn't kill her grandmother either." Jed eyed the father and wondered how his next question would be received. "Have either of you ever been involved with hoodoo?"

Ginger's head snapped up.

Her dad said, "What?"

"Hoodoo," Jed said. "Did you or Kristin study it in school or go to see a local conjurer?"

Ginger stared incredulously. "*No!* Kristin would never practice black magic. No way!"

The dad asked, "Why would you think the girls might have been involved in hoodoo?"

"Your daughter mentioned that Kristin told her that her family was cursed.

There are plenty of folks living in these parts who still believe in hoodoo curses. We also found signs of hoodoo ritualism at both crime scenes."

Silence billowed in the room. The father leaned back against the sofa.

Ginger shrugged. "She never mentioned it if she did."

"You're sure?"

"Yes . . . yes."

The father stood. "I think that's enough. I don't know where all of this is headed, but I know my daughter, and she and her friends aren't into weirdo practices that summon up spirits from another world. She's answered all the questions she's going to, so it's time for you to leave."

Ginger didn't budge. She stared at her hands as she rubbed and squeezed them.

"I understand," Jed said, grunting as he stood from the chair's deep seat. "I'm not accusing your daughter of anything but being a good friend to Kristin. I know she's in pain over what happened, but she might have helped, in some small way, to find Kristin's killer. I think we all want that end."

Ginger looked up. "That other deputy said he couldn't rule out suicide, but I know Kristin wouldn't kill herself. She loved life too much."

"I can rule it out," Jed said with a sympathetic smile. "Kristin didn't kill herself."

"Is my daughter in danger?" the father asked.

"All I can tell you is that I don't believe Kristin's murder was a random act. She was sought out and killed for a reason. We just don't know why yet."

The father's pale face grew even more so. He looked at Ginger. "We'll be going back home as soon as she's able to get the things she needs. I can't leave her here."

"Dad!"

Jed said, "For what it's worth, sir, my instincts tell me she's not in danger."

"Your instincts aren't worth risking my daughter's life."

Jed nodded, thanked Ginger for her time and help, and left the apartment. As he climbed into his Volvo, he thought about the grandmother's car wreck. Nothing made sense about why she would have been driving that car if she always depended on Kristin to take her places. There had to be a reason the woman set out on her own when she was not known to venture out like that.

He pulled out his cell phone to call Jake and noticed a missed call. About to check for messages, he stopped. Jessie, as Kristin's godmother, might know what Kristin's grandmother had told the girl to upset her. He retrieved the card Jessie had given him, stared at it as he wondered if this was such a good idea.

Minutes later, after speaking with Jessie, Jed snapped the phone cover closed. Soon he would know if he had made a mistake.

* * *

On the way to Jessie's, Jed retrieved the voice message left on his phone. Jake had been the missed caller, and he sounded pissed off. Jed dialed the sheriff's office number, and to his surprise, Jake answered on the first ring.

"Armistead," the growling, tired voice said.

"Damn, Jake. You sound like you're mad at the world."

There was brief silence, followed by a deep guttural noise like someone clearing their throat. "Where the hell have you been?"

The hairs on the back of Jed's neck bristled. "Diggin' up them bones. Why?"

"What kind of answer is that?"

"The only kind you're going to get using that tone with me," Jed said. "Who the hell licked the red off your lollipop?"

"A bastard used to getting his way, that's who."

"Oh, and who is this bastard?"

"Senator Bain Granville. You remember the Granvilles don't you?"

Jed rolled his eyes. The Granville family was to Sweetgrass and Indigo County what the Borgias were to Italy in the 1400s—powerful and hated, and feared by many. Nobody dared to cross them. Theirs was not a family easily forgotten.

"I remember," Jed said. "What's the senator's beef with you?"

"You."

Jake's answer came as no surprise. "I suspected as much. What the hell did I do to him?"

"You mean other than breathing lowcountry air? Probably nothing. But his cousin Parker called him and told him about you being involved in this investigation."

"Hell, I haven't seen the senator or his spineless cousin in over thirty years. Wait a minute." Jed's forehead wrinkled as he recalled seeing Stump talking to the pear-shaped man in the rumpled suit near the courthouse.

"Maybe I have seen him," he said, "out talking to Stump as I left your office day before yesterday. If that was Parker, he ain't aged all that well. So what's his beef?"

"They know about your phone calls and questioned how you've come to be chosen to receive them. In fact, the good senator as much as demanded you be brought in for questioning. He claims you have the best motive of anyone for coming back up here and killing folks."

"And that would be?"

"Payback for what happened to your brother."

Jed's forehead grew hotter than his grandmamma's breakfast griddle. "Where does he come off making demands like that?"

"He knows Sadie Dunlap was kin to Willie Sims, and he deduced you could have killed her to get back at Willie for what he did to your brother."

"That's bullshit. What's my motive for killing Kristin Clay?"

Jake clucked at Jed's response. "I asked him that very question."

"And?"

"He said you likely killed her to make it look like a serial killer is on the loose. He suggested that with your experience, you'd be able to concoct a way to take any focus off of yourself as a suspect."

Jed tried to unravel the senator's illogical premise. "What about Parker? Abby Granville was his sister."

"They apparently chose to overlook that connection," Jake said.

"And just how in the hell did they know about my phone calls?" Jed thought about Hap Gentry. "That SOB reporter didn't write a story in the paper about them, did he?"

"Not exactly."

"Then exactly how?" Jed asked.

Jake's voice soured. "Stump is Parker's nephew."

"I'll be damned. No wonder I don't like the bastard." Jed inhaled and then exhaled slowly to calm down. "So, Stump decided to get me out of this investigation by having the state senator force you into arresting me for the murders."

"Look." Jake's voice sounded sharp and angry. "Ain't nobody, especially Bain Granville, forcing me into arresting you or anybody else until I'm convinced about their guilt. I'm still sheriff in these parts, and I decide when I have enough evidence to make charges."

"I'm thankful for that." A hint of sarcasm laced Jed's words.

Changing the subject, Jake said, "Heard you were looking for me."

"Yeah, earlier. I found Willie Sims and talked to him."

"I heard that too."

Something in Jake's tone signaled a problem. "What are you not telling me?" Jed asked.

"It's Sims. Old man Rifkin saw the two of you talking. He also said when Sims came back inside the store, he was visibly shaken and shortly afterwards Sims left, saying he'd be back. Rifkin ain't seen or heard from him since."

"We just talked about Sadie. When I asked about any connection she might have had to hoodoo, he got all rattled. That's when he went back inside and I left."

Jed heard a long sigh come through the receiver. "So, you haven't seen him since, right?"

"Right."

"Rifkin's convinced something's happened to Sims, and he thinks you had something to do with it."

"Sounds to me like the whole damn town thinks I'm running around killing folks. Stump didn't happen to go out and interview Rifkin, did he?"

"As a matter of fact, he did," Jake said. "By the way, the senator said Parker told him he saw you talking with Jessie out in front of the courthouse."

"Yeah. Did he find something wrong with that too?"

"Just that he found it interesting you were meeting with a shrink. He suggested I might bring her in for questioning."

Jed laughed out loud. "If that's the case, she just might have to claim doctor-client privilege. I'm on the way over to her place now. You want me to tell her she's wanted for questioning?"

"That won't be necessary, Jedediah, but you be careful. You need to be watching your back. Given somebody's already gone and blown up your house, you need not let your guard down."

"I know that better than anybody, but thanks." Jed realized that Jake might be the only person in Sweetgrass who believed in his innocence.

"What's with you and Jessie?" Jake asked. "I thought those flames got a good dousing years ago."

"Purely business, old friend. Turns out she's Kristin Clay's godmother. I'm hoping she can clear up some details from my interview with Kristin's roommate. Say, have you found out any more about the boy killed with Sadie Dunlap?"

"Not much I didn't already know. His daddy, Trent, used to manage the sawmill down by Crescent Landing. After Trent's death, the boy's mamma moved and Lamar stayed here in Sweetgrass. He lived by himself."

Jed asked, "How did Trent Lassiter die?"

"Used a twelve gauge to splatter his brains all over his office."

"Sounds like he wanted to make sure. Leave a note?"

"Nope," Jake said. "No real explanation. He just up and offed himself. His widow took his death hard, blamed herself. As could be expected, she took her son's death pretty hard, too. He was all she had left."

"She know of any reason Lamar was out with Sadie Dunlap? Any history of drug use?"

"Not that she knew of. She hasn't seen him in over a year; hadn't talked to him lately. Him being found with a black girl, especially a junkie, came as a big shock to her, though. She couldn't offer an explanation."

"I'm almost at Jessie's now," Jed said. "You'll let me know if anything else develops?"

"Will do," Jake said. The conviction in his voice sounded weak. "Tell Jessie I said hello," he said before hanging up.

# CHAPTER · 14

Following the directions Jessie had given him, Jed turned off the paved road onto a sandy drive and entered an arbor tunnel where live oak branches twisted overhead, clasping one another like giant hands joined together. The driveway looked like a postcard photograph.

A few hundred yards ahead, he saw a pristine, white antebellum home with tall columns and a sprawling front porch. Off to his right, a pond's silvery surface shimmered in the dimming light of dusk. Jed craned his neck and looked all around the plantation estate, which, he imagined, appeared as it must have looked over a hundred years before. Jed pulled around the circle drive and parked at the base of the long stairway.

The heavy oak door opened as Jed stepped up onto the broad porch. Behind Jessie he saw a gleaming crystal chandelier lighting the entrance hall, but for all its brilliance, Jessie's welcoming smile shone brighter.

"Wow, Jes! I half expected Scarlett O'Hara to come gliding out onto the porch to greet me."

"You've been watching too many old movies," she said. "You can come in, but jokes about Tara remain outside. I've heard them all."

"Yes'm," he said with a wink as he walked by her.

Jed's eyes drank in the home's exquisite interior, from the ornate detail of the crown molding, to the Persian runner stretching the length of the dark, hardwood hallway. A spiral staircase corkscrewed down from the second and third stories, and he could almost imagine Jessie decked out in a vintage gown with a wide-brimmed hat as she descended to receive guests. The walls of the living room to his right were covered with tapestries and paintings, the tables with expensive crystal, china, and silver.

"Jes, you live in a museum."

"Sometimes, at night, it seems that way. If I didn't love it so much here, I'd move somewhere smaller." A look of wanderlust fell over her as she closed the door behind Jed.

"It's so peaceful out here," she said. Her eyes sparkled. They revealed the fanciful quality of a child at Christmastime. "I just can't imagine living anywhere else."

"I can understand," Jed said, thinking back to his small Atlanta apartment and to the modest home of his parents before the explosion.

"In the summertime I love sitting out back, listening to the bullfrogs croak and the cicadas sing. And when it gets real dark, you can watch the lightning bugs flash or count the stars in the sky. The creek out back is full of oysters and clams and shrimp. At low tide I can wade out and catch my supper."

Listening, Jed realized Jessie was living his fantasy life. "This is wonderful."

"Enough of my goings-on. I've fixed us some sandwiches. They're out back on the porch. I keep it enclosed in the winter so I can enjoy the view without freezing."

"Sounds great," Jed said, guarding against feelings he hadn't experienced in thirty years.

"What would you like to drink? Iced tea, water, a Coke, beer? You name it; I'll see if I have it."

"What? No mint julep?"

She wrinkled her mouth. "Funny. I do have a little bourbon—but no mint, I'm afraid."

Unpleasant memories of his recent morning hangover made his choice of beverage easy. "Tea would be great," he said.

Jessie disappeared through a doorway, leaving him to stroll down the hallway toward the back porch. Along the way he stopped to admire the artwork hanging on the walls. On the brightly colored canvases he recognized the scenes as being of New Orleans. Several were of jazz musicians performing in the nightclubs there. *Whoever painted these is pretty good,* he thought.

When he reached the end of the hallway and stepped out onto the back porch, his eyes bugged. The porch was bigger than his house had been. High-back rockers—seven of them—lined the wall. Three fans hung evenly spaced from exposed beams dissecting the ceiling into four equal parts.

Jed opened the storm door leading outside and breathed in the cool brackish air blowing off the tidewater creek out back. He saw a dock and a pier stretching out into the water, disappearing beyond the glow of the spotlights mounted at the corners of the home. A boathouse stood next to the dock, and he could just make out the surface of the high tide lapping against the sides. *Beautiful,* he thought, *absolutely beautiful.*

"Shadrach found this place soon after we married," Jessie said, stepping onto the porch with tall glasses of iced tea. "We both fell in love with it at first sight. It needed a lot of work, so we kind of stole it and then fixed it up. That was fun."

A mirthful glow illuminated her face as she handed Jed his tea. "It's way too big for just me, but like I said earlier, I love it too much to leave."

Jed thought about the paintings he had seen in the hallway, especially the ones of the jazz musicians. The one of a pianist in a smoky nightspot settled in his mind.

"Green?" he said, staring at Jessie. "Shadrach Green, the jazz legend?"

"The one and only," she said, smiling.

"Wow, Jes. I've got his CDs."

"He didn't just play the piano and the sax. Those made him famous, but he could take almost any instrument, even ones he hadn't played before, and in no time he'd create a sound straight from heaven. He even painted. Those you saw in the hallway were done by him." She looked out at the stars in the dark sky. "Now his audience is celestial and holy."

"Best I recall, he wasn't that old. How did he die?"

Jessie mashed her lips together, and Jed could tell she did so to gain her composure. "Cancer at age sixty-three," she said. "He took to coughing and couldn't shake it. He blamed his allergies, and I couldn't talk him into going to see a doctor. He flat refused to slow down, to give his body time to heal. When he did go in for a checkup, it was too late." Her voice trailed off as she spoke.

Over the next several minutes, Jed and Jessie rocked in their rockers, staring out toward the creek. Jed wondered what occupied her thoughts but didn't feel he had the right to intrude.

Jessie broke the silence. "When you called, you said you needed to talk about Kristin."

"I spoke with Ginger Lane," he said.

Jessie sat her tea on the glass-topped, white wicker table between their chairs. She eyed him with a look of renewed interest. "How is she holding up? I meant to call her but just haven't."

"She's understandably shaken, but her father's with her. She came back to get a few things, and he's pretty insistent she return home with him until the killer is caught."

Jessie shook her head as she rocked. "She's a good kid."

"Yeah, seemed so. She mentioned Kristin's relationship with her grandmother. Can you tell me about her?"

"Nell? Sure. What do you want to know?"

"I guess for starters, what do you know about her accident?"

"Not a lot," Jessie said. "According to what Carol Ann told me, her car went off the causeway bridge into the water, and she drowned."

"Interesting. I got the impression from Ginger that the grandmother was a bit of a recluse."

"She was. That's what's so strange about her accident. She never drove by herself. Usually Kristin would drive her where she needed to go."

Jed stared out toward the canal behind Jessie's house. "Carol Ann? That's Kristin's mom?"

"Uh-huh, that's right. Don't you remember her from high school?"

Jed's forehead wrinkled as he tried to recall a Carol Ann Clay in high school. "No, I don't think so."

"She was Carol Ann Renfrow," Jessie said with a smile that told Jed she had picked up on his confusion.

"As in Sheriff Renfrow?" he asked, startled at the obvious connection to Bobby.

"Yes, Cletus Renfrow was Carol Ann's daddy."

As Jed rocked back in his chair, the branches of two family trees sprouted in his head—one white and one black. The revelation shocked him speechless.

"Jedediah, what's wrong? You look like you just saw a ghost."

Theories and what-if scenarios swirled like tiny tornadoes inside the veteran investigator's head. "There's something very obvious in all of this," he said, "and I'm missing it."

"You look and sound like you're under a spell."

Jed glanced over at Jessie. "What did you just say?"

"About what?"

"You said I looked like I was under a spell."

"Yeah . . . so? I just meant—"

"Do you believe in hoodoo, in the power of the root?"

Jessie laughed. "That's a strange question. Why would you ask me that?"

Jed stroked his chin as he tried to mentally sort out the pieces of the murderous puzzle. "Seriously, as a doctor, a psychiatrist, do you believe in hoodoo?"

Jessie twisted her mouth. "As a psychiatrist, I certainly believe there's a connection between a troubled mind and a sick body. So yes, I can believe a mojo or potion conjured by a root doctor could probably work when people believe it will work. Providing, of course, there isn't a more organic cause of the ailment."

"You're hedging."

"No, no, I'm not. Hoodoo is deeply rooted in spirituality, just like modern-day religions are. I know a lot of folks believe in the power of hoodoo, and their beliefs can have an effect on them. But do I believe a root doctor can put a curse on me or have hags chase me around and take over my body? No, I don't believe that."

"So what you're saying is that a root doctor doesn't necessarily have any power, but if folks believe he does, then what that root doctor does can affect them."

"Yes, I think that's true, but there are plenty of people who would argue the root doctor controls the power instead of it just being a mental thing. The human mind is our most powerful organ," she said. "It can control our physical ailments as well as our mental ones. If we could harness all the capabilities of the human brain, we could overcome any illness and accomplish any feat, just by willing it to happen."

Jed nodded. "So if a person is a believer in hoodoo, a root doctor could probably convince them an evil spirit has taken over their body."

"If you're asking if our minds are capable of making us hear voices and see things that don't really exist, the answer is yes. Clinically, we might interpret those symptoms as indicative of schizophrenia. . . . What's this all about?"

"I don't quite know," Jed said, feeling bewildered. "Sadie Dunlap is the granddaughter of Willie Sims, the man convicted of killing Bobby. And Kristin is the granddaughter of Cletus Renfrow, the man who investigated Bobby's death and arrested Willie Sims. I just don't believe those relationships are coincidental."

"And the hoodoo?" Jessie asked.

"Signs of it were found at both crime scenes." Jed sighed. He tapped his finger on the arm of his rocker. "There's something I haven't told you."

Jessie's expression revealed her intense interest in what he was about to say. She barely blinked.

"Prior to or soon after both murders, the killer called me and told me where to find the bodies."

Jessie's hand flew to her mouth. "Oh, my!"

"I'm convinced all of the killings have something to do with Bobby's death, and I fear more may die."

Jessie stared wide-eyed at Jed. She said nothing.

"The only plausible reason for him calling me," he said, "is because I'm Bobby's brother."

"Did this killer mention Nell when he called?" Jessie asked. "Is that why you asked about her?"

"No, but I have to admit that the circumstances surrounding her death cause me to wonder if there's a connection there too. The reason I came by this evening is because Ginger mentioned that a few months ago, Kristin returned from visiting her grandmother, very upset about something Nell had told her. I was wondering if you knew what she may have told Kristin."

"I have no idea, although I did notice Kristin seemed distant and preoccupied on the few occasions I saw her after Nell's death. I chalked it up to grief, figuring we'd have other opportunities to talk."

"I saw her on campus the day the school dedicated a music rehearsal hall in memory of Shadrach. I went to unveil the plaque." Jessie gazed thoughtfully out the back windows. Emotion coated her words. "It was a beautiful day, quite an honor. . . . Anyway, Kristin came to the dedication. When I asked about her mother and expressed sympathy about Nell's passing, she came across as cold and distant. I was surrounded by friends and admirers of Shadrach, so I didn't have a chance to find out what was wrong."

Jessie closed her eyes for a brief second. When she opened them, moisture was visible. "That was the last time I had a chance to talk to my goddaughter."

Jed waited as Jessie sipped her tea. Her hand shook. He listened to the tinkling of the ice against the glass, wondered if continuing with questions now was such a good idea.

"We can do this another time," he said.

"No, I'm fine—really."

"If you're sure," he said, "I'd like to hear more about Nell and why she became a recluse."

"Really, I'm okay," she said. "But I'm not sure I can help you with why she shut out the world."

"Yet, she chose to go out the night she drove off the causeway bridge."

"Yes. . . . If that's what happened."

"You don't believe the official story?"

"I don't know what to believe. I do know Nell almost never left home, and when she did, Kristin drove her. Other than the night of the accident, I don't ever recall hearing about Nell driving, much less seeing her behind the wheel of her car. Even the times when Kristin drove her were rare and usually involved necessary trips to the doctor or dentist—in Savannah. She avoided locals with a passion."

"Any idea why she didn't like being around people from her hometown, people she grew up around?"

"Not really. It all started around the time her husband died. Before that, I'd see her and Carol Ann out and about in the community fairly regular. After Sheriff Renfrow passed, she got to where she wouldn't have anything to do with anybody. Her shades stayed pulled down, and her curtains remained drawn. She verbally abused anyone, including the mailman, who dared to try to be sociable. Rumors spread she had gone crazy. Neighbors warned their kids to stay away, and of course you can imagine what the children did with that information."

"I can indeed," Jed said. "How did the sheriff die?"

Jessie blinked with surprise. "I thought you knew. He committed suicide."

Jed gaped in stunned silence. "Seems we have an epidemic of folks taking their own lives around here. When?"

Jessie shrugged. "I don't know exactly. I know Carol Ann and I were living in an apartment near the Charleston campus when the police came by and delivered the news. She had a car at school, and I drove her home."

Visions of the sheriff's granddaughter sitting beside a tree with a bullet hole in her temple occupied Jed's thoughts. "Do you know any details?"

"No, not really. It's been so long ago, but if it's important, I can call Carol Ann."

"If she's up to it, I'd like to talk with her about Kristin's last conversations with her and how her father died. She might also be able to shed some light on why her mother isolated herself from her friends and neighbors."

"I'll ask," Jessie said. "She may be full of grief, but she wants answers too. And if what she knows can help catch Kristin's killer, I'm sure she'll be willing to share it with you."

Jed stood and walked across the porch to look out the windows. "I was thinking," he said. "Do you think Carol Ann would be willing to drive down and let us look through Nell's things?"

"Yes, if you think it's important. She was impressed when I told her what you did in Atlanta and that you were looking into Kristin's death. She'll come. I'm sure of it."

"I was wondering if Nell kept a diary. Maybe she wrote down the secret she told Kristin."

Jessie smiled. "That's pretty good. Did they teach you that in detective school?"

"No. As the old saying goes, I learned it in the school of hard knocks." Jed laughed, glanced at his watch. "I guess I ought to be going. It's getting late, and I'd like to talk to Jake if I can get up with him."

"Let me try calling Carol Ann before you leave." Jessie hurried back inside the house.

Minutes later she returned. "I got her on her cell phone. She's in Charleston, where they took Kristin for autopsy. She's pretty torn up, but she agreed to meet us at Nell's sometime midmorning."

"I can understand how hard it must be for her, but I think it's important she come," Jed said. "Call it an educated hunch, but I believe something in that house will shed some light on what's been going on around here."

Jessie walked with him out onto the front porch, where she smiled softly. "I'm glad you came by. It's been real nice seeing you again."

The porch light shined down on Jessie's face, just as the porch light had on that night thirty-five years before at her mamma's house. "Me too," he said and hurried down the steps.

# CHAPTER · 15

The chatter of the wildlife foraging in the forest's darkness reminded Buckra Geechee of home. He heard an owl screech somewhere off in the night, the shriek of a bobcat, the hush that followed the blood-chilling cry.

He listened with an intent ear, visualized the night stalkers. The great horned owl with its massive wingspan soaring through the cypress high above the glistening surface, its keen eyes peeled for dinner scurrying across a peat bog; the lynx with its reddish brown fur, stealth in its hunt, lethal in the attack. They were killers with a purpose, just like he was.

Growing up in Granny Leech's swamp, he had become familiar with all of the animals living there, their calls from the depths of the darkness, the way they hunted, and the tracks they left in the loamy soil. He had learned from them, considered them his kindred.

He knew from the bobcat's caterwaul whether the animal was male or female. He could tell when it wanted a mate and when it wanted to signal a nearby deer of its imminent demise. He longed to be back out there with them, matching wits, hunting, and yes, even being hunted.

Now, however, he had come in search of other prey, a two-legged treacherous variety. This animal and others like it were responsible for his never being able to know his grandpa. And for that misstep, they would pay with their lives.

The first three to die weren't personal; they were necessary. They were what the military referred to as collateral damage, the deaths of innocents to achieve a mission. They died so he could be the bobcat sending a warning of imminent demise.

The victims who would come next were another matter altogether. He cherished the thought of watching their eyes fill with terror, their throats constrict until they couldn't cry out for mercy.

He laughed out loud. Mercy! Would they really expect he would show any?

He knelt and scooped up a handful of forest humus, held it close to his nose, inhaled through flared nostrils. He loved the smell. It reminded him of home.

Walking to the edge of the forest, he looked across the road to where his next victim lived. Unlike the first three, the thought of bringing down tonight's prey excited him.

Granny Leech had promised him he would come to this time and, when he did, the spirits would be with him to protect him from those wanting to do him harm. He gripped the amulet hanging around his neck. He feared nothing, as long as the spirits were close, and Granny Leech promised they would be there until his job had ended. Then he could come home.

He walked back to his truck, which he had parked in a thick mix of pines and oaks bordering the field across from the house. He picked up the pistol off of the seat.

Over the past year, he had come to this place often. He had watched the strikingly beautiful woman who lived in the modest home go about her chores, and he had watched her small daughter play as the mother worked. In the summer he even witnessed the death of the woman's husband when the tractor the man rode in the field turned over on top of him.

Buckra Geechee alone saw the accident, and he alone could have tried to save the man. The instinct to do so gripped him at the time, but he couldn't allow anyone to see him, for fear his mission would be compromised. He left the man there alone in the field, pinned underneath his green tractor's engine, until the woman came home and found him. By then her husband had died.

He glanced at his watch. He had waited long enough for the woman to leave with her daughter, didn't understand why she hadn't. Every Tuesday and Thursday afternoon, she drove her daughter into town, where the little girl studied to read Braille. He knew, because he had followed them on several occasions, and when he had asked around, he found out the woman who lived in the home they visited taught children to read in Braille. The child wasn't completely blind. He had watched her play in the yard, but she did wear glasses—thick ones, he presumed—even though he had never risked getting close enough to see for himself.

He began walking toward the front of the home. He hated he would have to deal with the woman and child, but some things couldn't be helped. *Collateral damage,* he reminded himself. Granny Leech had warned him of times when things wouldn't go as planned. He couldn't let those distractions deter him from his mission, she had told him. He had to do whatever necessary to ensure completion of his mission.

He walked up the wooden steps, stopped on the porch, and looked up and down the dark and deserted road. Now was the time of destiny.

Callie Hart leaned against the pale blue ceramic tiles covering her kitchen countertop. She smiled at the shine sparkling from the freshly mopped floor.

When she and Ronnie had decided to remodel the rundown farmhouse before their wedding, they agonized over the slightest detail. The colors in the kitchen needed to be just so, and the draperies throughout the house had been meticulously selected. In the end, all of the hours spent studying every sample at the Savannah home decor store had been deemed well spent. The home had turned out just as they had dreamed.

Callie dried her hands with a blue-plaid dish towel and reflected on that brightest of times. She sighed. Ronnie would love how she had refinished the cupboard that sat in the corner.

Restoring the old house became a labor of love for the young couple. Ronnie refinished the hardwood floors, repaired the damaged walls, and replaced doors and windows. He remodeled most of the kitchen himself. Callie did the scraping and painting, and she even helped with the plumbing, something she had learned from a do-it-yourself book she checked out of the local library.

After their wedding, they lived in two rooms in the back of the three-bedroom home for almost a year. She cooked on a borrowed Coleman camping stove, and the outhouse behind the barn became their bathroom until they completed the one downstairs.

That first year had been both hard and wonderful. Ronnie had always wanted to be a farmer like his grandfather, so he managed to find time to plant peanuts on the fifteen acres across the road from the house. Callie recalled how proud he had been after his first harvest.

The birth of Megan came that first year, too. With her brown eyes and a dimpled smile, everyone remarked how much she favored her father.

Callie threaded the towel through the brass ring next to the sink. Tomorrow would be Megan's fifth birthday, exactly eight months since the tractor had turned over on Ronnie, crushing his chest, killing him.

"Mamma! Mamma! Some man's at the door." Little Megan's loud drawl flowed from her cherub lips like thick molasses. "He says he needs to talk to you."

Callie frowned. She cast her pale-blue eyes up at the ceiling and then glanced into the mirror hanging on the wall. Beads of perspiration dotted her reddened forehead, and her sun-bleached, honey-blonde hair hung in limp, damp ribbons across her face.

She frowned, thinking she didn't look presentable enough to be welcoming a visitor. She wiped the moisture from her face. With a flick of her weather-chapped hand, she moved the wet strands of hair from her eyes. *Who could be calling so late?* she thought. *Salesmen never come out this far, and all of my friends know my routine. If Megan hadn't been running a fever earlier today, she'd be in her Braille class now.*

Callie said to her daughter, "Coming, sweetheart, but don't yell. Remember, Gramps is sleeping." Callie cast one last critical look into the mirror. She tucked her denim shirt into her jeans.

As her bare feet stepped onto the glistening hardwood of the hallway, she could see the image of a man on the other side of the screen door. Megan, standing near the threshold, held a cloth doll with mismatched button eyes and lips sewn with red thread. Callie had cherished the doll when she was Megan's age. Now she drew joy in watching her own daughter do the same.

"He said he needs to talk to you, Mamma."

Callie held her finger to her lips. "Shhh. All right, dear, but not so loud. You run in the other room. Put Dolly to bed."

She patted her daughter's back and then watched the ringlets of naturally curly hair bounce across the girl's shoulders as she danced into the family room. Callie turned and faced the vaguely familiar man standing at her front door. "Hello. How may I help you?"

# CHAPTER · 16

Jed pulled his Volvo in front of the courthouse, hopped out, and headed up the steps to the Indigo County Sheriff's Dispatch Center. He glanced at the AUTHORIZED PERSONNEL ONLY sign just before he turned the doorknob. As it had been earlier, the door was unlocked, and as he had earlier, he received a less than friendly welcome.

"Git out," the dispatcher barked without looking to see who had entered the small and dimly lit room. "Ain't got time for no visitors."

Before Jed could respond, he heard the frantic treble voice of a male deputy stammer from the radio speaker.

"10-4, units are on the way," the dispatcher said. Her voice was strained but calmer than the deputy's.

Aware something urgent was taking place, Jed didn't speak. Instead, he shuffled over to a dark corner to listen to the radio and watch the woman managing the flow of sheriff's cars to what had to be a serious incident.

She pushed a button in the center of her console, setting off a high-pitched tone. The alert sounded several times before she keyed the microphone to speak. "We have an officer down and a 10-67 at the Hart residence on rural route 1530. That's the old Lassiter Sawmill Road. The driveway leading to the house is in the first curve beyond Wilson Creek Bridge."

Jed didn't wait to hear more. He hurried back out the door of the dispatch center and scurried down the steps of the courthouse. He repeated out loud the directions he had heard. He repeated them again as he climbed into his Volvo, then he reached for a pad to write them down while they were fresh. Before he could finish, his cell phone rang.

He answered without looking to see who had called. Only Jake and Jessie knew the number, and with all the commotion in the dispatch center, he figured his caller had to be Jake.

"I just heard you have an officer down," he said. "Your dispatcher gave out an all-response call to the Hart residence. Are you headed there?"

"Bradley?" The voice didn't belong to Jake.

"Who is this?"

"Gentry. Did you get another call?"

"How the hell did you get this num—? Never mind. What do you want?"

By this time, Jed had steered onto the highway, speeding in the direction he hoped would take him to the location given by the dispatcher. He didn't know the Harts or where to find their house, but he vaguely remembered where Trent Lassiter's sawmill had been located. His father had taken Bobby and him there to get scrap lumber for their tree house. He figured once he got close enough, he would see the flashing emergency lights and they would lead the way to the scene of the crime.

"Did you get another call from the killer?" Gentry asked.

"No," Jed said without trying to hide his annoyance for being bothered at such an inopportune time. "The telephone he called me on was the phone in my house, and, like my house, it blew up."

But as the reporter's question penetrated his wall of irritation, Jed realized the man must already know about what had happened. "Has there been another murder, Gentry?"

"Yeah, but more than that," he said with a hint of distress in his voice. "The sheriff's been shot."

Jed heard his own gasp. "How . . . how do you know? Are you sure it's Jake and not a deputy?"

"I was listening to my scanner. I heard the original call go out. A few seconds later I heard the sheriff call to say he was close by and would check it out. After the sheriff called in to say he had arrived, I didn't hear him again. About five minutes went by before the dispatcher tried to raise him. She couldn't. Another few minutes passed. Then I heard a deputy screaming into his microphone. He said the sheriff had been shot."

"Oh, no!" Disbelief shrouded Jed's thoughts.

"The killer must have still been there and shot him when he arrived."

"Thanks," Jed said as he mashed his right foot against the accelerator. Preoccupied with the news about Jake, he flipped the phone cover closed, reopened it, and dialed Jessie's number. "Hope I didn't wake you," he said before she got "hello" out of her mouth.

Jessie's voice soothed his tremors of concern for Jake. "I lived with a jazz pianist for ten years," she said. "Early to bed wasn't something we practiced."

"Jake's been shot." Jed blurted out the news, immediately wishing he hadn't.

Jessie drew a deep breath. "Oh, sweet Jesus! What happened?"

"Sounds like he was ambushed by the killer we've been after . . . at the scene of another murder. The killer must have been waiting on him. I'm on my way there now."

"Another murder?" The dread in her voice deepened. "Who?"

"Name's Hart. The house is off the Lassiter Sawmill Road."

Silence filtered through the phone, followed by Jessie's distraught recognition of who had been killed. "Oh, no, that's Callie's house."

"How well do you know this Callie?" Jed asked.

"Very," she said in a whisper. "She has. . . . What about Megan?"

"Who's Megan?" Jed asked, even though the concern in Jessie's voice already had answered his question.

"Callie's little girl. She's five." Jessie breathed heavily into the phone. "Are . . . are they all dead?"

"I don't know," Jed said. "Are others living in the house? Callie's husband?"

"He died last summer in a farming accident," Jessie said. "His tractor turned over on top of him."

"Damn." *Talk about star-crossed.*

"Callie's granddaddy lived with her and Megan. He moved in after his stroke a few years back."

A chill ran down Jed's spine. "Her granddaddy lived with her," he said. His next words came in a slow cadence. He feared the answer. "Who is her granddaddy?"

Jessie said, "Rembert Baker. You remember. He used to be a judge. . . ." She paused. "Oh, no."

She didn't have to finish her explanation. Jed knew from the sound of Jessie's fading voice that she also had made the connection. He drove in stone silence, almost paralyzed from speaking. Judge Rembert Baker had presided over the trial of the two men convicted of killing Bobby and Abby.

"Jedediah? Are you still there?"

"I'm here."

"Are they all dead?"

"I don't know. The dispatcher referred to a 10-67, which means there's at least one death. She didn't say how many. Let me call you back when I learn more." He glanced down at his watch. "It might be late."

"I don't care what time it is—call. I won't be able to sleep anyway until I hear about Callie and Megan."

A thick haze crept from the creek beneath the shadowy image of Wilson's Bridge just as their conversation ended. Up ahead, heavy woods on both sides of the road concealed any sign of emergency lights. Jed slid the phone into his shirt pocket and leaned forward to see where the road leading to the Hart home came out to meet the highway.

Too many coincidences, he thought, and he didn't understand most of them.

He realized the phone calls had been the killer's way to keep him involved. He didn't know why. But the imaginary appearance of Rascal and his late night rendezvous with Bobby's spirit weren't so easily explained. An overactive imagination, he thought. Maybe, but a gradual migration toward insanity seemed more plausible.

A mailbox with HART painted on the side in stenciled white letters came into view. Jed looked up to the fog-shrouded heavens. "If it really is you, Bro, keep showing me the way."

Rotating red and blue lights, their luminescence obfuscated by the thick soup, were barely visible until he pulled onto the dirt drive leading to the Hart home. The hazy glow of a spotlight lit up the entrance to a barn and a green tractor partially covered with a canvas tarp. He wondered if that had been the one Callie Hart's husband died under.

Jed counted six marked and two unmarked cars. Stump's Crown Vic was right in front. In fact, he thought, the entire force of the Indigo County Sheriff's Department must have responded.

An ambulance sat parked beside a plain blue van on the front lawn of the neat-as-a-pin home. He knew from the previous murders that the van belonged to Rutledge Funeral Home, the designated body removal service in Indigo County. The presence of the van sadly underscored that someone had died, but the ambulance gave hope that someone else might have survived.

The humanitarian in him felt good that a life might have been spared, but the cop in him took special notice of the ambulance's presence. Finally, there might be a surviving witness.

As he exited his car, Jed wondered where everyone was. He saw no one, heard no one, and their absence concerned him. Nowhere did he see a sentinel guarding the front entrance to the house, and nowhere did he see anyone searching the grounds of the home for evidence. The soupy mist crawling from the depths of the creek banks lent a sense of eeriness to the entire scene. "Spooky," he whispered.

He climbed the steps to the front porch, which was lit by two ceiling-mounted light fixtures. A green swing hung from chains attached to hooks in a crossbeam on one end; pots filled with pansies dangled from the overhang of the roof. His mamma used to plant pansies in the fall because they would bloom most of the winter; and even if they froze, they almost always came back out in the spring. Jed paused in front of the wide-open door, studied the big blue and yellow blooms peering over the lips of the containers. What a stark contrast they were to what he expected to find inside the home.

He thought he heard voices, but the longer he listened, the less sure he became. *Where is everyone?* The inside of the home was as still as a grave. He cautiously glanced all around. Seeing no one to stop him, he stepped through the doorway.

Regardless of how many times he had entered homes such as this one, he never got used to the anticipation for what he would find. Of the hundreds of deaths he had investigated over the years, most turned out to be homicides. Some were accidental, others self-inflicted, but regardless of the cause, none had been pleasant. The death of a child always tore at his soul more than the adults, but each victim had a story and, in most cases, loved ones who cared about them and who worried for their safety.

The first thing he saw was a bloody swath slithering down the middle of the gleaming, hardwood hallway like a ghoulish scarlet serpent coming to greet him. All the lights shined bright, spotlighting the mayhem, but it was the mind-numbing silence that seized his attention.

*Where are the investigators, the crime-scene evidence gatherers, the guards protecting the area from contamination?*

In the living room, to his left, he spotted two gnome statuettes with red cone-shaped caps sitting peacefully on a sculpted log. A small, navy throw pillow with a Bible verse embroidered on it rested against the arm of a green-and-navy striped sofa. Furniture and knickknacks in the room looked undisturbed, while out in the entry hall, a rug lay crumpled in a corner next to an overturned table. Framed photographs lay scattered across the floor.

Jed looked at the disarray. His eyes followed the bloody trail leading into the kitchen at the end of the hallway. He picked up a photo of a dark-haired little girl holding a Raggedy Ann doll. From the photograph, she smiled up at him. *Where's the girl? Where's her mother? What kind of animal are we dealing with?*

Jed thought about the unthinkable, about the Park Angel Murders. He shook his head. None of the victims in Sweetgrass had been children. Had the killer now taken that next step toward hell?

He started toward the back of the house, careful to keep close to the wall and out of the bloody stripe bisecting the hallway. At the entrance to the kitchen he stopped, stared in disbelief.

*Our killer is getting careless.*

Jed knelt down to get a closer look at a shoe print in the blood. Farther into the kitchen he saw another print, a better, sharper image of the pattern made by the sole. Both looked as if they came from a boot, maybe a size ten or eleven.

The kitchen was awash in fluorescent light. The shiny appliances sparkled, and the cherry-stained cabinets glistened. Across the room, bright lights from the backyard shone through a bay window. He saw shadowy figures moving about there.

*Could it be Jake's still alive? Is that why everyone is gathered out back?*

Jed took a quick step toward the rear door, his heart pounding with anticipation. Then he stopped.

A bare foot extending from the leg of a pair of blue denim jeans captured his attention. When he stepped around the blue marble-topped kitchen island, he saw Callie Hart, her honey-blonde hair pasted to the floor in a crimson coagulation. Her eyes were still open, staring in disbelief.

Jed leaned down beside her, thought about how this mother must have fought before succumbing to the inevitable, the totality of her mental acumen focused on the fate of her daughter. "She's fine," he whispered and brushed his hand across her eyelids to close them. "Megan's going to be just fine."

Of course, he didn't know if the girl was fine or if she had been taken by the killer . . . or if she was in the backyard with Jake, wounded—or worse, dead. He closed his own eyes and squeezed the bridge of his nose between his thumb and forefinger. For some unexplained reason, he believed telling her mother that everything was okay with the girl would help her to let go, allow her spirit to drift on to the next world.

Jed had never considered such a possibility before. Never at any other homicide scene had he allowed himself to consider the spiritual realm in his thoughts of the victim. *I really am losing it.*

"Return to admire your handiwork, did ya?" The voice came from behind Jed.

He whirled around to see Stump standing in the doorway leading from the front hallway. The barrel of the deputy's blue steel revolver pointed straight at Jed's head.

"Stand up, asshole. Keep your hands in plain view."

Jed eased to his feet. He stepped around Callie Hart's corpse.

"That's far enough. Don't be giving me a reason to blow your worthless head off. 'Cause it won't take much."

"Where's Jake?"

"Don't try that 'innocent' bullshit with me. He trusted your black ass, and now he's damn near dead. He's in back, right where you left him."

*He's still alive!* "I didn't shoot him. We're fr—"

"Yeah, yeah. Save it for the jury and judge. Not that I think it'll do you any good."

On the island counter Jed saw a wooden block with knives seated in slots across the angled top. His gaze stuck to it as if glued. For a fleeting second, he wondered just how good of a shot Stump would be if he grabbed for one of the knives.

The deputy stepped closer, cocked the hammer of his revolver with his thumb, and said, "Lessen you want to get dispatched straight to hell, you'd better be backpedaling away from the counter."

A siren blared outside. Jed took a quick step back. "You said Jake was near death. If he's conscious, he'll tell you I didn't shoot him." He backed up a couple more steps, all the while keeping a close watch on Stump's finger wrapped around the trigger of the revolver.

"Conscious? Shit, boy, I doubt he'll ever see conscious again. It's likely your shot minced his brains into mush. At best, he'll have the recollection of a radish. The EMTs done all they could out back, and now they're on their way to the hospital."

"Take me to the hospital to see him."

Stump laughed sarcastically. "So you can make sure he can't identify you as the killer? My mamma didn't raise no stupid young'uns."

As far as Jed was concerned, the deputy's conclusion about his mother's offspring was subject to debate.

"The only place you'll be going is to jail. 'Three hots and a cot' is our slogan." He grinned, no doubt considering his acidic remark clever. "After the trial, I'll personally take pleasure in delivering you to death row."

Jed responded through clenched teeth. "I didn't kill Jake any more than I did anyone else."

"You do have a way with words," Stump said. He pointed to Callie Hart. "Yessir, you stooped pretty low this time, killing the mother of a handicapped girl." He pointed to a door leading to a room off of the kitchen. "And old Judge Baker ain't been nothin' but a harmless old coot since his stroke."

"Rembert Baker's dead too?" Jed wondered if Callie happened to be a victim of circumstance instead of intent.

"You can drop the innocent act, Bradley. That dog don't hunt."

Ignoring Stump's remark, Jed said, "What about Megan? Where is she? Is she okay?"

"Oh, so you know the little girl's name. Now ain't that interesting." He stared at Jed, nodded his head. "Real interesting. Did her mamma scream it out before you shot her?"

"You son of—"

"No, you're the son of a bitch. That poor girl's at the hospital with her grandpappy Hart, who happened to show up just about the time we all arrived. Can't imagine how traumatized she is, what with seeing her mamma killed right in front of her and all. I'll credit you with having the decency not to harm her, though."

Roland, the deputy Jed had dubbed Elmer Fudd, walked up behind Stump. "Want me to take him on into town?" He seemed as concerned as Jed that Stump meant to carry out his own justice, an on-the-spot finding of guilty followed by instant execution for the crime.

"If Megan saw the killer," Jed said, "she'll tell you I'm innocent."

"Hmph," Stump grunted. "I doubt she can see well enough to ID anybody. She's legally blind, but that don't mean she didn't see some and hear a lot of what was going on."

Jed glanced at the bloody footprint on the linoleum. "The killer left a track in the blood. Take a look at the imprint on the tile over there. It doesn't match my boot."

Stump glanced over at the bloody print and shook his head. "Roland, you want to tell this ace detective how that boot print came to be there."

Roland's shoulders drooped. His gaze swept the floor before he looked up with a sheepish grin. "Reckon I got careless when I first arrived."

"That's your footprint in the blood?" Jed asked incredulously.

"Yep, that pretty much is mine."

"Okay, Roland, cuff him. Take him out of here before I do something I'll regret. Watch him, though. I don't trust him any more than I would a fox roaming around a henhouse."

Before Jed could protest, Roland walked up behind him and shoved him toward the kitchen island. "Spread your legs," he said, "and put your hands palms down on the counter."

Stump stepped closer and slid the block of knives away from Jed's reach. He grinned. "He knows the drill."

With his hands cuffed behind him, Jed sat in the backseat of Roland's patrol car and watched the deputy's eyes watch him from the rearview mirror. Neither man spoke.

Jed hated being the hunted, and he could feel the anger welling up inside. He shifted in his seat. The arch of the steel handcuff dug into his wrist. He grimaced, bit his lip, and closed his eyes, desperate to retreat to a peaceful place where he could block the pain.

He thought about the times his father got arrested. There was the time he drove all night to join Reverend King in Alabama. He spent three days in the Birmingham jail that trip. And there were the times he got arrested in Savannah and Charleston for leading protest marches, and right here in Sweetgrass when he refused to leave that restaurant. His father's sermons about those experiences made the preacher stronger and strengthened the faith of his congregation in their cause.

As the patrol car bumped over a rough piece of pavement and the handcuffs grated against his wrist bones, Jed wasn't so sure his experience would make him any stronger, but it sure was making him madder than hell.

# CHAPTER · 17

As with hospitals, jails often have a lingering, distinctive odor. When first walking into an emergency room, you get the sense of a sterile, clean environment. Alcohol and disinfectants permeate everything. Unfortunately, the same can't be said of jails, especially older ones like Indigo County's five-cell facility.

A hint of the fetid essence of rancid body odor attacked Jed as he entered the bleak front office. The gray concrete walls and worn wooden floors reeked of the stench that caused the bile rushing up his throat to curdle.

A wrinkled-face deputy with stooped shoulders and frail-looking limbs stopped sweeping to sneer at the newest prisoner. Without uttering a word, he leaned his broom handle against the edge of the desk and started toward a steel door behind a gray metal desk. On the way, he pulled a ring of oversized keys from his belt. The keys clattered as he held them close to his eyes, examining each until he found the one he needed to turn the lock's steel tumblers.

The deputy swung open the heavy door, unleashing a wave of the wretched odor that washed over all three men. Jed gagged. His eyes watered as he fought off the nausea rumbling deep inside his stomach. Even Roland emitted a strangled-sounding cough, but the elderly jailer continued inside, oblivious to the foul smell.

Beyond the threshold, a dimly lit hallway led to a row of smaller steel doors. The three men stopped at the first. Jed stared at the metal hatch covering a square window. He didn't have to imagine what awaited him inside. Jail cells such as these weren't all that different from the ones he had seen in Atlanta, no matter the sophistication or modernization of the facility. He glanced down at the food trap, where trays could be safely slid in to the prisoner. Jed grimaced.

Roland unlocked Jed's handcuffs while the old deputy utilized his oversized keys to gain access to the cell. Neither spoke.

"Don't suppose you have any air freshener?" Jed asked.

His glib remark went unanswered. Roland nudged him through the doorway into the small rectangular room. When the door slammed shut, darkness swallowed Jed. Hinges creaked as the cover over the cell door opened. Jed saw the piercing stare of the older deputy for a split second, then only dim light from the hallway filtering through the thick glass. Just enough light came in for him to make out his austere surroundings.

On a back wall, high up next to the ceiling, he saw a narrow window to the outside. Darkness deeper than night poured through the iron bars that divided the opening into three segments. He groped his way past a metal urinal and sink to the steel bunk attached to one wall, unfolded the plastic-covered mattress, and stretched out on his back with his hands cradling his head.

*Now what?*

As the minutes passed, desperation became his roommate. Stump had made it plain that he was hell-bent on hanging the murders on Jed, and arguably the deputy would likely be able to present a pretty good case for probable cause to hold him until trial. The calls he had received, though real, were suspicious and not provable. They alone might be enough to convince a judge.

Jed wrestled with how he could explain why someone he did not know, presumably the killer, would call him and volunteer where he could find three bodies. He sighed as he thought about how the judge would look upon his explanation.

Bain Granville had already postulated Jed's motive to be revenge against the descendants of the people who killed Bobby. Any reasonable judge would come closer to accepting that theory than believing what Jed knew as the truth.

As his eyes adjusted to the dim of his surroundings, Jed noticed the faint collage of graffiti gibberish scrawled in pencil on the light gray wall of chipped and peeling paint next to his bunk. He read a poem that made little sense and studied the phone numbers, dozens of them, written one after the other in a column. Based on one very detailed drawing of a man and woman making love, Jed decided one of the previous residents possessed a genuine talent wasted in criminal endeavors. It did cross his mind that this modern-day da Vinci might merely have been expressing a graphic opinion about lowcountry justice.

"Hey, bro, ain't you dat po-lice what moved here from Atlanta?"

The loud voice from another inmate down the hall awoke Jed. *I must have dozed off,* he thought.

Jed knew jailhouse communications were good, but he was surprised this inmate knew so much so fast. "How do you know me?" he asked.

"Everybody know da man what riled the conjurer's son."

"What conjurer's son?"

"Da hag ridin' you straight to jail, then to hell. You can't shake her. She done got your blood scent."

Jed sprang from his bunk and pressed his cheek against the window in his door. He tried to get a glimpse of the cell the man might be in. "How did I rile this conjurer's son?"

"You learn soon. 'Fore dayclean comes again, you know."

"What's *dayclean*? How will I know?"

The man said nothing. Silence fell on the hallway.

Jed hollered down the corridor again, repeated his call to the inmate. No response. When it became obvious no answer would come, he gave up and returned to his bunk.

The slam of the metal door at the end of the corridor awoke Jed again. Roland and the old deputy had taken his watch, wallet, cell phone, and other personal effects when they brought him into the front office of the jail, so he had no idea what time it was or how long he had been asleep. Outside, through the window, the moon illuminated the night. He remained on his bunk, still and quiet, waiting to hear from the person who had just entered his dark and putrid world.

Slow, heavy footsteps started down the corridor. Jed knew they didn't belong to the old deputy. By the time they stopped in front of his door, his gut had knotted.

"Hope I didn't wake you," Stump said as his beefy face filled the tiny window. The deputy's steely glare peered inside.

"How's Jake?" Jed asked.

The beady eyes narrowed. "Died an hour ago."

Jed sat up and staggered to his feet, feeling as if the concrete walls surrounding him had just collapsed onto his chest. He didn't want to believe the callous Neanderthal standing outside his door, but when he got close enough to see the ominous glint in the man's eyes, he knew. Jake *was* dead.

"Damn shame, too," Stump said. "He's the only eyewitness we had who could positively ID you as the killer."

Jed's back teeth ground together. "Have you even tried to talk to the girl?"

"Little Megan?" Stump clucked. "She didn't . . . *couldn't* see anything, and I ain't about to go upsettin' her more. Besides, according to her grandpa, she ain't uttered a word to nobody since he found her. The doctor said he don't have no idea how long she'll be that way."

"When do I get a phone call?"

"First thing in the morning. You ain't makin' one now."

"If Jake's dead, then I want to talk to the acting sheriff. Maybe he won't piss on my constitutional rights like you have."

Stump chuckled. "That's almost funny, Bradley. Unfortunately for you, you're talking to the acting sheriff." The man's proud and arrogant tone caused Jed's nausea to return.

"What about a new sheriff? When will they appoint one?"

Jed watched as smile creases surrounded Stump's round eyes. "Likely in the morning," Stump said. "Just as soon as Uncle Parker convenes the county board. He's chairman, and they'll select the person who'll serve as sheriff until the next election."

The knot in Jed's stomach tightened. *Of course,* he thought. *What else could go wrong?* He tried to look unmoved, but he knew he failed miserably. "What about bail? Don't I get a bond hearing?"

"Sure you do . . . just as soon as Judge Horne returns to town. Shouldn't be more than a couple of days, but don't go wastin' no time hopin' for miracles. Even given the fact your friend, Doctor Braddock, is right well off, I doubt the judge'll be settin' bail for you on these charges."

"And what exactly are the charges against me?"

"We're workin' on 'em," he said. "I'll be happy to take your statement, if you want." He stared silently through the window for a couple of moments. "You got anything you want to say?"

"Yeah, go to hell!" Jed's anger boiled, and he knew the deputy controlled him, but he couldn't do anything about it.

"I'll just put down that the defendant failed to cooperate." Stump's face disappeared from the small window.

As Jed listened to him walk away, panic began to take hold of his emotions. *With Jake dead, I'm fair game,* he thought. *And hunting season just opened.*

The steps stopped, followed almost at once by Stump's echoing voice. "By the way, Bradley, old man Rifkin said you came by and questioned Willie Sims."

"Yeah, so?" Jed shouted back. "That sure as hell isn't against the law."

"Nope, it's not. But kidnapping and murder are. Rifkin told me that soon after you left, so did Willie Sims and he seemed real scared."

Jed recalled Jake's warning: *Rifkin's convinced something's happened to Sims, and he thinks you had something to do with it. You better be watchin' your back.*

"I've checked around," Stump said. "Nobody's seen him or knows what happened to him—unless, of course, you do."

Jed didn't respond. Given who all had been killed and why, and given the direct tie of Sims to Bobby's death, he realized the old man might very well have fallen prey to the real killer.

"Suit yourself," Stump said. "After all, you do have a right to remain silent."

Jed heard the sound of the door open. He waited until he heard it slam shut before taking a breath and trying to clear his head.

For the next hour or so Jed paced back and forth. He needed to get out of jail, back on the trail of the killer. The question at hand was, *How?*

Breakfast came before sunlight sifted through the window slit on the back wall, and Jed had not slept since Stump's visit. When the elderly deputy's face appeared in the window of his door, he watched and silently waited for an opportunity to overpower the jailer. It never came. Instead, a thick brown tray slid halfway through the door slot.

"Get your breakfast, boy, or I'll dump it."

Jed swung his legs off the bunk and reached for the tray, but he didn't move fast enough. Before he could grab it, the man let go. Jed's breakfast splashed onto the dingy concrete floor.

"Sheriff Armistead was a good man," the feeble voice said through the door. "His killer don't deserve to eat nowhere but off the floor—like an animal."

Jed stared at the nearly indiscernible slop as he listened to the man cackle his way back down the hallway. Greenish powdered eggs swam in a soup of gray grits. The only thing recognizable was an unopened carton of milk, but when he picked it up, the carton felt warm. He opened it, smelled the milk, and after a cautious taste test declared it passable, if not tasty. After finishing the lukewarm drink, he tossed the empty carton into the middle of the breakfast sludge pooled on the floor.

He walked to the back wall and stretched up to look out the window. He saw the beginning of morning brightening the sky to a dull bluish gray. Along the horizon, he caught a glimpse of orange and red hues where the sun's rays streaked above the earth's curvature.

*This has to be my last day in this place,* he thought. *Having to spend more time here sure enough might turn me into an animal.*

Jed thought about the other inmate and what he had said the night before. Careful to avoid slipping on the putrid gruel, he hurried to the window and pressed the side of his face against the glass.

"Hey, what are you in for?" Jed asked.

No answer came.

He listened intently, thought he heard movement. "Are you still there?"

No one responded, so after one last attempt, Jed returned to his bunk. All he could do was wait.

"Bradley?"

Jed grimaced. He had heard the outer door open, then the heavy footsteps. The sound of metal pecking against the outside of his door told him someone was sliding a key into the lock. As he sat up and swung his legs off the bunk, he saw Stump's plump face framed in his door window. Morning light from the window slit now lit his cell.

"Stand against the back wall," the acting sheriff ordered. "I need to open the door, and I don't want you tryin' nothing stupid."

"What do you want? If you're not going to give me a phone call, just leave me the hell alone."

"I want to show you something one of my deputies found."

Jed stared at the face in the window, not liking where this visit was heading. Still, whatever Stump's men had found might be important, and if that was the case, Jed was still enough of a detective to want to know what it was. He slid off the bunk and positioned himself under the window slit on the back wall.

The key turned in the lock; the bolt slid back. Stump pulled open the door.

To Jed's surprise, the deputy did not enter alone. Behind him in the doorway stood a man with stringy blond hair splayed across his shoulders. He was the same man Jed had seen Stump talking to the morning he left Jake's office after discovering the bodies out by the church. *Parker Granville! No doubt about it. Stump's uncle and chairman of the county council.*

Father time had not been good to Parker, Jed noted. The frumpish man with a pear-shaped body and rosacea-ravaged complexion didn't look much like the arrogant, rich kid Jed had grown to despise. His wrinkled beige suit and shaggy hair made him look more destitute than privileged, but the beady, deep-set eyes were unforgettable.

A flashback to a summer day along the Tullifinny bobbed up from the morass of Jed's childhood recollections. Bobby and he had been swinging out over the river on thick vines, then letting go to see who could create the biggest splash, when Abby Granville and two of her friends drove up in Abby's bright yellow Corvair convertible. All three of the girls wore two-piece swimsuits, not bikini small, but enough to reveal their elevation to womanhood. Abby, the polar opposite of her enigmatic brother, dove into the water and swam straight to where Bobby treaded. Back then, you didn't have to be a detective to note electricity generating between the rich girl from the affluent family and Jed's son-of-a-preacher brother. Both were sixteen; both were experiencing changes in their bodies neither understood—nor seemed to want to.

Not long after the girls had joined the brothers in the river, Parker, driving a souped-up pickup truck with chrome tailpipes and flashy flames painted behind each wheel well, came sliding to a stop behind Abby's car. Rage masked his face; beer fueled his courage. A shouting match ensued between Abby and her brother, and if a couple of members of Jed's father's church, who had been fishing a few hundred yards downriver, had not come running when they heard the ruckus, the events of that day could have played out much differently. Parker and his two half-in-the-bag friends jumped into the truck at the sight of the two burly men running toward them, each with a tree limb the size of a ball bat in one hand, and left with a shower of gravel peppering the swimmers. Once the commotion died down, Abby and her friends left too, but by then her brother's defiance had melded a bond between girl and boy that only death would put asunder.

"Parker wanted to come by to let you know there's a new sheriff in town." Stump tittered like a school boy.

Florid-faced with fleshy cheeks that sagged into uneven pouches, Parker stepped up beside his nephew and threw his arm around the back of the stout man's neck. He patted Stump's shoulder and said, "That's right. I thought it so important, considering the state of crime around Sweetgrass these last few days, that I convened a conference call of all the board members about an hour ago. Unanimously, we decided to name Stump sheriff."

Jed bit his lip to prevent his expression from rewarding their less than surprising announcement. "Why come tell me? I'm a prisoner, not a voter."

Stump smiled at Jed the way Ulysses S. Grant must have smiled at Robert E. Lee when they came face-to-face at Appomattox Courthouse. He held up a black Glock pistol, one Jed recognized at once.

"Recognize this here firearm?" Stump asked.

Jed tried to read his expression, wondering what the new sheriff was up to. He didn't answer. The last time he had seen the gun was shortly after he moved back home, before the phone calls started, before Sadie Dunlap and Lamar Lassiter died. He had locked it in his glove compartment so he would have it if he ever needed it. With it locked up, he had not violated any concealed-carry laws, so he had given little thought to the weapon of late.

"Let me help you," Stump said. His voice heavy with sarcasm, he read the inscription engraved on the side of the weapon: "For twenty-six years of service—APD."

Jed stared at the gun, then at the two men. His lips pressed together, his silence continued.

"I figure *APD* stands for Atlanta Police Department, and this is the gun your department presented to you when you retired. How am I doin', boy?"

"What did you do—search my car?"

"Your car?" Stump hooted. "No, we searched around where we found Willie Sims's cold dead body a couple hours ago—on an embankment alongside the Tullifinny River. I'm betting ballistic tests at the state lab in Columbia will match this gun to the bullets we found at the Hart residence—ones recovered from Sheriff Armistead, Judge Baker, and Callie Hart. I'll even bet it'll match the bullets that killed the first three victims and the one we hope to recover from Willie Sims."

A trapdoor in the pit of Jed's stomach dropped open. "Do you think, with all my experience, I'd leave the murder weapon near the body of someone I killed?"

"I pondered that notion, I really did," Stump said, grinning. "And you know what I decided?"

Jed didn't answer.

"I decided you just might and then claim the gun was stolen. I think you thought we would be stupid enough to fall for that notion."

Stump pulled the slide back on the gun and looked down inside the top. He released the slide and pulled the trigger. Parker flinched at the sound of the loud metallic ping of the firing pin.

"You know, I think even your old friend, Jake, found it harder and harder to believe you, much as he might've wanted to. Once he saw the articles and notes we pulled from Kristin Clay's backpack . . . well, he just couldn't deny those."

"What articles? What notes?" Jed asked. Neither Jake nor anyone else had mentioned finding anything except textbooks and school information in the backpack found in the girl's car.

With his lips pressed together, Stump smiled. "Oh, I bet you know. I'll even bet Jake told you. He might've even asked you to surrender to him. I figure he phoned you and the two of you set a place to meet. But instead of meeting him, you went to the Hart farm, knowing that was close to the place y'all had agreed on. You knew Jake would be near and the first on the scene when the call went out about another murder. I figure you surprised him there and killed him."

Jed's head swam in disbelief of the absurd but believable theory Stump put forth. "I don't know what you're talking about."

"Of course you don't," the new sheriff said, showering Jed with sarcasm. "Deny everything; admit nothing. Once you've seen what we've got, I figure you'll change your tune to avoid the needle." The man disclosed a truly sinister grin. "But since your defense attorney will get it in discovery anyway, I'll go ahead and tell you what we found in the backpack."

Jed looked at Parker, thought he detected the odor of alcohol cutting through the jailhouse stench he had somehow grown accustomed to. The attorney's bloodshot eyes danced with glee; he seemed to be enjoying his nephew's performance.

Stump said, "We found newspaper articles written after your brother and Abby were killed, and there were even a couple of articles about the killings down in Atlanta. Your name was circled in red. Along the sides of the articles, she had scribbled notes. Among them were the words *find the killer,* written with the same red ink, and a bold red line was drawn from the word *killer* to your name."

As preposterous as all of it sounded, without seeing the articles or reading

Kristin's notes, Jed couldn't respond to Stump's allegations. As for the gun, someone had to have taken it from his glove compartment. But who?

He stroked the back of his neck with his hand. "I don't suppose you thought to try to lift fingerprints off the murder weapon before you brought it here for show-and-tell."

Stump smirked. "Nope, sure didn't. Funny thing, we found it in a puddle of water, so I figured prints were useless. I'm sending it to the state lab today. With any luck, we'll get it back in time for your probable-cause hearing."

Before leaving, Stump looked down at the mess in the middle of the cell floor. "I'll have Sylvester bring a mop back for you to use. We don't allow our prisoners to be sloppy."

He nodded to his uncle, and both men left the cell. Just before Stump closed and locked the door, Jed said, "What about the phone call? Don't I get one?"

Stump didn't try to hide his good mood. "Why, sure. I'll have Sylvester take you to the phone after you've cleaned up your mess. But you won't be getting out until the judge comes to set bail.

Stump slammed the door shut and spoke in a voice he knew Jed could hear. "I've got to get back down to the Tullifinny to see how our investigation is going."

# CHAPTER · 18

Anyone who has ever hunted a raccoon knows that when backed into a corner, this cute and fuzzy creature wearing a Lone Ranger's mask becomes a fierce adversary and will fight to the death, if necessary, to escape. It was about the time the elderly deputy, the one Stump had called Sylvester, opened Jed's cell door and rolled in a wheeled bucket full of water and disinfectant that the prisoner realized just how much like that cornered coon he had become.

"Sheriff said you're to mop up your mess. I'm to see you do it and to see you get a phone call once you're finished." He pulled the mop from the bucket and thrust the handle in Jed's direction.

Jed glared at the man with the frail, age-worn physique, knowing he could overpower him with little effort. Somehow, that seemed way too easy. He wondered who else might be outside the corridor waiting for him to try something stupid and desperate.

"Hurry up, boy. I got more chores to do around here than there's time in the day." The deputy pulled a short wooden club from his belt and leaned back into the corner by the door. He propped his right foot up against the wall behind him and began pounding the round stick against the palm of his hand as if to say, *Don't even think about messing with me.* He watched his prisoner with an intense stare, and Jed wondered what the man would really do if he moved toward him.

"Stump called you Sylvester," Jed said as he took the mop and began swirling the head back and forth in the frothy breakfast mix. "How long you been a deputy, Sylvester?"

The old deputy pushed away from the wall and gripped both ends of the club. "Just mop up your mess so we can get your call made. I need to get back to work."

Jed plunged the mophead into the bucket. An almost welcome pungent aroma of pine needles flooded his nostrils.

"You'd think the new sheriff would leave me some help," Sylvester said. "But instead he sends everyone out to where they found that dead ex-con. Then before I know it, he goes and heads out there himself."

Jed swiped the mop back across the floor as he listened to the deputy grumble, telling him no one else was in the building. *Could this old man be really that careless and stupid, or is he just baiting the trap set by Stump and the others?*

"That's good enough," Sylvester said after a few more minutes of watching Jed mop. "Roll that contraption out into the hall, and we'll go get you your phone call."

Jed stuck the mop into the bucket and used the handle as a rudder to steer the container of grimy grits and egg-filled water out into the corridor. Sylvester followed a safe distance behind.

"What happened to the other prisoner?" Jed asked, motioning with his head down the hallway. "He get released?"

"There ain't no other prisoner. You're it."

Jed turned and looked back at Sylvester. "I mean the one in here last night when they brought me in. Did he already get out?"

The deputy's forehead furrowed. He cast the look of someone confronting a crazy man. "I'm tellin' you, boy. You're it. You've been it since you arrived. Ain't nobody else been in any of these cells 'cept you. Understand?" Poking Jed in the back with his round stick, he nudged him toward the door leading to the outer office. "Come on, let's get this call of yours made so I can get back to my chores."

Jed shot a last glance toward the other cells. Jessie did say the mind was powerful enough to make a person hear voices. He chewed on that thought as he walked.

She'd also said that hearing those voices might mark the onset of insanity. He scratched his head. *If hearing voices is a sign of insanity, what does carrying on conversations with them mean?*

Sylvester poked Jed again with his club and then pointed toward a deep metal sink near the door. "Park the bucket in the corner over there." As Jed went about doing as the jailer instructed, the old man pulled the ring of keys from his belt to unlock the door. "Then follow me."

The two men stepped through the doorway into the sparsely furnished office. Morning sunlight flooded the room through three windows. Jed's quick glance confirmed no one else was around. He looked out the nearest window, searching for deputies out front. None were in sight. Stunned by his good fortune, he shook his head. *Can you beat that?*

"Use this one," the deputy said. He pointed to the only phone in the room, a black, rotary-dial antique sitting on the solitary desk.

"I didn't know these still existed," Jed said.

Sylvester didn't comment.

Through the finger holes, Jed saw a worn semicircle where the numbers once were, the nine and zero still faintly visible. "The county must've bought this thing before you were born."

Sylvester glared. "You're on the clock, boy, and you've only got three minutes."

Back in Atlanta, all the jailhouse phone calls were recorded. Jed didn't know if that held true for Indigo County, but to be safe he reminded himself to be careful of what he said.

He lifted the receiver from its cradle and glared at Sylvester, who hovered over him. "Can I have a little privacy?" he asked.

Sylvester shrugged then walked to the opposite side of the room, where he leaned back and again propped his right foot on the wall behind him. Jed's every move remained the object of his rapt attention.

Jed dialed Jessie's number, turning his back toward Sylvester when he finished. Relief washed through him when she answered on the second ring.

"Listen carefully to what I'm about to say," he said in a whisper as soon as he heard her say hello. "I don't have much time."

"Jed!" She sounded excited to hear him. "I heard you were arrested. I was worried. Are you out? Where—"

"I'm okay, but just listen, please."

He waited. She didn't reply, so he continued. "Meet me where we discussed before I left your house. Go there now. Don't delay, or you might be followed. I'll explain when I arrive."

"Jed—"

He dropped the receiver back onto its cradle; almost immediately Sylvester pushed off the wall and started toward him.

"All right, back you go," the deputy said, pointing toward the open metal door leading into the cellblock.

Jed took two steps toward the door. *This is it.*

As the deputy drew close, Jed stopped, whirled, and grabbed the man in a bear hug, pinning his arms to his sides. Jed squeezed the frail body until he heard a loud *oomph* and the wooden club clattered to the floor. A rattle rolled from deep down in the man's throat.

Jed released Sylvester, sure he had squeezed the life right out of the old man. The deputy slumped to the floor in a heap, and Jed dropped to his knees to check for a pulse.

With his fingers on Sylvester's carotid artery, Jed waited several seconds before detecting a heartbeat. The color began returning to the pale and withered face.

Jed sighed. *Thank God.* His intention had been to temporarily disable the old coot, not kill him, but for a few tense moments, he feared Stump just might get his chance to charge him with a murder he really *did* commit.

Sylvester moaned. Regaining consciousness, he mumbled, "What happened?"

"You fainted and I grabbed you before you fell and hurt yourself," Jed said. "Here, let me help you get to where you can lie down."

Sylvester looked up at his prisoner with a woozy stare. "Huh?"

"It'll be okay," Jed said as he pulled the man to his feet and helped him down the corridor to the open cell. "Lie down and rest. I'll get you some water."

Jed eased Sylvester onto the bunk and removed the keys from the deputy's belt. The elderly man continued to look bewildered and disoriented. After checking to make sure Sylvester's pulse was beating strong once again, Jed walked out the door, shut it, and turned the key in the lock. "Hate to do this to you, Sly, but I've got a killer to catch."

In the outer office he rifled through the desk drawers and found a bulging brown packet with his name scrawled on the outside. Inside were his wallet and watch, some loose change, and his car keys. *That's everything but my gun,* he thought. *Must be locked up in the evidence vault.*

He saw a rack of shotguns and rifles mounted on one wall, but he didn't see a key to fit the chain lock running through the trigger guards of the weapons. *Screw it.* He figured if Stump knew he had stolen a gun and armed himself, the headstrong sheriff and his deputies would have one more reason to shoot him on sight, without warning.

Outside the jail, the escapee spotted a blue work truck with the keys in the ignition. He looked around, saw no one in sight.

Opportunity—the first element necessary for a criminal act—sat right in front of him. Jed glanced up and down the street again, jumped inside the truck cab, and started the engine. This was the first time in his career he had been glad to find keys in the ignition of an unattended and unlocked vehicle.

His foot mashed the accelerator as he drew a deep breath. His escape had been all too easy, so much so that he braced for the sound of a shotgun blast.

His mouth was dry, his breathing labored. Being the hunter came natural to Jed. Being the hunted did not.

Not only did he not hear the shotgun, no one even yelled for him to stop. A woman standing on the corner under a sign showing the time and temperature even nodded with a demure smile as he drove by. Jed nodded in return.

She had just witnessed a crime and yet she suspected nothing wrong. No wonder car thieves thrived back in Atlanta.

Crime had never been a problem in Sweetgrass, at least not before Jed's return. Before his arrival they didn't spend their mornings discussing the latest homicide or whether they should let their young'uns go out, with a killer running around. No wonder Stump and half the town suspected he was the reason all hell had broken loose in their usually tranquil county. He was beginning to believe it too.

Glancing into the rearview mirror every few seconds, he drove the speed limit, trying not to draw any undue attention from passing motorists. Stump would return to the jail sometime soon, Jed predicted, and when he did, word of the escape would spread like a wildfire through dry timber. Jed turned the radio on, twisted the dial, hoping to find a local station broadcasting the news.

*Shoot,* he thought, *news of the manhunt might even be important enough to preempt the local farm report.*

He tried to laugh at his little joke but couldn't. He could only envision hundreds of farmers who would be listening, all armed with shotguns, all eager to bag their first escaped murderer. *Today could turn out to be bigger than the opening day of deer season.*

He needed to ditch the truck. Assuming the driver had discovered his loss, and allowing time for him to stomp and cuss, his call to the sheriff's dispatcher likely had already triggered a broadcast alerting all deputies to be on the lookout for the escapee and the stolen vehicle.

Having parked the truck in woods deep enough to conceal it, Jed had walked what he estimated to have been a mile or more before kneeling down beside a stand of scrub pines behind Nell Renfrow's house. Jessie's BMW sat behind the house out of sight of the roadway. He could see her leaning against the front fender with her arms folded across the middle of her navy silk blouse. She looked bewildered, and he felt guilty for dragging her into the middle of his plight.

Jed's rational side wanted to rush up to her, tell her to drive away to avoid becoming an accomplice to a felony escape, not to mention an accessory to murder. His desperate side, on the other hand, wouldn't allow him to send away the only hope he had to avoid prison and very possibly a date with the executioner. He needed her to help identify the real killer.

"Jake's dead," he said as he walked out of the tree cover, through an overgrown vegetable garden filled with weathered-gray tomato stakes angling out of the ground.

Surprise, mixed with relief, appeared on Jessie's face. She pushed away from the car and brushed her hands against her beige skirt. "I'm so glad you're okay," she said. "I'd already heard about Jake. I also heard Stump's the new sheriff and that he's charged you with the murder."

"To name just one," Jed said. "News travels fast."

She looked past him to the forest. "How . . . how did you get here?"

"Let's just say I borrowed someone's truck and leave it at that for now."

She reached up and touched his cheek. "Oh, Jed."

He pressed his lips tight. For the first time, he felt the fatigue, the anxiety, and the anguish of his friend's death starting to overwhelm him. "How did you hear about Jake?"

"Radio. It was the lead story this morning as I was leaving the hospital. How did you get out of jail?"

"Don't ask," Jed said. "Why were you at the hospital?"

"I had to check on Megan. See for myself that she was all right."

"How is she?"

"Okay . . . for now."

"Did you talk to her?"

"No, she was sleeping when I arrived. Her grandfather was with her. We went out into the hall to talk so we wouldn't disturb her."

"Did he say if she told him what happened?"

"He said he found her hiding behind the sofa in the living room, clutching her . . . dolly." Jessie's words caught in her throat. "He did tell me how he found Callie, how gruesome her house looked."

"As bad a mess as any I've seen," Jed said. "I'm afraid the killer's becoming more violent."

"He said the killer dragged her up the hallway into the kitchen," Jessie said.

Jed nodded. "Did he mention seeing Jake or if he heard any shots?"

"No. He did say he went back and looked into the judge's bedroom. He found him shot in the head. His body was half in the bed, half out."

"Interesting," Jed said. "Judge Baker must have heard the shot that killed his granddaughter and tried to come to her aid."

"Despite his infirmities," Jessie said.

"That's right," Jed said. "Stump referred to him as harmless, as if he didn't present much of a threat to anyone. His stroke must have been a really bad one."

"Massive," Jessie said. "Callie told me shortly afterwards that the doctors said all those years of hard drinking likely caused it. She said they were surprised it hadn't happened sooner."

"Judge Baker was an alcoholic?"

"The worst kind. He lost everything to the bottle," she said. "Everything, that is, but Callie's love."

"Wow. He was a young man when he presided over the trial of Bobby's and Abby's killers. I remember Daddy talking about how fair he seemed, how someday he would be a big name around these parts."

"Your daddy was partly right," Jessie said. "He did become a big name, but for all the wrong reasons. I first heard about his drunken escapades while home from med school one year. He went from being judge to the town drunk in a few short years. Far as I know, nobody ever knew why."

Jed looked over at the old house with its rust-covered metal roof and screened-in back porch. It reminded him of the tenant house where his grandparents lived when he was little. "By the way, I really do appreciate you being here for me. I've put you in a precarious situation, but there was no one else I knew to call."

Jessie hit Jed with a scolding glare. "I would've been awful upset if you hadn't called me," she said, holding her gaze for emphasis. "I can't get over the fact that Stump and the others actually think you could have killed Jake."

Jed reached out, took her hand, and squeezed it. "Thanks. As for Stump's suspicions, given the circumstantial evidence, I guess I can't blame him."

"I can," she said. "You don't have any more motive than the Granvilles, especially Parker. He lost his sister that night, just like you lost a brother."

Jed picked up a piece of gravel from the drive and chunked it at one of the tomato stakes. "Funny you should mention Parker," he said. "He showed up at the jail with Stump. To gloat, I think. Parker may have motive, but the circumstantial evidence points straight at me. The most damning being the matter of my gun being discovered near where they found Willie Sims."

"Willie Sims is dead? When did that happen . . . and . . . how did your gun wind up near his body?" Her face twisted with her question, causing Jed to wonder if her faith in his innocence had just taken a hit.

"The worst is yet to come. My guess is that ballistics tests will tie it to all of the killings." He held his hands out with his palms up and shrugged. "See what I mean? All of the circumstantial evidence points to me as the killer."

Jessie raked gravel with her shoe. She looked at Jed and then walked to the rear of her car. She stood with her back to him for several seconds before turning around. "No, I refuse to see that," she said. "Where did they find Willie Sims?"

"Somewhere along the Tullifinny River. Stump delivered the news personally around daybreak. With my luck, time of death will be determined to have occurred before I was arrested."

"And you're sure your gun was the one they found?"

"Very sure. Stump brought it for me to see. He showed me the engraving on the side. It's mine, all right."

"How could someone have gotten it?"

"No idea. As far as I knew, it was still locked in my glove compartment, where I thought it had been since I moved back home."

"So you've been framed since the beginning."

Jed grinned. "I like the way you think. Want to be my attorney?"

"Sorry, that's out of my area of expertise. But we do have to show them all you're innocent. So what do we do first?"

"I've got to find proof and—" Hearing gravel crunching, the sound of a car coming up the driveway, he stopped talking and stared at Jessie.

# CHAPTER · 19

Terror masked Jessie's face as she turned toward the unmistakable sound of an approaching vehicle. Jed didn't know whether to run or duck behind the BMW, but before he could do either, a silver Mercedes rounded the corner of the house.

"It's Carol Ann," Jessie said. She sounded as relieved as Jed felt, if not more so.

Carol Ann Clay parked and stepped from her shiny car, wearing blue jeans and a red leather jacket over a taupe blouse. Jed recognized her as soon as he saw her, even though streaks of gray highlighted the short raven hair that once fell past her shoulders in high school. Dark shadows cupped her eyes. Her facial muscles sagged. He recognized grief when he saw it, and he saw its shroud draped over Carol Ann.

Jessie rushed to her friend. They hugged each other, and then Carol Ann looked at Jed. "Hello Jed," she said deadpan.

He said, "Carol Ann. Thanks for coming."

Her eyebrow arched. "Just as I drove into town, I heard on the radio that a fugitive had just escaped from the jail. The announcer called him dangerous. Then he said the fugitive was you, Jed."

Jessie said, "It's . . . a misunderstanding." She didn't sound convincing, even to Jed.

"I did escape from jail this morning," he said. "I'm accused of killing seven people—including your daughter."

He didn't know what he expected Carol Ann to do when he dropped that bombshell on her. Whatever he expected, he didn't see it. She walked to within a few feet of him and stared straight into his eyes.

"Why on earth would you want to kill Kristin?" she said with a slight edge to her voice. "You didn't even know her—did you?"

"No, I didn't know your daughter, and other than some very strange coincidences, I can't fully explain why I'm the prime suspect in her death or the deaths of the others."

"Who *are* the others?" Carol Ann asked.

Jessie said, "A girl named Sadie Dunlap, Trent Lassiter's son, Lamar, Callie Hart, Judge Baker, Jake Armistead, and Willie Sims."

Carol Ann said nothing. Her puzzled expression begged for an explanation.

"The only connections," Jed said, "are the murders of my brother, Bobby, and Abby Granville."

"I remember that," Carol Ann said. "Daddy investigated them."

"And Judge Baker tried the men your father arrested," Jed said. "Willie Sims was one of those men."

Carol Ann stood dumbstruck. She looked back and forth between Jessie and Jed. "Why Kristin? She wasn't even born—I wasn't even married. . . ." Her wall of stoicism began to crack. Tears leaked onto her cheeks.

"I'm not sure," Jed said, "but I have a couple of theories. I asked Jessie to call you because I believe the answer might be found in your mother's house."

Carol Ann turned to look at the aging structure. "Mother's?"

He nodded.

"Jed talked to Ginger," Jessie said. "She told him about Kristin being upset about something your mother had told her. Ginger said Kristin referred to it as a dark family secret."

Carol Ann nodded. "Yes, Kristin became very distant after Mother died. I thought it was because they were so close, so I figured she'd get past it soon. She never told me what was bothering her."

Carol Ann dabbed at her tears with her fingers. Jessie handed her a tissue.

Jed pointed toward the back door of the house. "I'd like to look around inside, see if anything there might explain what Nell told Kristin."

"Jed hopes your mother kept a diary," Jessie said.

Carol Ann shrugged. "If she did, I never knew about it. But sure, we can go inside."

She led the way into her childhood home. Jessie followed. Jed brought up the rear, but before he could clear the threshold, he heard a loud gasp from Carol Ann. Jessie started at the sound, and Jed stepped around her to see the kitchen in shambles.

Shattered dishes, silverware, and an assortment of utensils cluttered the floor. Canned goods and boxes of food were strewn across the countertops. Two of the seven white cabinet doors hung from broken hinges. All of the drawers were open and empty. The room looked as if a tornado had spent hours swirling around, destroying everything it touched.

Jed moved quickly into the other parts of the house. The dining and living rooms had fared no better. The wood frame was exposed where drywall had been ripped down. Edges of the carpet were pulled back, furniture was overturned.

Pictures had been pulled from the wall and smashed on the floor. Jed stood beside the china closet, a massive piece appearing to be over a hundred years old. Its glass doors were shattered. The antique dinner plates and crystal heirlooms looked like so much fine confetti on the plush carpet.

"Damn! This has to be the queen mother of all ransackings," he said. Someone had come searching for something. Question was, did they find it?

Carol Ann and Jessie crept in behind Jed. Neither spoke as both examined the chaos left behind by intruders. The musty odor of a dwelling closed to ventilation for an extended period of time hung in the air.

Jed wiped his finger through a layer of dust on an overturned end table. "My hunch is this happened shortly after Nell's death," he said.

Carol Ann dropped onto an ottoman. She buried her face in her hands. "I can't believe someone would do this. Why didn't they just steal what they wanted and leave? Why did they have to destroy everything?"

Jed glanced around, spotted several antiques that he calculated would garner a good price at a local pawn shop. "Whoever did this was looking for something in particular."

"What?" Jessie asked.

"Maybe the same thing we're looking for," he said. "Wonder if they found it."

"But what *are* we looking for?" Carol Ann pleaded.

"I'm hoping your mother wrote down the secret she shared with Kristin," Jed said.

"That damn secret!" Carol Ann's voice exploded in the quiet room. She began slapping her hands on the side of the ottoman. "My family was normal . . . at least I think they were." She looked at Jed with tears streaming down her face. "What kind of secret provoked someone to do this to my family's home and then kill my daughter?" Shock masked her face. "Do you think they killed Mother too?"

Jed looked at Jessie then Carol Ann. "I think it's possible, yes."

"Why wouldn't I know this secret, if it's so damn important to kill over?" She shook her head; her voice bordered on the edge of hysteria.

Jessie grabbed her friend and pulled her tight against her chest. Carol Ann mashed her face into Jessie's shoulder.

"We'll find out," Jessie said. "I promise you we will find out." She glared at Jed. "Won't we?"

He knew she wasn't asking, she was telling. He had seen the same look of determination on the face of other women, women back in Atlanta who vowed to see the animal who had killed their children pay with his life. Jed hoped Jessie's vow proved more successful than his search for that killer had.

"That's what we're here for," he said, walking over to pull open the curtains. Sunlight poured inside.

He pulled a picture frame from under a crocheted seat cushion. The broken glass fell out, but the photograph didn't seem to be adversely effected. He held it out for Carol Ann to see.

The distraught woman's reddened eyes cast an affectionate gaze. "That's Daddy. It was taken just before he died."

The image showed a man wearing a Stetson-style sheriff's hat with a star in the center. Jed placed the picture on a table he righted.

"Can you tell me about his death?"

Carol Ann stared past Jed at the photo as if she hadn't heard his question. "I really should box up the unbroken stuff and take it home. No sense leaving it for more vandals to destroy."

She walked over to another picture, one among three scattered along the base of the wall. "Someone at the courthouse took this of Daddy right after he was elected sheriff. I was only ten then, but I can still remember how proud he was to have gotten so many votes. We were all proud of him." She blew her nose into the tissue Jessie had given her. "Me more than Mother, I think."

Carol Ann ran her fingers through her hair. "Mother nearly drove herself crazy worrying about him. She didn't want him to be sheriff, but he always said he didn't know anything else. That was a lie, of course. He was smart and good with his hands. He could have done just about anything, but he wanted to protect people. He loved his job."

Jed bent down to see other pictures. In one Carol Ann couldn't have been more than three or four. In another, her parents appeared to be newlyweds. "They made a handsome couple," he said, placing his arm across her back and squeezing her shoulder.

The stricken expression on her face told Jed she didn't want to talk about her dad's death. Even so, he believed anything he could learn might be important.

"Jessie told me about your daddy's suicide. Do you know why he chose to take his own life?"

"I don't know how to answer that question," she said.

"What do you mean?"

"I knew your brother," she said. "And I knew he and Abby saw each other on the sly, even though they tried to downplay their relationship at school. Their love for each other was the worst-kept secret in Sweetgrass, and some folks accepted it better than others." She flashed a thin-lipped smile. "I remember the night Daddy came home and told Mother about finding their bodies."

"Do you remember what he told her?" Jed asked.

"Not exactly. Just that they were found murdered. Not much else, because he tried not to let me hear. But I did. I knew Abby, even though she was a couple of years older than me. Her death hit a lot of us girls really hard."

"I understand," Jed said. "But what does their death have to do with your dad's?"

Carol Ann touched the newlywed picture of her mother and father, and then she turned and walked away. She began picking up family heirlooms, pieces of broken china, a Bible. She didn't look at Jed when she said, "Daddy acted different after Bobby and Abby died. I don't think I noticed at first, but after a while it became obvious that his enthusiasm for being sheriff wasn't what it had been before the murders."

She turned toward Jed. She clutched an intact porcelain statuette of an angel. "You'd have to know how much he loved being sheriff before that night to understand the difference in him. Before, he didn't think of it as a job. He considered being sheriff a privilege. Everywhere he went, people—black and white—looked to him as someone they could trust to help them when they needed it most."

She frowned. "Jed, you know better than anyone that wasn't always the case with law enforcement back then."

Jed thought of Stump. "Or now," he said.

"I guess," she said. "All I know is that back then, some folks made a habit of running roughshod over others. Daddy considered it his duty to make sure everyone got a fair shake. He loved being looked on as the champion of the little guy. Before Bobby and Abby died, you could see the sparkle in his eyes every morning when he went off to work.

"But after their deaths something happened. The sparkle disappeared. Daddy became moody. He and Mother fought more, something I almost never saw growing up. Mother tried to get him to quit, and I think he considered it, but in the end, he claimed it was what he knew, what he did, and the people needed him. And they did need him."

Carol Ann leaned against the door frame leading into the kitchen. "Five years after the murders, Daddy was found dead. Coroner said he shot himself." Her steely stare locked on Jed. "I never believed it, though. Not for one second. Daddy may not have been as happy as before; he even may have been suffering from depression. But he wasn't suicidal. I don't believe he would go and kill himself."

To Jed the inference was obvious, if not surprising. "You think someone murdered him?" he asked.

Carol Ann glared. "He . . . didn't . . . kill . . . himself." She said each word with slow conviction.

"Do you have any idea why he seemed so despondent after Bobby and Abby were killed?" Jessie asked. "Arrests came fast. He did his job by catching the killers."

"None," Carol Ann said. "You remember how protective our parents got after the murders, don't you? It was the same all over town. But after Daddy and his deputies arrested those men a few days later, everyone seemed relieved. To many living in Sweetgrass, Daddy was a hero."

"You're right," Jessie said. "After the news of the murders broke, Mamma told us all that if anybody could get to the bottom of the killings, Sheriff Renfrow could."

Carol Ann nodded her head, looked pensive. "Everyone reacted the same way," she said. "A few months later, after the men were tried and sent off to prison, I saw the first signs of change in Daddy. I have no idea what happened."

Jed listened to her describe her father's love for his job. Like Carol Ann, he couldn't imagine what all of a sudden drove the man to kill himself. "To your knowledge, there were no changes in his health or the family's finances that might have caused him to think about taking his own life?"

"Nothing," Carol Ann said. "As far as I knew, Daddy was as healthy as a horse. And as for money problems, we were comfortable. Mother baked cakes and pastries to bring in extra money. And they were both frugal with their spending. No, I can't imagine money problems caused whatever troubled Daddy."

"Did he . . . die here at home?" Jed asked in as sensitive a manner as he could.

Both women looked at him with odd expressions.

"I thought you knew," Jessie said.

"They found him in the woods," Carol Ann said, "sitting at the base of a tree. He was shot once in the head."

The image of Kristin appeared in Jed's mind. He knew the way the killer had positioned her had been intentional, but until that very moment he had not realized why. *The bastard left her in the position her granddaddy was found after his death. Sins of the grandfathers. . . . The killer knew someone would make the connection eventually.*

"Who found him?" Jed asked.

"Bain and Parker Granville," Carol Ann said.

Noting a hint of resentment in her voice, he looked at Jessie. Judging from the surprise on her face, she had not known the Granvilles had been the ones who found the sheriff's body.

"What were they doing out in the woods?" Jessie asked before Jed could.

Carol Ann moistened her lips, took in a deep breath, and released it slowly before answering. "Hunting . . . at least that's what they said."

"You don't seem convinced," Jed said.

Carol Ann glared at him through her narrowed eyelids. "At first, I didn't know what to believe. Mother, on the other hand, didn't believe their story from the get-go."

"Did she say anything to anyone?" Jed asked.

"Oh, yeah," Carol Ann said. "She tried to get the new sheriff, one of Daddy's former deputies, to investigate more, but he refused. He said there was nothing to investigate."

"Interesting," Jed said, uttering the word half under his breath. He had experienced the same response from the sheriff when he had inquired about his own father's death.

"I'm not saying they killed Daddy or had anything to do with his death, but back then, if the Granvilles wanted to get away with murder, they could have—and everyone knew it."

"For the sake of argument," Jed said, "let's say they might have killed your father and staged it to look like a suicide. What would have been their motivation? They all got along didn't they?"

As he waited for Carol Ann to answer, he thought about his father, the burning of the church. He and Carol Ann shared a common distrust for how the deaths of their fathers had been handled by local law enforcement.

"Daddy got along with everybody, even the folks he arrested," Carol Ann said. "As for the Granvilles, I guess he got along with them about as well as anyone could."

"Were they friends?" Jed asked.

"Daddy recognized the political reality of not crossing the richest family in the county, but I don't know of anyone who claimed them as friends."

Jessie said, "What did your mamma do after the new sheriff turned down her request to investigate more?"

Carol Ann shrugged. "Not much she could do. She didn't have any clout."

"Was she bitter?" Jed asked.

"Oh, yeah. Wouldn't you have been?"

Again, he thought back to how the sheriff maintained that his father's death was an accident. "Yes."

"Mother grew very bitter. She soured on everyone in the county, because Daddy had cared so much for how the people were treated. After he died, no one seemed to care about what had happened to him. Time never healed that wound."

"That explains why she became reclusive," Jessie said. "Did Kristin know how her grandfather died?"

Carol Ann nodded. "She knew, and she knew her grandmother didn't believe the official version."

"Did your mamma have proof to back up her belief about your daddy's death?" Jed asked.

"I don't know," Carol Ann said. "We quarreled a lot after he died. I didn't want to discuss anything having to do with him dying. I especially didn't want to hear that somebody had murdered him and gotten away with the crime. I guess, looking back on it, I was in denial."

"Maybe Kristin listened," Jed said, theorizing out loud.

"Maybe," Carol Ann said, sounding a little resentful of his remark.

"I think what Jed meant," Jessie said, "was you were too close and you probably *were* in denial. When Kristin came along, your dad had been dead around twelve years. He wasn't someone she knew or was attached to. She only knew him through your stories about him and those Nell told to her. Your mother found someone who would listen and maybe someone who even grew very interested in what had happened."

Jessie turned to Jed. "Kristin was very idealistic. She wanted to save the wetlands, right the wrongs, and change the world. All kids are like that to some extent."

He nodded. "Maybe your mother did have proof. Maybe she showed it to Kristin."

"I suppose," Carol Ann said in a soft voice. "But what kind of proof?"

The former detective studied the disheveled room. "I don't know. But somebody came in here searching for something. Whether they found it or not is anybody's guess."

Carol Ann's face held a lost expression. "How would they know? Why would they come here looking for it?"

"After Nell's death, Kristin may have called someone or asked too many questions," Jed said. "She may have revealed the existence of the proof, and someone wanted to make it go away."

"Do you think that's why she was killed?"

"Maybe," he said.

Jessie shot to her feet. "If that's the case, then one of the Granvilles must be the killer."

"Maybe." Jed held up his hand like a stop sign. "We need to try to find out what Kristin knew and what the proof is—if it exists. Did your mamma have a special place to keep things, Carol Ann?"

She rubbed her forehead as she stood and surveyed the room. "She did use my room for storage after I left home. There's a lot of junk back there."

Jed motioned with his arm. "Show us the way."

# CHAPTER · 20

Carol Ann led them down a narrow, dark hallway to a closed door, where a straw doll dressed in a faded, pink gingham dress decorated the outside. The doll still hanging in place was a good sign to Jed. Maybe the intruders hadn't ventured this far into the house.

Carol Ann paused at the door, reached out to touch the doll. "It's been a long time," she said. "Have you ever wished you could go back in time and undo the hurtful things you did? I would love to have a chance to be with Mother again and to sit and listen to everything she had to say, to hug her and tell her how much I love her."

She turned, her eyes glistening. Jed nodded. Regret squeezed his heart, too.

Carol Ann took a noticeable deep breath. She turned the glass doorknob. Inside, stale air greeted the trio as they entered. Across the semi-dark room Jed could see ruffled pink curtains framing a single shade-covered window. Carol Ann flipped the wall switch, but nothing happened.

"No electricity," she said as she made her way across the room and raised the shade. Particles of dust danced in the sunbeams.

When Carol Ann turned around, she shook her head. "The bastards wrecked my room, too."

Jessie stepped deeper inside, joining her friend. Jed remained in the doorway. *Carol Ann's right,* he thought. *The intruders have indeed been here.* While the women sifted through artifacts from Carol Ann's past, Jed surveyed the disarray. Drawers were pulled out, their contents dumped onto the light blue carpet. Papers and books lay scattered across the bed. As he watched the two women pick up pieces of childhood memories from the bedroom floor, he noticed how Carol Ann's face revealed the strain of someone about to lose control of their sanity.

"Why would someone do this?" Carol Ann asked in a low voice, as if speaking only to herself.

"Someone wanted to find something in the worst way," Jed said.

"And when they didn't," Jessie said, "they pitched a fit."

He looked at her. "Interesting theory."

Jessie looked back with a puzzled expression. "What?"

"You said they pitched a fit because they couldn't find what they came for. I figured this was all a by-product of the search, but maybe not. Maybe they didn't find what they wanted. Maybe they truly did pitch a fit."

"Who really cares?" Carol Ann said. "They've destroyed or trampled on all of my memories."

Jed pushed wadded up quilts off the cedar chest and opened the top. "This is unlocked," he said.

"Mother never locked it," Carol Ann said. "I don't know if she ever had a key."

Jessie peered over Jed's shoulder and said, "Well someone's been through it, because everything inside looks like it's been ripped apart."

Inside the chest Jed saw torn newspaper articles and mangled letters. At least the cedar lining smelled refreshing. "Let's start reading through some of these to see what's here."

He held up a handful of torn papers and pictures for someone to grab. Neither Jessie nor Carol Ann stepped forward.

"You've got to be kidding," Jessie said. "Finding the proverbial needle in the haystack would have to be easier. At least you'd know what you're looking for."

"This is all we've got," he said, "and if the intruders didn't find what they came after, it might still be here."

The women exchanged glances. Jed grabbed up pieces of newspaper and settled back against the wall. The first headline he picked up announced the start of the trial for two men charged with killing two teens. The article had been torn away. He rummaged through the chest until he found part of an article he thought might go with the headline and began to read.

After nearly two hours of silent reading and tedious matching of bits of old letters and jagged-edged shreds of newspaper articles, the three searchers managed to create little more than incomplete journalistic jigsaw puzzles and barely legible mosaics of faded correspondences. They found nothing incriminating or remotely able to explain why someone would kill anyone or ransack Nell Renfrow's house.

Jed did find parts of news articles recounting the trial and sentencing of Willie Sims and Roy Nash, and he learned some of what had occurred behind the doors to the courtroom his father had prohibited him from entering. Another article of interest, written after Sheriff Renfrow's body had been found, described the sheriff's death as "a shocking tragedy, an act of depression no one really understood."

Maybe he was reading too much into what the reporter wrote, but Jed thought he detected doubt and wondered if the journalist believed the same thing Carol Ann did—that Cletus Renfrow did not die by his own hand. If the reporter, in fact, didn't believe the official version of the sheriff's death, Jed wondered if he had ever acted to try to disprove it. He also wondered if the Granville influence extended to the printed word. Without having to reflect very long, he was sure it did.

Jed leaned back against the wall and watched the two women. Jessie shuffled through a pile of torn letters, while Carol Ann had resorted to thumbing through an old and battered book.

"You're right, Jessie," he said. "This is worse than looking for that needle. I have no idea what we're looking for and even less of a clue if it could have already been found by those who came before us."

Jessie sighed. Frustration showed on her face as she nodded.

Just as Jed was ready to throw his hands up in defeat, Carol Ann said, "Look at this. I found it in the back of this old book of poetry."

Jed's legs were too stiff to spring up to his feet, so he crawled on all fours to where Carol Ann sat under the window. She handed him an intact letter written in broad heavy strokes that appeared to be a man's handwriting.

"Is this your daddy's?" he asked.

"Uh-huh." She nodded as Jed read.

The letter was written to Nell, who apparently had gone to visit her sister. It started off with her husband telling her how much he missed her and how he hoped her sister was feeling better.

*Nothing sinister or covert here,* Jed thought.

Most of the letter consisted of the usual spousal small talk about things around the house and town and what went on in church the Sunday before. But near the end of the letter, the tone changed.

Cletus wrote of experiencing bad dreams. He told his wife he thought the preacher had directed the sermon at him. He sounded like a man overwhelmed with guilt.

"Listen to this," Jed said.

Jessie eased close to Carol Ann, who seemed preoccupied with her hands.

"'Nell, darling, my insides stay tore up over what happened. What we did weren't right, no matter what the others say. I've got to do something. When you return, we have to decide how to go about setting right the wrong I've done.' He signed the letter, 'Love Cletus.'"

Jessie took the letter and began to read it herself. Her only response came when she finished. "Wow. What did he do?"

"I have no idea," Carol Ann said, her voice quavering.

"Where did your aunt live?" Jed asked.

"Atlanta."

He took back the letter from Jessie and glanced over it again. "Your daddy didn't mention you, Carol Ann. Were you already away at school?"

She nodded and looked over at Jessie. "Our freshman year, I think. Mother went down to take care of Aunt Bess after she fell and broke her hip. She was gone about two weeks, an eternity for Mom and Dad to have been apart."

Jed said, "That would make it three years after Bobby and Abby were killed. I wonder if the others referred to in the letter could have been Bain and Parker Granville. Judge Baker also could have been one of them."

Jessie's forehead furrowed. "Go on."

"What if, in all the frenzy surrounding the murders, they arrested the wrong men?"

"And convicted them?" Jessie said. "That came months later."

"Exactly. But maybe the sheriff uncovered evidence later on that cleared the men already convicted."

Jessie said, "If that's the case, why wouldn't they have just admitted the error and let the convicted men out of prison?"

"What if the sheriff wanted to do exactly that and the others wouldn't let him?" Jed asked. "Maybe he threatened to expose the cover-up. . . ." He mashed his lips together, stared wide-eyed at Jessie.

She said, "So you think the Granvilles might have killed Cletus to keep him quiet."

Jed looked over at Carol Ann to gauge her reaction. She glanced up from a high school annual and raked her teeth across her lower lip before she returned to leafing through the yearbook.

"If Sheriff Renfrow had proof of the wrongful conviction," Jessie continued, "why would the Granvilles care? And I find Judge Baker's complicity in a cover-up incomprehensible."

"That may explain why he drowned himself in alcohol all those years," Jed said.

Jessie's expression told him his speculation about the judge might have some merit. "But killing the sheriff is pretty out-there," she said, "even for bastards like the Granvilles."

Carol Ann remained disengaged from the conversation concerning her dad. She flipped pages, one after the other, without really taking time to look at the pictures of her former classmates.

"They *were* the ones who found him after he allegedly shot himself," Jed said.

"Okay," Jessie said. "Answer this. What new findings could Cletus have uncovered that would have prompted them to resort to murder to keep him quiet?"

Carol Ann looked up from her yearbook. "Here!" Her voice cracked like a rifle shot. "I know what he found."

"What?" Jessie sounded nearly as excited as her friend.

Carol Ann began to laugh. "I know why they came, what they wanted to find." She laughed harder. "I know their damn secret."

Jed stared at Jessie and then they both stared at Carol Ann.

"It's been here the whole time. Mother must have told Kristin about it, and she must have confronted them. They killed her and came looking for it, but the bastards missed it. It was under their noses the whole time."

Her laughter became hysterical, out of control. She pounded her fists on the pages of the open book.

Jessie embraced her friend. Carol Ann's laughter melted into breath-choking sobs. Tears poured from her eyes.

"It's okay," Jessie whispered. "It's okay, baby. Show us what you found."

Carol Ann raised her trembling hand, and in it she clutched a letter. "They killed him. They really did kill him. Mother was right all those years. The bastards killed Daddy."

Jed took the letter from Carol Ann's fist and pulled the high school annual from her lap. The book was opened to a page where an envelope had been taped. The faded ink on the yellowed paper was hard to read in places, but more than enough of it was legible, and what he read was incomprehensible.

# CHAPTER · 21

"This is an incredibly bad idea," Jessie said, grousing as she drove past the Optimist Club sign welcoming visitors to Sweetgrass. "If anyone sees you, they're sure to shoot you. You're a wanted man . . . a wanted *black* man . . . or have you forgotten that little detail."

"I haven't forgotten," Jed said. "How could I? You've reminded me of it at least five times since we left Nell Renfrow's."

Jessie scowled. "Apparently my reminders haven't sunk in yet."

Jed stared out the windshield at the white line in the middle of the roadway as it disappeared under the front of the low-riding sports car. "I have to confront him. I've got to see his expression when I tell him I know what he did."

Jessie cut her eyes at Jed. "Let me force another *little detail* inside that hard noggin of yours." Fear and anger swam together in the deep brown pools focused on him. "He just might kill you. You don't have a gun or anything to stop him. Have you even bothered to consider that possibility?"

"I prefer not to think about it, thank you very much."

"That's just great. You don't want to think about it." Jessie's grip tightened on the steering wheel. "Well, think about this. He'll probably get a reward for killing a dangerous fugitive. You're getting ready to make the son of a bitch a hero."

Jed motioned toward a tree-lined residential street two blocks from the courthouse. "Turn up here on Jasper."

Jessie jerked the steering wheel hard to the right. Her tires squalled. "What is it you want me to do while you're out committing suicide?"

"Go back and get Carol Ann," he said. They had left her resting at her mother's house after Jessie found a sedative in Nell's medicine cabinet and gave it to her. Once Carol Ann calmed down and began acting normal again, Jed talked Jessie into driving him into town.

"I don't think it's a good idea to leave her there alone," he said. "I want the two of you to take the letter to your office and make two copies like we planned.

Mail one copy to the SLED offices in Columbia. Lock the original in your desk and take the remaining copy to the sheriff."

"Do you really think Stump will pay it any attention?"

Jed sighed. "I don't know. I'm counting on him being a cop first and a bigot second." He winked. "But just in case, that's why you're mailing a copy to Columbia.

"Pull over there," he said, pointing to the curb.

As the car jolted to a stop, Jed said, "Hopefully, Stump will believe the letter and arrive before the gunfire begins."

A dark scowl fell over Jessie's visage. "Not funny. Not funny at all."

Jed winked again and crawled out from the small interior. He felt his uncoiling spine crack and pop. His muscles barked and he groaned. Upright, he pushed the door closed and blew Jessie a kiss.

She tossed a disapproving sneer in return. She mouthed *Men!* before squealing her tires as she pulled away from the curb.

Jed watched the BMW's taillights glow when she braked to turn onto the next street. "She took that well."

He realized the risk he was taking. But he feared waiting might allow others involved to manipulate facts and evidence even more than they already had. If they did, he would be the one going to prison. He was not about to wait around for that to happen, even if it meant risking being killed.

Seeing no one out in their yards, Jed broke into a jog and cut between two stately homes. The shortcut brought him out on Center Street near the law office of Parker Granville. He glanced up and down the street before stepping from the cover of a large rhododendron. Assured he could continue without detection, he hustled across the roadway to the brownstone building and climbed the stairs to the second floor.

Jed felt better already. Now, once again, he was the hunter.

He entered the law office, wearing a ball cap he'd borrowed from Jessie and dark glasses he'd borrowed from the Renfrow home. He hoped no one inside would recognize him. Relieved to find the chairs in the lobby empty, he walked straight to the receptionist's desk and asked to see Parker Granville.

"Mr. Granville's with a client," the woman said. "Did you have an appointment?" Her nose bridled as if she detected a foul odor.

"No, I'm an old acquaintance. I was just passing through town and thought I'd stop in to say hello." Jed smiled. "For old time's sake."

The woman reached up and patted the mousy hair clamped like a clamshell against her rouge-colored cheeks. She pursed her bright red lips, soured her expression, and cast a suspicious glare over the rim of her rose-colored, flattop spectacles. "Uh-huh," she said.

*Parker's receptionist obviously knows her boss well enough to know he doesn't have black acquaintances,* Jed thought.

"I'm afraid I'll need—"

The phone rang before she could finish. She grabbed the receiver and flipped Jed a harsh scowl as she pulled it to her ear.

He glanced around the office, spotted a door down a short hallway that he believed would lead into Parker's inner sanctum. The retired cop would have bet his pension that no one was inside with the attorney.

The receptionist covered the phone's mouthpiece with her hand and narrowed her eyes. "Excuse me, *please.*" She pointed a long thin finger toward the empty sofa and chair across from her desk. "Have a seat. I'll be with you in a minute."

Her tone reminded Jed of a stern teacher sending a pesky student back to his desk. He turned toward the sofa and chair and then shook his head. "That's all right," he said. "I'll stop by next time I'm in town."

The woman shrugged and with a tone of indifference said, "Whatever." She watched him walk toward the door. As he pulled it open, she whirled around in her chair and began talking into the phone.

A long-time believer in seizing the moment, Jed let the door close without exiting. He quietly stepped down the hallway out of sight of the receptionist and stopped in front of a door marked PRIVATE.

Jed glanced back. He could hear the woman chattering away and figured she had no idea he had never left. He pressed his ear against a door panel, and when he heard nothing from inside, he turned the brass knob and eased open the heavy wooden door.

To find the attorney's office plush and elaborately appointed came as no surprise. After all, the man did belong to the richest family in Indigo County.

Thick green carpet covered the floor, and the walls appeared to be paneled with mahogany. A huge desk built of the same material as the paneling sat at one end of the large room in front of a door in the corner. The wall behind the desk was filled with bookshelves overflowing with law books. The other walls were lined with framed photographs of Parker posing with presidents, governors, sports stars, and Hollywood personalities, most inscribed with autographs and personalized messages to the attorney.

*Impressive. These people obviously don't know the same man I do.*

On one corner of a polished wood table near the door stood a stuffed pheasant mounted on a large tree limb. A wild boar glared down from one wall, his snarl exposing long tusks. Across the room Jed spotted a largemouth bass mounted above a tan leather chair. The room reeked of runaway testosterone with all the trophies and symbols of power on display. But Jed saw no sign of Parker or his imaginary client.

As he prowled around, Jed instinctively kept an eye on the door he had entered and an ear out for any telltale commotion outside. If the receptionist had, in fact, discovered his deception and alerted Parker, who then left through the door beside the bookshelf, then he could expect Stump to arrive any second.

Jed listened intently but heard nothing. Unfettered, he continued his tour of the office. *As Daddy used to say, "You can't worry about what can't be controlled."*

He stepped close to inspect a photograph of two hunters kneeling down beside a felled elk. The animal was huge and its rack of antlers spectacular, but that wasn't what captured his attention. Jed recognized the hunter posing with Parker. Jack, his furnace-repairman-come-bomber, knelt with his rifle on the opposite side of the animal from Parker.

*Well, well. Parker Granville, hunter and world-class SOB, hired someone to blow up my house.*

Jed continued to inspect the quiet office, all the while searching for a quick exit should he need one. There was the door he had entered, and there was the row of windows leading to a two-story drop onto the street outside. He decided he was too old to play Spider-Man, so he returned his attention to the door next to the bookshelf. Did it lead out of the office, perhaps to a back stairway?

As he approached to investigate, a loud flushing sound came from the other side. Jed stepped back, but before he could duck out of sight, the door opened. Parker stepped into the office, zipping up his blue trousers and hoisting red suspenders up to his shoulders.

When the attorney saw Jed, his mouth dropped open. He stopped short. "Bradley, what th—" His question dissolved into one long gasp. Parker eyeballed Jed up and down and then looked around the room, as if others would be there, too.

"You expected someone else?" Jed asked.

"I expected no one," the attorney said. He began to show signs of recovery from his initial shock. A bright scarlet red colored his meaty cheeks as he glanced toward his desk. "How the hell did you get in here?"

Jed watched him gaze across the desktop. A silver tray held a half-empty decanter of what looked like bourbon and a highball glass with just a little of the amber liquid covering the bottom.

"The old-fashioned way," Jed said. "I walked through the door."

Parker staggered toward the desk. He was tanked, but Jed didn't think he planned on offering him a drink. *He must have a gun there somewhere*, Jed thought.

Parker angled toward the left side of the desk as he shuffled closer. Jed took a step nearer, ready to rush him if he lunged toward a drawer.

Deciding a bluff just might work on the alcohol-dulled senses of the man, Jed slid his hand around to his back and grabbed hold of his belt. "Don't do anything you might regret," he said and took another step forward. "I didn't come here to shoot you."

Uncertainty clouded the attorney's features as he stopped and stared at his intruder. "Wash do you want with me?" His slurred words were laced with a mixture of irritation and fear. "The sheriff's hunting for you right now, and when he finds you, he'll shoot first and ask questions later."

"I came for the truth, Granville. I want to hear it from your own mouth, in your own words." Jed stole a glance toward the door leading to the lobby. *So far, so good.*

Parker swayed back and forth beside his desk. "Truth about what? I don't know what in the hell you're talking about."

"Oh, I think you do. But for the sake of refreshing your pickled memory, why don't we start with recent events." Jed pointed toward the picture of the two hunters. "Why don't we begin with your old hunting buddy? Did you tell him to just blow up my house, or was I supposed to be in it?"

Jed noted Parker's squint-eyed assessment of the pictures on his office wall. "You're deranged, Bradley. You must be doin' drugs."

"Drugs, huh? Did Sheriff Renfrow do drugs? Is that why you killed him?"

"Wha . . . what're you gettin' at, Bradley? Everybody knows old Cletus got all depressed and went off by himself into the woods to end it all." Parker hung his head, shook it back and forth. "Damn shame too. Old Cletus was a good man."

"Spare me the sympathetic bullshit, Parker. We know what happened. We also know why."

Beads of perspiration popped out on the lawyer's forehead. His red face paled to a light pink. "Who's *we*?"

Jed smiled. He thought about an acronym some of his detectives used when they broke down a suspect in the interview room. *NIGYYSOB—Now I've got you, you son of a bitch.*

Jed looked at his watch. "Well, for starters, by now the US Postal Service is carrying a letter to SLED headquarters, so they'll know. And if he doesn't already, in a few short minutes, the new sheriff will know, too."

Parker's expression revealed his outrage. Hatred boiled his corneas. He began moving again, inching closer to the desk.

Jed considered overpowering the overweight slug before he could get to whatever he had concealed in his desk, but the former detective wanted answers first. He longed to see Parker's reaction when the attorney realized everyone would soon know the truth about what had happened on the night Bobby died.

"Why don't you tell me what really happened to your sister and my brother? Tell me the truth. As the Good Book says, it'll set you free."

Desperation began distorting Parker's features. He looked toward the door leading out of the office but must have realized he would have to go through Jed to reach it. He eyed the desk. Jed knew there would be precious little time to react if the man went for one of the drawers.

"Don't be foolish, Parker," Jed said, reissuing his bluff. "I'm a crack shot, expertly trained, and fast on the draw." He kept his grip on his belt.

Parker said, "If your damn brother hadn't taken her out there that night, them boys wouldn't have ever killed either one." Jed noted a distinct quiver in his voice.

"The truth, Parker. Tell me the truth. We both know Sims and Nash didn't kill them. They weren't even out at the church that night. But you were. Weren't you?"

"I . . . I don't know what. . . ." His glare shot past Jed toward the door.

Before Jed could turn, Stump uttered his warning. "Freeze, Bradley. Freeze right there!"

Jed gritted his teeth. *Shit!*

# CHAPTER · 22

The arrival of Parker's nephew washed the fear and trepidation from the attorney's face. He wiped his forehead with his shirt sleeve.

"Move your hands out where I can see them, Bradley," Stump said.

The sheriff's harsh tone, Jed decided, meant Jessie had not found him to give him the letter written by Cletus Renfrow. That or he didn't care.

Jed eased his hands out in plain view, held them up for Stump to see. "I'm unarmed."

"You bastard," Parker said, growling as he spoke. Turning to Stump, he said, "Watch him. You can't trust his kind."

Then he staggered to the desk and pulled open a drawer. He lifted a blue steel revolver with a pearl handle and pointed it at Jed. "I'm gonna kill your black ass right here and now."

Jed detected a glint in the drunkard's eye and started to dive behind a nearby leather wing chair. But instead of shooting, Parker reached for the glass and downed the remainder of the liquor inside.

"You're a fugitive wanted for killing seven people," the attorney said. "You broke out of jail, then broke in here and threatened me. Everyone will believe I shot you in self-defense."

Parker's scowl fell on his nephew. "You got that throw-down you carry?"

Stump didn't respond. His lower jaw convulsed beneath his gaped-mouth expression. For the first time since Jed had met him, the disagreeable bigot appeared at a loss for words.

"Your bastard brother caused me to lose a sister, Bradley." Parker said. "And losing her the way I did has caused me a life of torment. I ain't about to let you cause me no more torment with the lies you're trying to spread." He turned back to Stump. "You got that throw-down or don't you?"

Stump looked sheepish, uncertain as to what to do, which Jed considered a good thing. At least the sheriff was hesitant to go along with his uncle's murderous plan of planting a gun in Jed's dead hand.

Jed realized he had only seconds to decide on a plan of his own. Over his career, he had never encountered a situation quite like this one. He almost always had a way of fighting back—a gun, other officers with him, something. He had nothing right now, and his brain was on lockdown. Trapped between the two armed men, he could not foresee a favorable ending, and for some peculiar reason his only thought was of how truly pissed off Jessie was going to be when she heard he had, in fact, gone and gotten himself killed.

Stump finally spoke, but Jed didn't like what he heard. "I've got my other gun."

Jed glanced toward the windows. Did he want to die here from being shot or outside with a broken neck? As the teenagers back on campus might say, his choices sucked.

Momentary relief came when Stump said, "There ain't no need to shoot him, though. I'll put him back in jail. He won't get out this time."

"You don't understand, boy. He broke in here, came to kill me." Parker staggered backward. He reached out and propped his hand on the tall chair behind his desk to steady his balance.

"Uncle Parker, there ain't no need for no more killin'." Stump sounded nervous and, adding to Jed's concern, weak in his conviction.

The color in Parker's face had deepened from scarlet to purple. Jed expected him to explode any second.

Parker whipped his arm up and pointed the revolver at Jed. "Go to hell, Bradley."

The gun's thunderous roar in the closed office deafened Jed. His ears rang. He dove behind the wing chair. As he did, he saw Stump drop to the floor. A scream came from out in the lobby as the errant shot shattered a crystal lamp behind Jed.

Stump cried out from his prone position. "No, Uncle Parker!"

Jed peeked around the chair just in time to see Parker aim toward his nephew. "If you ain't part of the solution, you're part of the problem," he said.

Another shot rang out. The bullet hit the panel wall a few feet above Stump's head. Wood chips showered down on the new sheriff, sending him scurrying under the table near the door.

"You're the last of your vermin breed, Bradley, and I'm gonna make you extinct."

Jed heard another shot. The bullet clipped the top of the leather chair he was behind and slammed into a framed painting on the wall. When Jed looked up, he could see where it had torn a hole in the body of a black Labrador retriever with a canvasback duck in its mouth. The glass from the painting's frame showered down onto the carpet.

Stump yelled for his uncle to stop. "Don't make me shoot you," he said.

Jed wasn't ready to bet his life on Stump's professional sense of responsibility. He eased around the side of the chair to see where the attorney stood. Parker had moved in front of his desk with one hand on the top to anchor his swaying body.

Seeing Jed, Parker waved the revolver and fired another shot in the former cop's general direction. This one ripped through the arm of the chair and zipped past Jed's head, missing him by just inches. White cotton stuffing floated to the floor. The stench of gunpowder drifted through the smoky room.

Jed didn't know if Parker had been keeping count, but he sure had. Only two more bullets remained in the cylinder. If he could survive those, he had no intention of waiting for the attorney to reload.

Stump glared at his uncle from under the table. The stuffed pheasant above him stared straight at Jed. The idea that Parker might try to have Jed stuffed didn't seemed so far-fetched at the moment.

Jed said, "You've got to stop him, Stump. I'm unarmed, and if you let him kill me, you're allowing murder."

Stump appeared totally confused. His expression reminded Jed of a first-time visitor to Atlanta driving on the freeway during rush hour.

"Shut up, Bradley," Parker yelled. His voice sounded closer than before, but Jed didn't want to chance another peek.

He lowered his head to see if he could see the attorney's feet from under the chair. When he didn't see the man, Jed feared when he raised up, the last thing on earth he would see would be Parker's glowering countenance and the business end of the blue steel revolver.

He tossed a quick glance toward Stump. The sheriff continued staring straight ahead, so Jed figured Parker was still somewhere close to the desk.

Thinking if he could provoke the attorney to shoot wildly two more times he could rush the drunkard, Jed began recounting what Cletus Renfrow's letter had revealed. "Granville, is this how you gunned down your sister? Did you stalk her before you killed her?"

Stump flashed a wild-eyed glare at Jed. The attorney remained quiet.

Jed continued. "Or did you intentionally torment her with wild shots before you walked up and shot her point-blank in the face. That's a mighty powerful hate—to prefer your own flesh and blood dead as opposed to having her date a black man."

"You're a real smart nigger, ain't you, Bradley. I didn't kill her. Your son-of-a-bitchin' brother killed her when he took her out that night. If he'd left her alone, she'd be alive today."

Parker's voice cracked. Jed detected a hint of contrition bleeding through the anger and alcohol.

He glanced over at Stump, who still appeared dumbstruck beneath the table. At least the shooting had stopped for the moment.

"That letter I told you about tells the whole story, Granville," Jed said. "Cletus Renfrow wrote it to his wife, and she kept it all these years, hoping to show why you killed her husband. He planned on telling the truth, didn't he? Is that why you killed him?"

The attorney sniffed haughtily. "Cletus Renfrow was a whiner. He had no gumption."

"He had the guts to want to tell the truth, to try to get the men wrongfully convicted set free," Jed said. "He wrote how you went crazy that night when you saw them parked near the old church, and how you and your cousin Bain plotted to frame two innocent men so you could remain free."

Parker grabbed the decanter and swigged a mouthful of straight bourbon. Jed looked around the corner of the chair and saw him holding the gun with one hand, the decanter with the other.

"Weak man. . . ." Parker's words slurred to the point they were almost unintelligible.

"Did the sheriff tell you and Bain he was going to the governor to get the men released? He knew the judge wouldn't help," Jed said. "Baker was in on the frame-up, too, wasn't he?"

Parker slammed the decanter bottle down so hard that Jed thought it would shatter, but it didn't. The attorney wiped his mouth with his sleeve and staggered forward a couple of steps.

Jed decided to pepper him with questions, not giving him time to answer one before the next one came at him, anything to keep him distracted. "Is that when y'all decided to go hunting? Did Sheriff Renfrow know he was the hunted? Did you pull the trigger that day too?"

"Renfrow was weak," Parker said. From the sound of his words, the attorney was just before passing out.

Jed kept talking. "He wasn't weak at all. He was the strongest of all of you. You and Bain wanted him quiet, and to hell with those men in prison. The important thing was to protect the Granville name. You wanted to remain free, no matter who else suffered. That's how it was, wasn't it?"

Jed's mouth felt lined with cotton. He could barely moisten his lips, but he knew he had to keep talking. Stump remained under the table, staring out at Jed with disbelief.

Jed rambled on with the story. "Yes, sirree, old Cletus presented a real problem for both you and your cousin. If he went through with his plan, you would go to prison for murder. Bain would join you on a conspiracy charge. The Gran-ville name would be dragged through the mud, and everything would be lost, all because of your drunken rage and your hatred for my brother."

An eerie silence followed. Jed peeped around the chair to see Parker's red-dened face. The attorney's lethal glare honed in on him.

"Don't suppose it matters none now," Parker said with surprising clarity. "The hunting trip was Bain's idea. He needed to protect the family name after prosecuting them boys and sending them off to prison."

Jed watched the man's gun hand, ready to jump back behind the chair if he detected the slightest movement. He wanted to lure him into another wild shot and believed it could happen any second.

"Everything had been taken care of, you see," Parker said. "Bain worked it out. Sims confessed, so it didn't much matter what Nash said. Then Renfrow got righteous and decided to screw it all up. We couldn't let him do that. Even *you* ought to understand our position."

"How did y'all get Sims to confess?"

The attorney laughed. "Routine persuasion and a little money—of course. Everybody has a price, but the price for Sims wasn't all that high. Bain promised him he would only serve a few years if he fingered Nash as the trigger man."

"I suppose Bain arranged for Nash's death in the prison laundry," Jed said.

"None of that's important. Nash was a nothing, a swamp rat who worked for Bain. He was expendable."

"What's important," Jed said, "is that you killed your own sister. Did you do it just because she dated a black man?"

Jed thought he saw the gun hand twitch. His muscles tightened, ready to leap out of the way. Parker didn't move, though. He just glared, but he wasn't focus-ing on his quarry. He stared as if in a trance.

"That's it, isn't it?" Jed said. "You couldn't stand the ribbing from your bud-dies, so that night you drank and drank and drank. The more liquor you con-sumed, the madder you got. Is that how it went down? Did you kill her to save face?"

"She was so pretty and sweet." The attorney's voice lowered to a mourn-ful whimper. "She deserved better than your brother. Plenty of guys—her own kind—wanted to take her out, but not after she began dating him. They called her a nigger lover. She deserved more than a life of ridicule."

"Come on, Parker. It was you who worried about being ridiculed. Abby was in love. She didn't consider being with Bobby a bad thing, something to be ridiculed about."

"You don't understand shit, Bradley. Nobody could understand what we went through together. I had to protect my baby sister."

Parker's voice cracked with every word. Remorse choked him.

Stump shifted under the table. He drew the revolver from his holster and, judging by the look of determination on his face, Jed thought the sheriff might finally be ready to act.

"She wasn't supposed to be behind the wheel that night." Parker's voice now sounded heavy with guilt. "The car belonged to him. He was supposed to be driving."

The attorney's words stung with the cold reality of what had happened. Parker mistakenly killed his sister, and then in a rage gunned down Bobby. Sadie Dunlap's corpse in the driver's seat of the Studebaker filled Jed's mind. That's why the killer put her there; he knew the truth.

"You went out there to kill my brother, didn't you?" Jed could only imagine the shock Parker experienced when he realized the person he had just shot was his own sister. "But you killed Abby instead. You shot her dead."

The anger returned to Parker's voice. "Enough bantering, Bradley. The time has come for you to join your brother and daddy in hell."

"What do you know about my daddy's death?"

Parker laughed. "The mere thought of an uppity nigger preacher thinking he could bring down a powerful state senator is funny as hell. Your daddy was a dumb bastard who didn't know how to keep his mouth shut."

Jed clenched his fist. "Did Bain kill—"

Parker laughed harder, drowning out Jed's question. "You're dumber than your old man. Bain wouldn't have soiled his hands messin' with the likes of your kin, but he knew plenty of folks who'd welcome the opportunity."

As the attorney's guffawing faded, Jed saw Stump ease from under the table. At about the same time, he felt the floor tremble from Parker's heavy muted steps on the carpet and realized the time for reckoning had come.

"Uncle Parker, stop. That's far enough." To Jed's surprise, Stump had risen to his feet and was actually aiming his gun at his uncle.

A shot rang out. Stump dropped to one knee before collapsing. Blood stained the front of his shirt.

Before Jed could dive for the fallen sheriff's gun, a voice from the doorway cried out. "Granville!"

Jed turned and saw Cory Layton, the young former Marine he'd met at Sadie Dunlap and Lamar Lassiter's crime scene. The barrel of his pistol was trained on Parker.

"Drop the gun, sir," the deputy said.

Layton presented his request much too politely to suit the circumstances, Jed thought, but for a fleeting second he believed it might be effective.

Parker appeared stunned. His revolver fired.

Layton's gun roared.

The bullet from Parker's gun hit high on the wall beside the young deputy. The former Marine's bullet found its mark, however, hitting the attorney in the right shoulder. Parker dropped with a thud.

Jed hurried to the fallen attorney and kicked away his revolver. Parker moaned as Layton approached.

Jed tore away the attorney's shirt to reveal a bloodied hole in the flesh. *Unfortunately, not that bad,* he thought. He looked up at the young deputy. Feeling sinister, he winked. "Appears to be the end of the road for this one."

Parker gasped, then moaned louder than before. Jed fought to suppress a laugh.

The deputy nodded and turned away. He hurried to check on his sheriff, who had managed to pull himself up into a seated position. Stump breathed hard and seemed in a fair amount of pain, but Jed figured he too would survive.

Layton lifted his walkie-talkie to call for help.

"Your timing sure did cut it awful close, son," Jed said. "Who called you, the receptionist?"

"No, sir," Layton said. "Doctor Braddock flagged me down. She showed me the letter that old sheriff wrote, and then she told me you might be in trouble in here. I didn't know the sheriff was here too."

Stump sneered at Jed. "This might clear up those old murders, but as far as I'm concerned, you're still a suspect and an escapee."

Jed shook his head. "You don't give up, do you?"

"Cuff him," the wounded sheriff said in a raspy voice.

Layton winked at Jed, then gestured toward the open door with his head.

Taking that as his cue to leave, Jed stood and patted the deputy on the shoulder. "Sure glad you came when you did."

Parker groaned. Stump craned his neck to catch a glimpse of his uncle.

"Reckon you ought to check on Parker," Jed said to Cory with a wink. He spoke loud enough to ensure the attorney could hear him. "Listen for his dying confession. He might want to set the record straight with the Almighty."

Layton smiled and nodded knowingly. He hurried to Parker, and when Stump leaned forward to watch, Jed eased past him. As he rushed through the door, he heard the deputy calling for help on his walkie-talkie.

"Headquarters, we need an ambulance to transport two gunshot victims from Parker Granville's office. One's critical."

"You say Parker Granville's?" the dispatcher responded in a tone of disbelief.

"That's right, ma'am. And tell them to hurry."

Just outside the door, Jed paused when he heard Stump holler. The new sheriff sounded like he was gargling gravel. "Where . . . where the hell is Bradley?"

Layton's voice echoed. "He was right beside you, Sheriff. I thought you were watching him."

Stump's pained voice bellowed out into the lobby. "Sombitch! Go find him."

# CHAPTER · 23

Jed nearly collided with Parker's receptionist as he ran from the wounded attorney's office. She stood between him and the exit, and when he approached, she tried to grab hold of his arm.

"Stop!" she screamed. "Where are you going?"

Jed shrugged her off with one swipe, sending her tumbling backward into a waiting-room chair with her legs splayed out in front of her. Her sour expression wrinkled more than normal. She reached up with one bony finger and hooked the top of her glasses, sliding them down her nose out of her line of sight.

"Sheriff, he's escaping." Her shrill shriek sounded like a smoke alarm going off. "He assaulted me, Sheriff. Arrest him! Arrest him!"

Jed picked up his pace, and by the time he reached the steps leading down to the outside door, he was at a full jog. His breath labored as he hit the panic bar opening the door to the dimming sunlight. Once outside, he bent over, rested his hands on his knees, and sucked air into his burning lungs.

His heart pounded; his head ached. *I'm getting way too old to have to keep running away from trouble,* he thought. Every muscle in his body screamed.

A horn honked to Jed's left. *Jessie.*

He spun around, but as soon as he saw the car, his shoulders slumped. He stood immobile, breathing hard and staring in disbelief.

"You look disappointed," Hap Gentry said, leaning across his front seat and peering out the window of a weather-faded, pale green Ford Falcon. "Expecting someone else?"

Jed glanced back at the brownstone. A siren wailed in the distance. *Now is not the time to be picky.* "Hoping, more than expecting," he said as he grabbed the door handle and jumped inside.

Gentry's gaze lingered on the door of Parker Granville's building. "What happened in there?"

"I'll tell you later. Now, just drive."

As Gentry pulled away from the curb, Jed turned back to watch for pursuers.

Just as he expected, the door flew open and Cory Layton appeared. The deputy gave Gentry's Falcon a long hard look, then went back inside. Jed thought he saw a smile on the deputy's face.

"I owe you, son," Jed said. He turned around in his seat, leaned back, closed his eyes, and tried to catch his breath.

"What?" Gentry asked.

Jed shook his head. "Nothing. Now, tell me exactly how you came to be waiting when I came out."

"Easy," Gentry said. He pointed to a police scanner mounted under his dashboard. "I was just down the block talking to this poor guy who had his truck stolen early this morning, when I heard 'em say something about shots fired at Parker Granville's. I figured you'd be smack in the middle. Want to tell me what's going on?"

"Truck, huh? That's tough."

"Yeah, we don't have many stolen vehicles around these parts. Now, tell me, what went down in the attorney's office?"

"Guess you already know I'm a fugitive," Jed said.

"Oh, yeah. Everybody knows. Your name's been all over the radio. I suspect you'll be front page in tomorrow's newspaper, since we don't have all that many desperados running loose. You're more famous than Bonnie and Clyde."

"Terrific. Aren't you concerned you'll be charged for aiding an escapee?"

"Not especially. I'll tell 'em I was interviewing you. You know—anything for a story." Gentry winked. "You going to tell me what happened back there, or do I have to turn around and go get it straight from the sheriff?"

"You're a funny man," Jed said. "Let's just say Parker took exception to my accusing him of killing my brother and his sister."

"I can't imagine that bothering him."

"I also accused him of killing Cletus Renfrow."

"Ah, now there's an accusation with some meat."

"You don't seem surprised."

Gentry laughed. "When rumors hang around long enough, they become legend, and the one with the Lowcountry's longest tenure is the one about old Sheriff Renfrow."

The Falcon rattled out of town. It crossed Interstate 95, which split Indigo County into nearly equal halves.

Gentry said, "Nobody ever truly believed he killed himself, but nobody ever had the moxie to try to prove otherwise."

"Nell Renfrow did," Jed said.

"Yeah, but nobody listened. She was the widow. Nobody expected her to admit her husband would kill himself."

"But you just said nobody believed he killed himself."

"That's right, they didn't. Because the Granvilles were the ones who found him, speculation always has been they had something to do with his death. Nobody pushed it, because nobody wanted to take them on."

"That's insane. If that many folks suspected the Granvilles killed their sheriff, why didn't someone do something about it?"

Gentry pointed to a thick file folder on the seat between them. "Some tried."

Jed took the folder, flipped open the top, and began pulling handwritten notes from inside. "What's this?"

"Notes belonging to Dick Rison, a reporter who used to work for the *News*."

"He doesn't work there now?"

"He doesn't work anywhere now. He's dead."

Jed looked up from the sheaf of papers. "Natural causes?"

"Hardly. According to the Coast Guard report—you'll find a copy of it in there somewhere—his boat capsized in rough weather. Only one problem with that account. He was a skilled sailor who was smart enough to check out the weather forecast before putting out to sea. His body was never found."

As Gentry drove, Jed scanned the handwritten scrawl that resembled a doctor's illegible script. "Says here that Bain Granville operated an import/export business."

"Yep, of sorts. You'll also notice that several months before your brother's death, Willie Sims and Roy Nash, who had met in prison, came to work for Granville."

Jed looked over at Gentry with heightened interest. "What did he import and export?"

"Rison believed drugs were the import and laundered money the export, but he didn't live long enough to prove it."

Jed stroked his chin with his thumb and forefinger. "So that's how the senator knew the two men. He must have threatened Sims into testifying against Nash to cover up for what Parker had done."

"The oldest persuasion of all: my way or the dead way," Gentry said.

"So, how did you happen to come across these notes?"

"A story I've been working on. I don't happen to believe the senator's illicit business dealings are all in the past."

"You think he's still smuggling drugs?"

"Pretty sure. He oversees an operation bringing them in through Savannah and Charleston. Runners transport the goods straight up I-95 to the Big Apple. It's a very lucrative business."

"How close are you to breaking the story?"

The reporter shook his head. "I don't know. I keep thinking about those notes and the guy who made them. Then I get to thinking about becoming shark food."

Jed knew about fear. During his time with the Atlanta PD, Georgia had had as many corrupt politicians as there were water moccasins in the lowcountry swamps. They lurked in a morass of bribery and self-indulgence, and at least twice in his career he had been threatened by a couple. Even so, he was able to experience the pleasure of putting them in jail.

"Why don't you just turn over your information to the FBI or DEA and let them take it from there?" Jed said. "The feds love public corruption cases."

"It's more personal than that. Dick Rison befriended me when I was just a paperboy. He's the reason I became a reporter."

"I can understand that," Jed said. "Maybe after I clear my name and we find out who the real killer is, we can pool our resources and go after Bain Granville together." He couldn't believe he had just offered to work with a reporter, but in this case they had a mutual interest.

The Falcon passed a sign indicating they were thirty miles from St. Helena Island. "Where are you taking me?" Jed asked.

"A place of interest," Gentry said. "If I'm right, we just might learn the identity of the killer."

Thick forests loomed amid dark and swampy wetlands on both sides of the car. Gone were the flat fields of peanuts and cotton they had passed after crossing the interstate. The road narrowed.

Jed looked toward the heavens. "Father," he whispered, "guide this car and keep it on dry land." He closed his eyes.

# C H A P T E R · 2 4

Stretched out on the cold, uncomfortable metal bed with his eyes closed, Parker Granville pictured his hands wrapped around his nephew's meaty throat. His head ached and his chest burned, but the doctor at the hospital had refused to admit him. He couldn't even talk the SOB into giving him pain medicine until the alcohol had been flushed from his system. Now he faced the degradation of being treated like a criminal.

"Your wound is superficial," the physician had pronounced after probing and pushing on Parker's chest.

"Bastard!" The attorney's scream bounced off the concrete walls, out into the dim light of the cell block.

Before the doctor had come in to check him, he had thought he was about to die. And the young deputy questioning him did nothing to dissuade him from that opinion.

He groaned when he thought of how he had confessed to everything he had done since childhood. He wiped his mouth with his hand. *That confession won't hold up in court,* he told himself. Even so, he had confessed to things he knew he shouldn't have, and Bain would be furious when he found out. *How can I explain my gullibility?*

Adding to his misery, he thought back to how Bradley had barged into his office earlier in the day. He hated how he had allowed the bastard to take advantage of his drunkenness, how the son of a bitch needled him until he revealed the sordid details of what had happened to Abby. And worse, he confessed it all in front of Stump, who now believed he had an obligation to lock up his own flesh and blood. *Sanctimonious fool.*

Bain would get him out of this mess, just like he always had, but what would the senator do when he learned of the confessions? Parker drew a deep breath, flared his nostrils. A hundred years of sweat and urine imbedded in the bowels of the old jail assaulted his senses. He gagged and coughed and then spit onto the grimy gray floor.

*Everything will work out,* he promised himself as he wiped tears from his eyes. *Bain will handle everything, just like always.*

Since his arrival, the tiny cell had steadily grown darker as the sunlight outside diminished. The only other light came from the corridor, leaking through the window in the door. He widened his eyes, hoping they would pull in every bit of illumination, but with each passing minute, he felt himself growing more and more anxious.

What he really wanted was a drink. He hated the dark, and if he allowed the truth to be known, he feared it with every fiber of his being.

He stared at the gray cell wall, imagining being back in the root cellar where his father used to take him to punish him for the myriad of minor misdeeds he committed as a boy. His father had never been one to spare the rod, and Parker still despised the Scripture verses the fanatical man quoted while he beat him. After the beating, his father would leave him locked in the pitch-black underground room for hours.

Entire days had been spent in that abyss, listening and fearing the scratching and chirping of unseen rodents and vermin. At times he felt the creatures tug on his clothes and brush against his arms and legs. He would scream and flail to drive them away, but he knew he couldn't rest, for like the dirt and mold and the unforgettable musty odor, the creatures were always there, eager to forage on his stilled body.

The cellar became a special hell. One only Parker knew.

After his father died, just prior to his thirteenth birthday, Parker nailed the outside doors to the old cellar shut and never opened them again. He never talked of his experiences in the darkness with anyone, not with his mother, not even with Abby, who, as far as he knew, had never been forced to endure the horrors of that hellhole.

Memories from the night of his sister's death claimed him, just as they had over and over again every day since. He closed his eyes, squeezed his temples between the heels of his hands.

"I hate you, Bradley," he whispered.

The sound of a key turning the lock in the outer corridor door filled him with both anticipation and dread. *Bain's here.*

He swung his legs off the bed as the groan of the thick metal hinges signaled the outer door's opening. A loud boom came when the door slammed shut.

*Thank God,* he thought as he brushed whatever had been on the bed off of his clothes. "Get me out of here, Bain. And if Stump's out there with you, tell him to stay the hell out of my sight."

No one responded to his call. He heard the bolt being thrown on the outer door lock.

"Don't leave. Bain, is that you?"

No one answered.

He listened to the echoing sound of footsteps coming down the hallway. Slow, steady steps headed toward his cell.

He leaned toward the window in the door but saw no one. He pressed his cheek against the opening, trying to angle his head to catch a glimpse of who was there. He saw no one, not even a shadow on the floor. The footsteps stopped.

"Who's there? I know someone's out there. I heard you walking."

He stepped back from the window. The hallway light faded as first one bulb went out, and then another, until only the strained glow of a single bulb seeped through the opening in his cell door.

In the quiet of the darkness around him, he heard his heart beating inside his chest. He felt it too and tried to calm himself. He drew in a deep breath.

"Stump is that you? . . . Who's there?" This time his voice cracked. His hands shook; his body trembled.

Not a sound penetrated the thick walls.

A soft, hesitant cry leapt from his throat. "Who's there?"

His mouth became like sandpaper. He tried to moisten his gums, but all he could muster was a deep guttural cough.

Two eyes appeared in the door's window.

Parker gasped.

He couldn't see a face, only the piercing glare framed in the window. "Who . . . who are you? What do you want?"

"Hag be angry. Conjure man die for your crime. Hag come to set tings straight."

Warm urine streamed down both legs, puddling around Parker's feet. He moved away from the door, turned his head so he couldn't see the red-rimmed eyes fixed on him.

"No . . . no. I—"

A yellowish, pungent smoke wafted up from beneath the door. Fetid vapor stung the jailed attorney's eyes. He coughed and flailed his arms.

"What . . . are you doing? Stop! Stop!" His cough grew harsher with each word. The smoke grew thicker. "Someone . . . help . . . me."

"No one will hear you. The hag, she blocks the cries of the guilty. Retribution must be met for your sins."

Visions of the root cellar filled Parker's mind. He tried to draw in a clean breath but could only inhale the yellowish smoke as the rotten stench engulfed his nostrils.

An eerie chant came from the other side of the cell door. It began as a whispered, unintelligible noise but grew steadily until the rhythmic shouting deafened him.

His chest tightened. He felt a sharp pain, a fist squeezing his heart.

The rhythmic incantation continued. It grew louder and louder, came faster and faster.

Ribbons of yellow smoke slithered into the room. One by one they wrapped around the prisoner's head.

Parker grasped his chest, squeezed his breasts. A rattle rolled from his throat. His body collapsed in a heap on the cold concrete floor.

He smelled the old cellar. The chanting stopped.

# CHAPTER · 25

Jostled from a brief nap, Jed cracked open one eye. All he could see was inky black, putrid-looking water. The car dipped and swayed, and for the briefest of terror-filled moments, he feared Gentry had driven the Falcon off into a swamp.

He sat bolt upright and stared out the windshield. In the dim of twilight he saw a road, of sorts, in front of them, but on both sides of the car he could see only an endless black sheen dotted with cypress stumps. Taller trees, all cloaked in tufts of gray moss, formed a surrealistic canopy over the scenic horror.

"Where the hell are we?" His eyes searched the dark surface of the morass for signs of creatures that he did not even want to imagine living there.

"Relax, friend. You know, for a cop you're a bit edgy in a crisis."

Gentry wasn't driving the Falcon, he was fighting it, twisting and turning the steering wheel, holding on with a viselike grip as the car dove in and out of craters in the road. His face held the appearance of a kid at an amusement park. *The SOB is actually enjoying himself,* Jed thought.

The car dipped into a pothole deep enough to bottom out the frame. Jed felt the thud against his feet. "What the. . . ." His words drowned in a loud gulp.

Visions of godforsaken landscapes described in stories about witches and goblins told to him by his grandmamma nestled in Jed's head. He eased his cheek against the window and peered straight down, desperate to know good old terra firma lay beneath them. What he saw didn't lend him much comfort. The ribbon of roadway was barely wider than the car.

Jed looked out the windshield to where the road appeared to be running off the edge of the world. "I said, where the hell are we?"

"Relax, we're almost there. It should be just around the bend up here."

"What should be around what bend? There ain't nothing as far as the eye can see but swamp and what lurks beneath it."

Another pothole jarred the car. "Hmph." Gentry grunted. "Need a four-wheeler," he said.

"You need a boat." Jed glanced back out at the dismal surroundings, his interest drawn there like steel to a magnet. Again, he checked for eyeballs peering just above the surface of the black water.

"Here we go," Gentry said.

Sure enough, as advertised, the road turned and began to widen. A small shack came into view.

Built from warped boards and cypress shingles, the gray, weathered building stood on a peninsula surrounded on three sides by a piece of mother earth only reptiles and mosquitoes could love. Sprigs of fernlike plants sprouted in the sandy soil, and ground fog sifted through the trees from deep inside the swamp. Yellow smoke billowed from inside a black steel pot hanging from a tripod hook over an open fire in front of the cabin. The humid air reeked of the stench of rotten eggs.

"Humor me," Jed said before grabbing hold of the door handle. "Why are we here? I don't do spooky locations."

"We came for answers, I hope. We know from Rison's notes that Roy Nash had been in prison when he met Willie Sims. But Rison didn't know much about Nash prior to that first prison sentence."

"Yes, but—"

"I did some digging of my own into Nash's past. According to someone I trust a great deal, this is where we needed to come to find out about him."

Jed wondered if that someone might be a favored relative who was also a conjurer. "Nash is dead," he said. "He died in a prison fight. What do I care about where he came from?"

Gentry didn't answer. "Stay here while I check to see if anyone is home."

As the reporter strode toward the porch, he didn't seem to be the least bit apprehensive, so Jed gladly conceded it made sense to let him pave the way for their visit. After all, because of Gentry's relations, he likely knew how to converse with root doctors—a skill Jed had no interest in learning.

Jed pulled on the door handle, but the door latch didn't release. "Damn it!" He opened the window, reached through, and grabbed the outer handle. With a hearty push, the door groaned and creaked open. Relieved he wouldn't be trapped inside the aging vehicle, Jed stepped out onto the sandy loam.

The smoke from the burning sulfur stung his eyes. *This has to be what the hunters described smelling just before they found Sadie Dunlap and Lamar Lassiter,* he thought.

Before Gentry could step up onto the rickety porch, the door to the shanty flew open. Flickering light danced out into the gloom. Taken aback at the suddenness with which the door had been flung open, Jed inched closer.

The skeletal figure of an elderly black woman appeared in the doorway. Her tightly stretched, leathery skin looked like she had pulled it off of one of the swamp reptiles and then molded it to her frame. "Who disturbs the spirits this night?" she said.

Gentry spoke to the old woman in a low, whispered voice; Jed couldn't hear the conversation from where he stood. He crept closer, heard the reporter say they meant her no harm.

Gentry added, "Doctor Leopard sends her regards to Doctor Leech."

The woman's head tilted. Barefoot, wearing a dress made from burlap, she walked around Gentry, sizing him up. When she finished, she stared out through blue-tinted glasses toward Jed. Her gaze seem to streak right through him and off into the swamp.

"Another be with you. Who dat?"

"A friend," Gentry said. "He's a friend of Doctor Leopard's, too. We'd like to talk with you about a matter of great urgency."

The conjurer motioned for her two visitors to come inside. Gentry stepped through the door first. Jed followed, but not before noticing the old woman's eyes up close through her glasses. They were milky white, obviously sightless, yet she seemed to see everything going on around her.

The woman grabbed Jed's shoulder with the suddenness of a viper's strike. Her distinctive eyes bulged from her skull. Jed started, felt as if the old gal could see straight through him into his soul.

"You th' law?" she asked.

Gentry and Jed exchanged worrisome glances.

"We're not the law," the reporter said before Jed could answer.

"Hmph." With a look of disbelief, the woman pushed the door shut and walked toward a table brimming with lit candles fused in puddles of wax. Her necklace of tiny bones clacked with each slow and feeble step.

"Who be afflicted?"

Jed glanced at Gentry, who once again responded before the former detective could. "He is." The kind of boyish grin a kid would reveal when trying to deflect blame, while casting it upon another, inched its way across the reporter's face.

"How so?" she asked.

Gentry said, "We think he's been rooted. An evil spirit drove him here."

*A very evil spirit did drive me here,* Jed thought. He glared at the reporter, wondering what he was up to.

Undaunted by Jed's best attempt at casting an evil eye, Gentry continued his charade. "We were hoping you could conjure up something to drive that spirit away."

He winked at Jed, mouthed the words *play along.* Jed frowned.

The woman, blind as she was, looked back and forth, holding her sightless gaze on each man for longer than Jed's comfort allowed. She displayed the cynicism of a veteran cop.

"Actually," Jed said, drawing a disapproving leer from Gentry, "there have been several folks killed from where we're from. We thought you could help."

"Dat so?" the woman said. "How could it be I might help?"

Jed said, "We found a mojo near one of the bodies, sulfur powder sprinkled around another. We were told those were hoodoo signs, so we came here to see if you could help us sort out what those symbols might mean."

The woman turned to Gentry and said, "Why not ask your Doctor Leopard this question?"

Gentry stammered.

"We hear you're the wisest of all the root doctors," Jed said, making up anything that sounded good. "Doctor Leopard referred us to you."

"That's right," Gentry said, chiming in at last.

Jed glared at the reporter. Gentry shrugged and looked away.

Doctor Leech stepped to within inches of Jed. She glared straight into his eyes. Her head tilted back and forth. She didn't blink. "You sho you ain't the law?"

"I'm not the law," he said in a firm, somewhat agitated voice. "I'm the brother of a man who died almost forty years ago, and I think the murders happening now are related to his death."

A knowing smile slipped across the woman's pressed lips. She nodded her head. "He murdered too?"

"Yes."

The old woman stepped back and drew a symbol in the air. Her mouth made a clicking noise. "I see." She sounded and looked as if she had just discovered a missing piece to a puzzle.

Jed glanced at Gentry. Judging from the reporter's expression, he didn't understand any more about what this mystical root doctor was doing than Jed did.

"What you described," Doctor Leech said, "be used to help protect folks from evil spirits, not kill them."

"But these were found around those already dead," Jed said.

"Then maybe they not be for those killed. Maybe they be for others."

"Like the killer?" Jed asked, suddenly interested in the theory proposed by the woman.

"Maybe," she said. "Spirits know da heart. Maybe da killer's heart be good, his killing be to right a wrong."

Now she had his attention. She used the same words used by his caller the night before finding the first two bodies. "What do you know about these killings?" he asked.

The woman shook her head, became mute. She turned to walk away but spun around after a few steps. "You seem good. You want protection from the spirits?"

Jed figured the time had come to cut to the chase. *We came to this godforsaken place to learn about Roy Nash, so why not just ask the question.* "No, I want—"

"Actually, yes he does want protection," Gentry said. "That's exactly what we want for him. Can you conjure a mojo or something for him to wear to protect him during his search?"

Jed gritted his teeth. Gentry pointed to a shelf holding pictures and candles and dolls. Jed remained silent, but the urge to hold the reporter's head under the black swamp water outside was almost more than he could control.

The root doctor seated herself at the table. She motioned for Jed to join her. "Very well," she said. She pointed to a high-back chair directly across from her.

Jed hesitated.

The glow from the candles danced in the woman's milky orbs. "Sit," she said.

She sprinkled powders across the candles, causing their flickering flames to crackle. Sparks leaped into the air, and the stench of sulfur filled Jed's nostrils.

He pulled out the chair and plopped down, looking up to register his contempt with Gentry. The reporter turned away, seemed to suppress a grin, before settling back against the wall near the shelf of knickknacks and photographs.

"Give me your hands," the woman said.

Jed lifted his hands from his lap and extended his arms across the table. The woman took his fingers, squeezed them just behind the knuckles. Pain shot past his wrists and up his arms.

She continued to hold on, squeezing his knuckles as if trying to dislocate them. The flames licked the soft skin under his arms.

Jed began to fidget. The pain became intense.

Just as he was about to jerk loose, the woman let go and fell against the back of her chair. Her hands lifted above her head. "Spirits came wit you. Strong spirits, evil spirits."

Jed rubbed his arms and massaged his sore knuckles. The woman wiped her mouth with her thumb and forefinger. "They ride you hard?"

Jed looked back at Gentry. The reporter gestured, urged Jed to accept what the conjurer had told him.

"Yes . . . I suppose," Jed said.

She frowned. "You not believe mojo work, mojo won't work."

"He believes," Gentry said, pushing away from the wall. He kneed the chair, jolting Jed. "Don't you?"

Jed's jaw tensed. "Yes . . . I believe." He was fast growing weary of the charade and wanted to press the woman for answers before more people died in Sweetgrass. He drummed his fingers on the table, watched as she picked up a piece of scrap paper and scribbled on it with a small yellow pencil. She slid the paper across to Jed.

He took it and looked up in disbelief. "You want one hundred dollars?"

The woman didn't react to the obvious tone of disdain in Jed's voice. "Da spirit what wants you harmed be powerful. You need powerful medicine to keep it away."

Jed wadded the paper in his hand.

"He'll take it," Gentry said before Jed could get up. "Give her the hundred dollars."

Jed whirled around to stare at the madman beside him. He silently mouthed *What?!*

"You *need* the medicine," Gentry said. "He's like this with other doctors too. He never wants to do what's best for him."

Doctor Leech locked her sightless stare on Jed. She rocked back and forth, hummed a tune he vaguely recognized as a hymn.

"Okay," Jed said, reaching into his back pocket. He pulled out his wallet and plucked out five twenties. Three one-dollar bills remained.

Gentry wasn't a killer. He was a con artist, and Jed decided that if the old woman and the reporter were in cahoots, there would be hell to pay. He held out the twenties, wondering if he gave her just one bill, telling her it was a hundred, would she believe him.

Before he could act on his scheme, however, Gentry snatched the bills from his hand and gave them to the woman. "Thank you for helping my friend," he said.

She took the five bills, slid her chair back, and stood. "Now, give me a coin from your pocket."

Jed leered at Gentry but nevertheless dug out a dime from his front pants pocket and handed it to the woman. "Anything else?" he asked in the harsh tone of someone knowing they were being fleeced.

"Your brother's name," she said.

"Bobby," Jed said.

"And yours?"

"Jedediah."

"I'll be back," she said, rising from her chair to walk into the dimly lit back part of the cabin beyond the glow of the candlelight.

Jed could make out a small bed and a curtain draped across one corner. The old woman pulled back the curtain, stepped through the opening, and pulled the curtain closed behind her. As she did, Jed popped out of his seat and came nose to nose with Gentry. "You bast—"

"Later," the reporter said, holding his finger to his lips. Whispering, he said, "Help me look through the pictures and papers here on the shelf." He picked up a stack of photographs and handed them to Jed, while he began thumbing through another stack. "With any luck," he said, continuing to whisper, "we'll find a picture of Nash here. Then we'll know for sure."

"Know what for sure?" Jed asked.

"That she's the same woman in a picture Rison had with his notes. If she is, we have a connection."

"We have a connection," Jed said. "She spoke the same words as my caller the morning we found the bodies. She knows the killer, and I think somehow she's involved."

"Yeah, but if we can find something here, we can pressure her to tell us what she knows."

"She doesn't strike me as the type to be pressured about anything." Jed shook his head. "You just cost me one hundred hard-earned dollars. Why go through all that hocus-pocus?"

"To buy time, so we can look through this stuff. What kind of a cop are you, anyway?"

"An aggravated, impatient, retired cop who'd rather ask her direct questions about who the killer is and why he's killing people."

Sounds of bottles clinking drifted from behind the curtain. Jed leafed through a stack of photos, not seeing anything he found particularly interesting or germane to the investigation.

"HAG!" The scream from behind the curtain startled both men. Gentry dropped his stack of pictures, and as he knelt to pick them up, he looked like a kid caught stealing money out of his mamma's pocketbook.

"HAG, HAG, HAG." Each time the woman chanted, her voice grew louder.

Quiet seconds followed, and then the curtain pulled back. The woman stepped back into the light. She wore a mask of serenity as she held out her creation, an almost exact duplicate of the pouch found under Lamar Lassiter's body.

Jed slipped a handful of unviewed pictures into his shirt pocket and returned to the table. Gentry continued his search.

"Dis protect you," she said, handing Jed the red flannel pouch.

He felt a hard object inside. "John the Conqueror inside this?" he asked.

"Potions. But don't open it, or you'll destroy their power. You wear it for three days. While you're wearing it you will be safe. After sun sets on third day, you throw it in the water. It will bring you luck."

Jed watched the eerie reflections of the candlelight flicker in the woman's clouded eyes. She seemed to see everything, know what was happening around her. He wondered how.

"Doctor Leech," Gentry said, "I'm holding a picture of a man I found on your shelf. He appears to be about thirty. I know him as Roy Nash. Can you tell me why you have his picture?"

A pained expression fell over her face. "Leave my pictures alone." She reached her hand out to take the photo.

Gentry stepped back, pulled the photo away. His tone turned harsh. "First, tell us how you know him."

The woman's face showed the fierce determination of a mamma protecting her young. "Time you be leavin'." Her voice hissed like a snake.

Believer or not, Jed found the woman's dark glower disturbing. Earlier she had seemed frail and vulnerable. Now she reminded him of a wild animal about to attack. Jed decided not to give her the chance. "Let's go," he said to Gentry.

The reporter flashed a look of dismay. "Nash lived here didn't he? You raised him as your own."

"You be gone now or I'll call the hag on you."

Her screech caused a shiver to rattle down Jed's spine. The same must have happened to Gentry, because he paled and said, "We mean you no harm. We just—"

"Be gone!" The woman's shrill voice sounded like a rifle shot. She snatched the photo from Gentry, hissed at him again.

Already in the doorway, Jed nodded for Gentry to follow. The air outside had thickened with the sulfurous smoke rising from the kettle in the yard. The swamp had grown eerily quiet, amid a deepening darkness.

"Let's go," Jed hollered. "Now!"

# C H A P T E R · 2 6

As Gentry hurried to turn the Falcon around, he came dangerously close to sliding off into the black muck. Jed barely noticed. His attention was firmly fixed on Doctor Leech's wrathful visage standing on her front porch. She had followed them out of the cabin and lingered there until they had gotten into their car.

Jed watched as the hoodoo root doctor gestured at the retreating car. Smoke roiled from inside the pot, and as the woman lifted her arms to the sky, Jed swore he heard thunder rumble from deep in the swamp. He clutched the mojo hanging from his neck.

"When we're very far from here," he said, "I want you to tell me why I shouldn't kill you and leave you to rot in this hellhole."

Jed said nothing else until they had cleared the ribbon of road leading through the wetland and he could see solid ground on both sides of the car. When he did, he asked, "Just exactly who is Doctor Leopard?"

"An acquaintance," Gentry replied without taking his eyes off the road. He seemed subdued after his encounter with Doctor Leech.

"Your aunt?"

Gentry cut his eyes toward the former detective. His eye twitched, reminding Jed of Jake's affliction. The reporter did not reply.

"I ain't ever seen a real-life place like what we just saw," Jed said. "It's straight out of some scary hoodoo tale my kinfolks might've told to keep us young'uns from going somewhere they didn't want us to go." He stared out the window and shook his head in disbelief. "I'm waiting to turn into a toad."

Gentry said, "Doctor Leech is Etta Turpin. She's Roy Nash's foster mother."

"Foster?"

"Yeah. I'd say it's pretty obvious she's not his birth mom, but she did raise him."

"How'd you learn about her?" Jed asked.

"Rison's notes." He motioned toward the thick folder. "He's got a whole section in there on Nash, who grew up as mean as a snake in those swamps. Bar-room legend has it he once set a man on fire for drinking the last of his beer."

"We've already established Nash wasn't a pillar of the community," Jed said.

"From what I've been able to verify through police records in Charleston, the stories about Roy Nash were more fact than legend."

"Just goes to show, even the meanest and toughest legends can fall victim to someone meaner and tougher." Jed yawned, patted his mouth with his hand. "So, what else haven't you shared with me about Nash and his venomous foster mom?"

"Before prison, before going to work for Granville, Nash met a woman named Cora Capers. I think he was in his late teens at the time. Their brief union produced a son, Lincoln, who took his mamma's name because Nash split as soon as he learned about Cora's pregnancy."

"Not surprising for a pillar like Nash," Jed said, resting against the doorpost. Gentry looked over. "Am I boring you?"

"Not at all." Jed punctuated his remark with an exaggerated yawn. "I'm all ears."

"Cora lived near Sumter. She worked in a textile mill. When Lincoln grew up, he joined the army at eighteen and met a girl from Fayetteville, where he was stationed at the time. A year or so later she got pregnant. About the same time, Lincoln got transferred to Fort Jackson, in Columbia. Lincoln proved to be more honorable than his pappy, so he married her and took her with him. He never got to see his son, though. A training accident claimed his life before the baby was born."

Jed's thoughts drifted to the manhunt back in Sweetgrass and to Jessie. He wondered how she was holding up. "Hang on a second," he said. "Let me bor-row your cell phone to call a friend. Maybe she can tell me what's happening back home."

Gentry flipped Jed the cell phone. "You might have a hard time getting ser-vice out here," he said.

Jed looked at the dial face. Not even a hint of a signal. "Damn." He stuck the phone in his coat pocket. "You said Lincoln got killed?"

"Yeah, a grenade exploded next to him. Anyway, Lincoln's wife didn't want to raise the baby by herself. Guess it cramped her style. She abandoned him. Lincoln's son grew up with a foster grandma."

"Another foster?" Jed asked, rolling his eyes.

"Nope, not another one, the same one—Etta Turpin, alias Doctor Leech." Jed sat up straight. "Go on."

"The way I see it, Turpin taught Nash about conjuring, and there's no reason to believe she didn't do the same for his grandson," Gentry said.

"You thinking she taught him something else . . . something other than how to put a hex on someone?" Jed thought back to the visage of the angry root doctor. He remembered her words about the killer righting a wrong. "That's the missing piece," he said. "Etta Turpin—Doctor Leech—wants revenge for what happened to Roy Nash, and she sent his grandson out to exact that revenge." Jed thought about how long she must have brainwashed the kid. "He was an infant when his mamma abandoned him?"

"That's right."

"Did you see any pictures of the kid in the stack you went through?"

"No. What about you?"

"I didn't. . . ." Jed patted his pocket. The pictures he had slid in there when the woman came back from behind the curtain were still there. He had forgotten to put them back. "I don't know. I didn't get a chance to look, but I will now."

Gentry laughed when he saw the stack of pictures in Jed's hand. "I'll be damned."

"You got a flashlight? I can't see a damn thing in the dark."

"Glove box."

Jed opened the cluttered compartment, pulled out a pink plastic flashlight. "You spare no expense, do you?"

"It works. What else do you want?"

"The killer, not the victim, believed in the power of the root," Jed said, shining the light on photo after photo. "He carried it to ward off spirits working against his cause."

"You catch on pretty quick for a cop."

"Former cop," Jed said. He squinted to make out a face on one of the photos. "My skills have rusted a mite."

*A former cop who just might end up in prison,* he mused. The unpleasant thought loomed over him. He knew if he ever got locked up in a maximum security prison with society's more violent rejects, he wouldn't last as long as Nash did.

"Why do you think he called you?" Gentry asked. "Surely he didn't want to draw the interest of a former homicide cop?"

"He just might be smart enough to have figured my showing up like I did with a story about mysterious phone calls would make me a suspect and take the focus away from him."

"That or he read the press clippings from Atlanta and figured it didn't matter if you knew." Gentry chuckled.

Jed stopped leafing through the pictures to glare at the reporter. "How does that old saying go? Twenty thousand comedians out of work, and you want to be funny?"

"Something like that," Gentry said, smiling. "Find anything yet?"

As Jed leafed through the old photos, he thought about how crafty the killer had been to methodically take out victims, each one being a descendant of the principals behind the injustice done to Nash. He wondered about Lamar Lassiter. What was his connection?

"Nothing. . . ." He held a picture close to the flashlight beam. "Then again, maybe I have. Take a gander."

Gentry gave the picture a glance. "It's old. Who is it?"

"Yes, the photo's old. It looks to be of Nash when he was around twenty or twenty-one. He's clean shaven with short hair. Remind you of anyone?"

Gentry slowed the car as he turned his head to see the faded picture illuminated by the flashlight Jed held. "Yeah, he does . . . damn!"

"So you do recognize him."

"Recognize him? If two generations didn't separate them, I'd swear they were brothers."

Jed said, "Now I know how he was able to keep up with everything in the investigation. He knew when to dial up the heat and when to plant evidence pointing at me as the killer."

He pulled the phone from his coat pocket. "Shit, still no signal."

"Do you think you can convince Stump before he locks you back in that cell?" Gentry asked.

"Stump will have to believe me," Jed said. "If I'm right, Parker and the senator are next. They don't have kids, so their numbers just floated to the top of the hit list. He plans on killing them, just like he did Judge Baker and Willie Sims."

As they drove out from under the thick canopy of the forest, moonlight covered the countryside like a huge spotlight. A road sign indicated they were back on Highway 17 headed back to Sweetgrass.

The Falcon's engine whined as Gentry pressed the accelerator. He said, "Just for the record, you now know my source for all the information about the investigations, including your calls."

"He wanted to make sure the attention stayed on me," Jed said. "So, who better to tell than a reporter in search of a story?"

Gentry pursed his lips. "Yes, who better?"

The signal returned to Gentry's cell phone thirty-six miles outside of Sweetgrass. Jed dialed the sheriff's emergency number and listened to six rings before a woman's voice crackled through the static-filled phone. "Sheriff's emergency."

"I need to talk to the sheriff," Jed said, trying his best to sound urgent in his request.

"He's not available now, sir."

"He'll want to talk to me."

"That may be, sir, but he's unavailable at the moment. If you'd like to leave a number, I'll have him call."

"Listen, I—"

"Sir, don't use that tone with me. I'll hang up if you do."

Jed fought to control his anger. Gentry's eyebrow lifted.

"You need to leave a number," the woman said in a voice so sugary it made Jed even angrier. "The sheriff will return your call as soon as he can."

"Call him now," Jed said, raising his voice. "Find him. Tell him I know who the killer is."

"We know who the killer is," she said with an air of indignation. "We've been hunting for him all day."

"Damn it, woman—"

Jed heard a click and then silence. Gentry looked amused.

"The bitch hung up on me."

Gentry chortled. "You're surprised? Now what?"

"We've got to find Stump and let him know what's going on," Jed said, drumming his fingers on the closed phone. "As much as he's not one of my favorite people, I don't want him being surprised and killed by one of his own."

"Like what happened to Sheriff Armistead."

Somehow, amid all of the mayhem, Jake's death had taken an emotional backseat to Jed's escape and search for the real killer. He stroked his forehead with the tips of his fingers. "Yeah, like Jake."

Jed glanced at the speedometer. The needle quivered just beyond sixty miles per hour. "Can't this bucket of bolts go any faster?"

"My foot's all the way to the floorboard now." Gentry's voice was barely discernible over the whine of the straining engine. "Any faster and the whole thing will fall apart and collapse around us."

Jed picked at the torn vinyl on the armrest, at first thinking he should try the dispatcher again. Instead of acting on his instinct, he allowed the image of Parker shooting Bobby to overtake the urgency of the moment.

"Tell me," Gentry said, "how is it Parker came to kill your brother and his sister?"

Jed coughed to clear the clabber forming in his throat. "You read minds as a hobby?"

"Huh?"

"Never mind," he said, rubbing the top of his shaved head. He detected stubble needing a razor. "Parker spent most of that afternoon and night drinking with his highfalutin friends at the country club. They were all drunk, all white, and all angry about a black man dating one of their women."

"Volatile mixture," Gentry said.

"Yep. On the way to the gathering, one of Parker's buddies saw Bobby's car pull into the church driveway, and he watched as it pulled around back."

"They knew his car?" Gentry sounded mildly surprised.

"He worked on the grounds crew at the country club after school. Besides, they made it their business to know about the *black boy* dating one of their own." Jed fought the bitterness creeping into his storytelling.

"The guy who had seen them went straight to Parker, who was well past being drunk and on his way to comatose." Jed bit his lower lip. "You can imagine the reaction of everyone gathered around him."

"Mob violence at its finest," Gentry said.

"Exactly. You can only imagine how they goaded Parker and challenged his manhood. Nothing would do but for him to go rescue his sister. I'm convinced he went out there with murder on his mind."

"But just your brother's murder; surely he didn't plan on killing his sister."

"Right," Jed said. "He wanted to end the romance the only way his pickled brain knew how."

"So how did he wind up killing Abby?" Gentry asked.

Before Jed could speak, they drove past a billboard advertising a bed-and-breakfast in Sweetgrass. Gentry pointed and said, "Almost there."

Jed nodded to acknowledge seeing the sign. "That's really the tragic part for Abby. Parker's friend had seen Bobby's car pull behind the church, and everyone assumed Bobby was driving."

Gentry shot a glance at his passenger. "Oh, wow, she was driving."

"That's right, and Parker went there with the expressed purpose of killing Bobby. Drunk and unsteady, he probably couldn't see all that well in the dark. He shot through the driver's side of the windshield and hit his sister in the face. She died instantly, as far as anybody knows."

"Oh, man."

"My theory is that Bobby jumped from the car to run. Parker saw him, realized what he had just done, and lost it at that point," Jed said. "Bobby was shot multiple times. Parker just emptied the gun in him when he realized he had already killed Abby. That's why Sadie Dunlap was left in the driver's seat and Lamar Lassiter was found shot outside."

"Creepy. No damn wonder Parker lives in a bottle."

Jed smirked. "Knowing that his life has been a living hell since isn't much consolation."

"Guess not," Gentry said as they drove past the Sweetgrass town limits sign. "Where to now? Hospital or courthouse?"

"Jail," Jed said. "Parker's wounds weren't serious enough for him to be hospitalized. He should be there, and if we're not too late, I may just be able to keep the son of a bitch alive."

"That's noble, but you're nuts to go there. You'll have to talk damn fast to keep one of them yahoos from shooting first and asking questions second."

"That's a risk I have to take," Jed said.

Lights inside the century-old jail building came into view just as steam and smoke began pouring from under the car's hood. The engine sputtered, groaned, and then died in the middle of the road with a big gush of steam.

"She finally blew," Gentry said, sounding as if he had lost his best friend. "Go find Stump before it's too late."

Outside the Falcon, fumes from burning oil and the spewing radiator blasted Jed's senses. The image of Doctor Leech standing beside the bubbling black kettle with serpentine swirls of sulfur smoke surrounding her head came back to him. She had pointed and gestured at them as they drove away. *Could she? Did she?* He didn't want to think about it.

He yelled back at Gentry. "Get out of there before she bursts into flames. I want you to live long enough to write this story."

The blue paneled van that had carried off the dead from the other crime scenes sat in front of the jail when Jed jogged up out of breath. Stump's black Crown Victoria was parked in the spot designated for the sheriff, and two marked patrol cars sat at odd angles on either side, as if the drivers had slid to a stop and jumped out in a hurry. Chaos reigned on the front steps. Jed spotted Stump just before the new sheriff saw his escapee.

To Jed's surprise, Stump didn't draw his revolver from its holster. He didn't jump down the steps and run toward him or order the two deputies leading a gray gurney with a black body bag bouncing on it to arrest him. He stood akimbo and stared, and then he pushed the bill of his ball cap up from his eyes.

"Before you arrest me," Jed said, walking up to the base of the steps, "there's something you need to know."

"Where you been, Bradley?" Stump rubbed his meaty hand across his face.

"Looking for the killer."

"That so? If you'd been here earlier, you'd have found him."

Jed glanced over at two men in gray coveralls loading the bulging bag into the back of the van. "Parker?"

"Yep."

Jed looked to the ground, realizing an ocean of mixed feelings. "How?"

"Doc says heart attack."

"You don't sound like you believe him." Jed started up the jailhouse steps.

"Come in and see what you think," Stump said.

Jed felt uneasy about Stump's uncustomary acceptance of his presence. The sheriff's usual arrogance had been replaced by a puzzling reticence.

When Stump stepped out of the doorway, Jed saw the reason. Behind him, on the floor in a pool of blood, lay a deputy sheriff. A camera flashed as another deputy photographed the crime scene.

"Who. . . ." Before he could finish his question, Jed saw the high and tight haircut, the creases in the pants. "Oh, God. No."

He knelt beside the former marine, who, even in death, managed to maintain the military bearing that had set him apart from the rest. Jed looked up at Stump's hangdog expression and asked, "What happened?"

"We think he walked in as the killer was leaving. He didn't have time to draw his gun."

"Or he didn't think he needed to," Jed said. He showed Stump the photo he had taken from Etta Turpin.

Stump showed no surprise. "How'd you come across this photo of Roland? Layton ID'd him as the shooter before he expired."

"That's not Roland. It's a picture of Roy Nash taken years ago. Roland is his spittin' image—and his grandson."

"I would have never figured him to possess the gumption to pull off all of those killings," Stump said.

"Ever since he was a baby, all he's heard about was the injustice done to his granddaddy. The woman who raised him is a bona fide Gullah root doctor. She might be bona fide crazy too. She brainwashed the boy, convinced him he could kill with impunity. She taught him the spirits would protect him."

"All the killings were about vengeance for his grandpa?" Stump asked, plopping down on top of the gray metal desk.

"That's right. I think the first three were killed to send a message to those he really wanted to repay. He wanted them to know he was coming for them. He wanted them to be terrified."

Stump glared at the photo. "Parker and Bain."

"I think he knew we'd make the connection that Sadie and Kristin were granddaughters of men involved in the conspiracy to wrongfully convict his grandfather. I also think he intended me to be the focus of the investigation long enough for him to complete his mission. If I ended up being charged and sent to prison, no concern there. His primary targets were Willie Sims, the partner who committed perjury; Rembert Baker, the judge who sentenced his granddaddy; Bain Granville, the prosecutor; and of course Parker, the real culprit who should have gone to prison for murdering Bobby and Abby. But what I can't figure out is Lassiter's connection, why Roland chose him."

Stump grimaced. "I can help you there. Parker wanted to cleanse his soul after being shot. Among other things, he told me Trent Lassiter was the foreman of the jury that found them boys guilty. He was in on the conspiracy, but unlike old Sheriff Renfrow, Lassiter's remorse did lead him to suicide."

They walked to the concrete corridor. The stench of sulfur lingered in Jed's former cell, overpowering the rancid body odors he had earlier endured. Stump raked his hand through his close-cropped hair. "How in blue blazes did he cause Parker's heart attack?"

"Roland wasn't who he appeared to be. He spent his entire life learning the hoodoo ways, and he learned his lessons well." Jed thought about Gentry's car. "One thing I've learned over the past twenty-four hours: don't underestimate the power of hoodoo."

Jed told Stump about his trip with Gentry to the see Doctor Leech. "Making people believe in his powers became Roland's strongest weapon. Parker was already under a lot of stress after our encounter. He was ripe to be terrorized by an expert, and what better place than locked alone in a cell with no way to escape, no way to know who was outside the door, no way to know what was coming next."

"Hard to believe," Stump said. "I suppose Layton must have walked in and Roland caught him off guard."

"Layton had no reason to suspect Roland," Jed said. "By the time he realized what was happening, it was too late."

"Any idea what my renegade deputy might be up to now?" Stump asked.

"There's one more person left before his mission is complete, so I'd bet my pension he's gone after the senator."

"Parker called Bain after we brought him over from the hospital," Stump said. "I'm surprised you didn't hear the explosion."

"I can imagine," Jed said. "What did the senator do?"

"I was out, but from what I hear, he cussed a lot at first. Then he demanded we release Parker."

"Does he know Parker named him as a coconspirator in Cletus Renfrow's murder and the framing of Nash?"

"He does now." Stump pulled out a pouch of chewing tobacco and scooped some of the gummy leaves into his jaw. Jed watched him work the wad with his tongue.

With the tobacco positioned so he could talk, the sheriff said, "He called back later, and I talked to him that time. When he told me he was on his way to get Parker, I told him I'd be waiting with a warrant for his arrest. That wasn't one of my smarter moments, but I couldn't resist." Stump motioned toward the empty cells. "Reckon you can figure out he didn't show up."

"Anybody out looking for him?"

"We put out a BOLO but ain't heard nothing yet. He doesn't know about Parker's death, so he's likely decided he has to disappear."

Jed mused at what he was hearing. Never would he have imagined the day he'd be listening to Stump talk about arresting his own kinfolk. Parker didn't realize it—nobody did at the time—but by appointing Stump sheriff, Parker transformed a disgruntled, half-ass investigator into someone who had the makings of a decent lawman.

"Where do you run when you're as visible as a state senator?" Jed asked.

"If I know Bain, he'll be calling in some markers from folks and trying to get out of the country. He'll need transportation, but that might take a while."

Jed thought about the senator's business dealings. "I'm not so sure," he said. "Sun'll be coming up in a few hours. Think he's crazy enough to be at his home?"

"Nope, done checked." Stump spit an amber stream toward a trash can sitting beside the desk. He centered it. "I sent a deputy out there to look around. Bain's a widower who lives alone. His Cadillac wasn't there, and there were no signs of life inside the house."

"Think he knows Roland's after him too?"

"Doubt it." Stump unleashed another stream of tobacco into the center of the trash can. "I don't think anybody suspected Roland until the shooting here. When you showed up with that photo, you pretty much cinched it. I reckon Bain's still convinced you're the wacko hell-bent on killing anybody who might've been involved with your brother's murder."

"We need to find him and get him back up to Columbia for safekeeping in the prison there. You won't want a repeat of what happened to Parker."

"What if Roland kills Bain before we can find him?"

Jed thought about Etta Turpin's shanty, the dense swamp surrounding her place. He thought about water moccasins and gators and how Roland likely could maneuver through that bayou blindfolded. "If Roland gets back to his childhood haunts, we might never get him out."

The phone rang. Sylvester answered. He hadn't said a word since Jed had arrived, and Jed couldn't blame him. If Jed had been embarrassed by being locked in one of his own cells, he wouldn't be very friendly either.

Sylvester handed the phone to Stump. "It's for you, Sheriff. It's Bernice in dispatch."

Stump's conversation with the dispatcher was short. When he hung up, he looked at Jed. "You'd better sit down."

# CHAPTER · 27

The sheriff's dour expression alarmed Jed. "What is it?" The trapdoor in the pit of his stomach dropped open in anticipation of bad news.

"The deputy who went out to check on Bain made another stop on his way back to the office." Stump remained quiet for several seconds, breathing deeply and staring straight at Jed. "I sent him out before you arrived. I told him that if he couldn't locate the senator, to go by Jessie Braddock's to see if he saw any sign of you hiding out around there. I had been by earlier, and she didn't exactly roll out the red carpet for me. I wanted him to tell her that if she saw you to let you know we weren't after you anymore."

Jed wanted to smile at Jessie's tenacity, but Stump's grave expression stopped him. "What did your deputy find?" he asked.

"Bain Granville's Cadillac."

"The senator was at Jessie's?" That made absolutely no sense to Jed. "Why the hell would he go to Jessie's?"

"A few days ago, when Parker appointed me sheriff, he told me about watching you and Doctor Braddock from his office window. He also told me he had told Bain about seeing the two of you together."

"What's that got to do with the senator's car being at Jessie's?"

"The senator's not stupid. If he thinks you're coming after him, he wants an advantage, a way to keep you at bay. My guess is that he took Doctor Braddock as insurance against you trying to kill him."

"Did . . . did your deputy see the senator or Jessie?"

"Nobody's there. The house is dark." Stump sighed. "He did find signs of a struggle."

"We need to find them," Jed said. "Can you think of a place he would've taken her?"

"One," Stump said.

Stump barked at Sylvester to clean the floor as soon as the other deputies were finished with the crime scene. He seemed cold and detached, but Jed knew what the sheriff was feeling inside. He had buried three officers during his career, and each one had taken a piece of him with them into the grave.

Jed grabbed Stump's shoulder. "Any chance I can get my gun out of your evidence vault before we go?"

Stump shook his head and chuckled. "City folk. We don't have vaults in Indigo County. We have drawers. Anyway, I sent your weapon up to the state lab." He walked to the gun cabinet, pulled a stainless steel Smith & Wesson pistol and a holster from inside. "You can borrow these," he said, tossing them across the room.

Jed took the pistol, checked the magazine. What a difference a few hours made. He had started out the day as a fugitive and now he was joining the High Sheriff of Indigo County in hunting down a state senator and a rogue deputy.

As Jed threaded his belt through the holster straps, Stump went to the metal desk and pulled open a drawer. "Now let me get your personal belongings back to you."

"Uh . . . that won't be necessary," Jed said with a smirk. "I've already helped myself."

"Hmph, so I see."

"How did the senator's wife die?" Jed asked as they sped out of town.

"Coroner ruled it an accident—overdose." Stump shot a glance in Jed's direction, caught the veteran cop's sidelong look. "I know what you're thinking," he said. "Hell, given everything else going on, I'm wondering the same thing."

Jed said, "Sure does give you pause to speculate." He wondered if the coroner had been the same tire-recapper coroner Jake had told him about.

Stump rolled down his window, hooked the wad of tobacco inside his jaw with his index finger, and tossed it out onto the asphalt. "Yep, sure does."

The black Crown Victoria zipped past shuttered roadside vegetable stands surrounded by plowed-under fields waiting to be planted. The moonlight made the night bright. Even so, the job of hunting for Roland and the senator in the dark would be difficult.

Jed thought about losing Bobby, then Jake, and prayed Jessie wasn't about to join them. "Where is this place we're headed?"

"A place few folks know about."

Jed said, "Hap Gentry's been digging into the senator's import/export business. Says it's a front for drugs being brought in through Savannah and Charleston. If he's right, Granville just needs a place to hole up until his cronies can help him escape."

"Bain's been smuggling drugs all these years, right under our noses?" Stump looked dumbstruck. "How the hell could that be?"

"I guess the same way he kept his murders a secret."

"I guess." The usually boisterous voice of the sheriff came out muted.

"Got any suggestions for a location he might hide out until he could arrange to get away?"

After a lengthy silence, Stump said, "Where we're headed would be the perfect place to wait for someone to take you out of the country."

"Where is it?"

"Not far," Stump said. "It's a hunting cabin the Granvilles own. Been in the family for years, and it's right on the sound. Somebody could come in by boat or seaplane to pick him up. He could disappear from there with ease. That's got to be where he's going."

"Then that's where we need to be," Jed said.

Hidden amid dense forests, surrounded by vistas of marsh grass, where white herons perched high in trees and unconcerned cranes stood on one foot, the wilderness surrounding Senator Bain Granville's cabin provided the perfect outpost to await a clandestine escape.

Stump drove slowly across a narrow, bumpy log bridge. A murky tidal creek lapped against the sides, up onto the logs in places. Jed sensed the timbers give beneath the car's weight.

"Are you sure these bridges are safe?" he asked, feeling more timid than he would ever admit.

"Most of 'em," Stump said. His words lacked reassurance. "The water ain't all that deep through here, though, so you don't need to worry much about drowning."

Jed rolled his eyes and spoke with lightly veiled sarcasm. "That's good to hear."

"Welcome to the best-kept secret in South Carolina," Stump announced like some adventure guide. The Crown Victoria rolled past a sign displaying a painted skull and crossbones. Beneath the symbol, PRIVATE PROPERTY was painted in blood-red letters. "The timber out here is as thick as fleas on a hound dog, and you can fish or hunt any damn thing you want, anytime you want. The local game wardens know better than to try and enforce wildlife laws on Granville property."

"Terrific," Jed said, deadpan.

"You can hunt pheasant and quail, deer or boar. If it's wild and natural to the Carolinas, you can usually find it in here. You might even find some game not so common to this part of the country—or world, for that matter." He turned to Jed with a look of pure devilment. "Rumor has it that Bain transplanted some big cats and other wildlife for them to feed on."

The car stopped. Stump shoved the gearshift into park. "We'll have to hike a spell to get to the cabin."

Jed gave a start of surprise. "Walk? How far do we have to walk?" His thoughts hung on the yellowed glare of a lion or cheetah or whatever vicious predator Stump had referred to earlier.

"Oh, a little more than a mile would be my guess."

Jed resisted the overwhelming urge to reach over and slap the silly grin off the man's fat face. "And why wouldn't we drive closer and then walk?" he asked.

Stump pointed out the windshield. "See that tall grass at the end of this road?"

Jed sat forward and peered into the dim of twilight. "Barely."

"We wouldn't get ten feet before we sunk down to our axles."

Jed looked around the sandy road. "Is this the only way? There's got to be more solid ground around here."

"Oh there is—if you've got four-wheel drive, which we don't. Or an ATV." He shrugged. "We ain't got one of them either. Even if we did, we'd still have to walk a half mile or so through swamp where even an ATV can't go."

"Why the hell didn't we get one of those before we came out here?" Jed asked. "You knew about this place."

"Yep, I knew, but there used to be another road over there, beyond that pile of downed trees. I thought we could go that way, but obviously we can't."

Jed thought about Jessie's low-to-the-ground BMW. "Then they can't be at the cabin. If they're in Jessie's car, they couldn't get through there either."

Stump sighed. "Nope, they couldn't. There's another way to the cabin a few miles back, but if we come in that way, Bain will be able to see us, especially with daylight on its way." He pointed up at the lightening sky.

"How so?" Jed asked, eager to find any alternative route than through the bog and forest."

"The cabin sits up on a knoll. You can see clear back to the highway if you're watching. That's the way he'll expect us, so I'm sure he'll have an eye peeled for visitors. He won't be thinking we're dumb enough to try coming in this way."

Jed surveyed the area. The thought of having to hike through the morass of wild beasts and slithering vermin in the dark caused the hairs on his arms to stand at rigid attention atop rows of goose bumps. "Dumb is right," he muttered under his breath.

"If we don't surprise him, he might just kill your lady friend. This is our best chance at sneaking up on him." Stump's words held a hint of resignation. "If you want to risk going in the front, I'll radio back and get as many troops as possible headed this way. We'll need the backup."

Jed tapped his fingers on the dashboard as he continued staring out at the foreboding forest. "No, surprise is our best chance to keep Jessie safe. Besides, if you alert the others to our location, and Roland still has his walkie-talkie, he'll know too." He threw open the car door and jumped out onto the spongy ground. "Let's go."

Visibility became difficult as they entered the thick forest. Towering trees whispered overhead, and gnarly underbrush crept around their feet. Jed could hear unsettling sounds coming from all directions.

"As lush as the vegetation is in here this time of year," Jed said, "this place would be impenetrable in the summertime." He stopped to catch his breath and to give the overweight sheriff time to catch up.

"Worse than that," Stump said, puffing, "the mosquitoes have been rumored to be big enough to carry off small animals."

"Funny," Jed said. "How much farther?"

"You don't really want to know." Stump's face appeared more flushed than normal as he bent over to rest his hands on his knees.

"You okay?" Jed asked.

The big man blew out a cloud of air. "Yeah . . . I'm okay. Just out of shape, but I appreciate your concern."

Jed presented a fiendish grin. "Concerned is right. If you drop dead on me, I have no idea where the hell I am or how to get back."

The sheriff's face contorted. He shined his flashlight beam off to Jed's right. "What the. . . ?"

Jed followed the sight line lit by the sheriff's flashlight. Hidden in the forest, a black pickup truck sat behind a thicket of vines and evergreen shrubs.

The pair quietly crept through the bramble to the rear of the truck. Both men drew their weapons. Stump approached along the driver's side; Jed came up the other.

"Empty," Stump said. He opened the door. "Sombitch, it's one of our walkie-talkies."

Jed placed his hand on the hood of the truck. "It's still warm."

"Dammit! Roland must have followed Bain out here. He came in over the rough terrain and likely is already up at the cabin."

"We've got to get movin'." Jed's sense of urgency heightened.

Stump shrugged. "Maybe he'll get sick of slogging through the smelly muck between here and the cabin."

"Not a chance. He grew up a swamp rat. He's probably more at home right now than he was back in Sweetgrass. We have to hurry."

Stump nodded. "We also better be careful."

"Ain't this just swell," Jed groused. "Not only do we have to worry about displaced man-eaters and who knows what else, but now we've got a killer out in the darkness waiting to snipe at us."

"Yeah, but if you're right about him, he won't be aiming to mess with us, when Bain is his target. One shot out here sets off nature's alarms. Bain would know someone was coming."

Jed hoped Stump's logic had merit, but it didn't afford him much comfort. For the next twenty minutes, as they trudged through muck and thicket, Jed jumped at every sound, flinched at every squirrel leaping through the treetops. *Get a grip,* he implored himself.

# CHAPTER · 28

"We'll be able to see the cabin any second now," Stump said.

Almost as soon as he spoke, a two-story structure of brick and cedar loomed in the early morning dawn outside of the forest. Jed saw three chimneys extending from the roof. A broad deck circled around to the front of the house.

"You call that a cabin?" Jed said. "Where I come from, we call a wilderness home that size a hunting lodge."

Stump put his finger to his mouth and whispered, "The Granvilles call it a cabin. Look." He knelt and motioned for Jed to do the same.

Jessie's silver BMW was parked under the deck, out of sight of the road leading to the home and unable to be seen from the air. No one was around the car. A quick glance to the deck above revealed no one there.

"Any sign of Roland?" Jed asked in a whisper.

Stump shook his head.

The land sloped away from the back of the structure. Only a couple of the high windows afforded a view of the forest.

"We ought to be able to sneak close to the building without being seen," Jed said. "How close is the nearest SWAT team?"

Stump eyed him with curiosity. "Savannah has a group, but they're in Georgia. It would take hours to clear the paperwork for them to come into South Carolina. Charleston's would come, but they're more than an hour away. "Whoever Bain has coming for him will be here and gone before any of them could arrive."

"Okay, I'm going out there," Jed said. "Maybe I can force Roland to make a move if he thinks we'll get to Granville first."

Stump's expression begged for reason. "You think we can stop him and get Bain too?"

"There's two of us and two of them. Even odds, I'd say."

Stump frowned. "And I'd say we'll be caught in the middle when the shooting starts."

"I'm guessing that the senator's attention is focused on his rescuers, and they're likely coming in by water. By coming at him from two directions, one of us might get to Jessie alive."

Stump looked thunderstruck. "And the other one?"

Jed shrugged. "Without a diversion, he's going to get a shot off at one of us. What happens then depends on how good of a shot he is."

Stump shook his head. "I hope you have a Plan B. Bain is a crack shot—with both a rifle and a handgun. And there's an arsenal inside that house, so he won't be running out of ammunition."

The sound of a boat engine rode the wind blowing off the sound. The pair exchanged glances.

"Plan A. Call for backup," Jed said. He raced out of the woods toward the house as Stump pulled the radio from his belt.

Jed hit the brick foundation with a thud. His heart pounded. His lungs felt like he had been breathing fire. He had misjudged the distance of his sprint— badly. Still, he knew he had to find the energy to keep going. Sweat poured from his forehead as he knelt on one knee and sucked air like a thirsty man drinking cold water. He couldn't get enough.

A loud rustling came from the dark forest just before Jed saw Stump explode from the tree line. The overweight man's speed amazed him at first, and then Jed saw him slow, and continue to slow even more. By the time he reached the knoll behind the lodge, Stump was running as if his shoes were made of concrete. Finally, the heavyset sheriff collapsed beside Jed.

"We're a fine pair," Jed said. "Are you all right?"

Stump held up his meaty hand, motioned for Jed to go on. With the color bleached from his face, the new sheriff didn't look good, but Jed knew the man was right, they had to keep moving. Even if Bain Granville hadn't seen them come out of the woods, Roland probably had. If not, he must have heard the approaching boat engine, too. Either way, the killer needed to make a move to complete his mission very soon, and Jed needed to be prepared to stop him—at least to prevent him from harming Jessie.

Jed reached Jessie's car and peered up through the spaces in the deck flooring. As he did, a door above him opened. He heard footsteps start across the wooden planks.

Jed backed against the foundation. The footsteps quickened as two people started down the stairs. Jessie led the way with the senator behind her. She carried a duffel bag. He wore a backpack.

Stump crawled to his feet. Jed caught a glimpse of him as he rounded the opposite corner toward the front of the house.

Jessie and the senator stepped to the ground and started toward the water. Jed braced his Smith & Wesson against the post. He waited for the senator to walk into his line of sight.

There would be no warning, no hollering "Freeze! Police!" like in the movies. There would be no chance to surrender. Too much was at stake with Jessie. In Jed's mind, one clear shot and the senator was going down.

Jessie came into full view, and a split second later so did Bain. Jed's finger tightened on the trigger. He wanted the senator positioned so if the bullet passed through him, it wouldn't strike Jessie. Jed released a breath. His finger squeezed slowly, not wanting to jerk even the slightest amount.

Stump's shout stopped him. "Bain, this is the sheriff. Let your hostage go and drop your weapon."

*Shit!*

In the instant it took for Jed to glance toward Stump, the senator grabbed Jessie and pulled her tight against him.

Jed's jaws clenched. *Damn it.*

Bain yelled out, "Stump, you dumb ass. If you don't back away, I'll kill her, and then I'll shoot your lard butt full of holes."

Jed stepped out from under the deck to where he had a clear view of the senator and Jessie, but the moment to shoot had passed. Jessie could be hit. He held the pistol out in front of him, gripped it with both hands. "You can't kill her and get both of us," Jed said.

Surprised, Bain turned his head. "Stay back, or your sweet little mammy is dead." He pulled her closer, dragging her as he moved. "Let me go, and when I'm out of your range, I'll put a life jacket on her and drop her in the sound."

The once powerful senator pulled his hostage toward the crown of the knoll. Jed followed. Down below, bobbing by the dock, was a cabin cruiser waiting to spirit Bain Granville to freedom. Across the lawn, Stump angled his way in front of the senator and took cover behind a brick well house.

Bain saw the sheriff. "I'm warning you, boy. Try to stop me, and you'll die along with her."

As if to punctuate the threat, a shot rang out from the boat. The bullet clipped a corner of the brick well house, and Stump fell out of sight. The source of the gunshot was a man standing on the bow of the cabin cruiser with a rifle trained on the well house.

The sound of the first shot had barely faded when Jed heard a shriek come from the woods beside the house. A plangent declaration followed. "The plat-eye will avenge Roy Nash!" And then a shot roared.

Jed saw Jessie slump to the ground, pulling Bain down with his arm still around her neck. Roland rushed from the woods; his gun barked a second time. Dirt from beside the senator and Jessie exploded into the air.

Jed turned. He dropped to one knee, fired as the killer closed to within a few feet of his latest victim.

Hit by Jed's round, Roland spun around. Surprise plastered his face. He lifted his pistol and pointed in his attacker's direction. Just as he fired, his knees buckled. The ensuing shot flew errant.

Bain pushed to his feet. He abandoned his hostage and raced toward the dock, carrying the duffel and backpack.

Jed ran toward Jessie. When he reached her, he shielded her from any return fire and shot at the fleeing senator.

Bain dropped the rifle, ran several yards, then fell to his knees. He tried to get up but stumbled when he reached to pick up the duffel and backpack.

Down at the dock, the boat's engine revved. The vessel turned out to sea and sped away, leaving the senator to fend for himself.

Stump crawled from behind the well house. He looked around as if he expected someone else to start shooting, but when he saw no one but Jed brandishing a firearm, he started after the senator.

Jed leaned close to Jessie's ear. He whispered her name. She didn't answer.

He checked her to see where the bullet had struck. As he did, he half prayed, half demanded she be okay. "Damn it, Jes, I'm not losing you again. You have to be all right."

A cough sputtered from her throat. "That's the most romantic thing I've ever heard," she whispered and opened her eyes.

Jed detected the beginnings of a tight-lipped smile but saw it vanish in a grimace of pain. "Easy does it," he said. "Where did you get hit?"

She swallowed hard. "I'm okay. And for the record, I'm not planning on losing you again either."

She held out her hands as she struggled to sit up. They were bound by an electrical cord. "What hurts most are my wrists. Can you get this cord off?"

Stump reached the senator, who offered token resistance before acquiescing. Slapping handcuffs around both wrists, the sheriff jerked his prisoner to his feet and started back toward Jessie and Jed.

"Let me go, you fat bastard," the senator said. He yelled as if he hoped his colleagues back at the state capital would hear him and come to his rescue. "I'm injured, you arrogant prick. Let me go."

Jessie mustered enough energy to laugh as Jed loosened the cord around her wrists. But before he got it off, a bloodcurdling wail pierced the air.

Jed twisted around in time to see Roland back on his feet, charging straight for them. The killer's eyes were glazed, his expression demonic.

He screamed as he ran past Jed and Jessie, toward Stump and Bain. "The plat-eye avenges all."

Wide-eyed, Stump released the senator, stepped back, and drew his revolver. He fired.

The bullet hit Roland in the center of his chest, staggered him, but he kept charging. Stump fired again and again. Every bullet found its target, but the crazed man kept coming.

Like a lion pouncing on its prey, Roland leaped, landing with his hands tight around the senator's throat. Both men tumbled to the ground. Roland screamed unintelligible gibberish. Bain kicked his feet and flailed his arms.

Stump aimed for another shot, but the fracas stopped before he could fire. Roland lay still on top of the senator.

Bain no longer cursed or moved. His terror-filled, popeyed gape fixed on the heavens.

Jed jumped up and ran to grab Roland, but as he neared the fallen killer, he realized the grandson of Roy Nash had completed his mission. Jed rolled Roland off of his final victim and felt for a pulse. When he detected none, he shook his head. "He's done."

Stump tended to the senator. He jostled him, trying to wake him. When the crooked politician didn't respond, Stump said, "I think he broke his neck."

Stump fell back on his haunches. Wearing a stunned expression, he said, "How many times did I shoot Roland?"

"Enough," Jed said. "I was too busy to keep count."

Stump said, "No normal human could take that many direct hits from a .357 hollow point and keep coming. But *he* did."

Jessie limped over to where the dead men lay. She leaned on Jed, who grabbed her around the waist and said, "Killing the senator—the mastermind behind his granddaddy being framed—fulfilled his destiny. He believed the spirits protected him, that they would aid him in carrying out the conjurer's legacy."

"You don't believe that hoodoo BS, do you?" Stump asked.

Jessie coughed. "Never underestimate the power of the human mind. Roland willed himself to be successful in carrying out his destiny. Someone that determined can accomplish almost anything and overcome most physical limitations."

"She's right," Jed said. "Doctor Leech summoned the spirits for him, and he believed they made him invincible."

"Doctor Leech?" Stump and Jessie spoke the woman's name in unison.

The sound of distant sirens rode the wind. "Here comes the cavalry," Jed said. "To explain Doctor Leech would take longer than we have. I'm taking Jessie to the hospital to be checked out."

"Wait a minute," Stump said. He knelt down beside Bain's body, foraged through the dead man's pockets. "Here," he said, tossing Jessie's set of keys to Jed. "You can take the road this time."

# CHAPTER · 29

Jessie peppered Jed with questions on the drive home from the hospital. She quizzed him about every detail of the day's bizarre events, and each time she asked him something, he considered it a blessing.

Earlier, while the emergency room doctor treated the cuts on her wrists where the electrical cord had dug through the skin, he had worried about her being in shock. None of Roland's shots had hit her, but his concern centered around the near misses and her kidnapping. She hardly spoke after leaving the hunting lodge, and the way she had stared out the window seemed almost catatonic. Jed took some comfort when, after relaying his observations to the hospital staff, no one appeared overly concerned.

"Normal reaction," the doctor said. He also told Jed he had known Jessie for years and didn't anticipate any long-term effects. "She'll be fine," he had said out of Jessie's earshot. "Yes, she's been through quite an ordeal, but she's reactive to all of the stimuli I presented."

He had rattled off the tests he had run on her, as if their names meant anything to a former cop with zero medical training. Then he told Jed how she had reacted to each one. The explanation had been a bit taxing, but Jed had not said a word, appreciative of the attention Jessie was receiving from the entire staff. She was one of their own, and that fact clearly stood out. The doctor ended by saying, "All she needs is a good night's rest."

Jed understood those last instructions, and once they left the hospital, Jessie seemed to snap out of whatever funk she had been in. The better she got, the faster the questions came.

"Who is Doctor Leech?" she asked before Jed could back out of the emergency room parking place.

He told her of his journey with Hap Gentry to the swamp and about the elderly root doctor who had raised Roy Nash. Jessie listened intently as Jed described the picture he had taken and how Roland had killed Parker by literally scaring him to death with a hoodoo ritual outside the attorney's jail cell.

The sequence of events that had occurred over the past few days had been tantamount to living in a nightmare world. Jed and Jessie rode the last few miles in silent reflection of the unusual week.

"I need a hot bath," Jessie said after entering her home. "I feel dirty."

"That sounds like a great idea," Jed said. "I'll fix you some coffee. . . ." He then remembered that the doctor told him she needed rest. "Or would you rather I leave and come back tomorrow after you've had a good night's sleep?"

Jessie started toward the stairs. "Stay . . . please. I don't want to be alone, and I'd prefer a glass of red wine to coffee."

She stopped midway up the steps and turned. Jed saw her smile for the first time since the shooting.

"I won't be long," she said.

"Take your time." Jed watched her ascend the stairs to the landing. She took slow and deliberate steps, gripping the banister for balance. He whispered a prayer of thanks, realized how fortunate both had been to come through the day's events with no more than sore muscles and stiff joints.

He grabbed a broom and dustpan from the pantry and swept up glass from the hallway. Apparently, Jessie had put up quite a fight before Bain overpowered her. Jed stacked broken frames and pictures, and he thought about the future. Maybe someday he could talk Jessie into introducing him to her friends, musicians he knew only as legends.

Several bottles of wine lay on their sides in a wrought-iron stand in the kitchen. Jed selected a Zinfandel, poured their glasses, and carried them to the enclosed back porch to wait on her.

He set down the wine and walked out of the storm door into the yard. Thankfully, Bain's Cadillac was gone. One of Stump's deputies must have towed it as evidence and Jed was glad. *One less unpleasant reminder for Jessie,* he thought.

He followed a stone path that wound through the yard toward the dock and boathouse. Three herons flew from a treetop when they saw him encroaching on their domain.

Bright sunshine punctuated the serene landscape. A crisp breeze rippled shallows left by the ebbing tide.

Jed's nostrils flared. The low tide exposed beds of oysters, clams sticking up from the muck. He found the briny stench refreshing, reminiscent of the times Bobby and he had spent seining for shrimp and crabbing in the tidal creeks near their house.

Jed wondered how different his life would have been had Bobby not been killed. Would he have ever moved to Atlanta? Would he have become a cop?

Maybe everything would have been different; maybe he would have settled right here in Sweetgrass and farmed.

He picked up a piece of broken shell, flipped it into a brackish puddle.

Or maybe he would have become one of Jake's deputies or even the sheriff.

He remembered his old friend, how hurt Jed had felt that afternoon after finding the horrendous scrapbook in Jake's home. That day had haunted both men all of their lives.

He wondered if Jake had time to recognize Roland as the killer. Did his hesitation, even his disbelief, cost him his life?

When Jed returned to the porch, Jessie was there waiting. She sat in a rocker with her hands clasped around her knees, a bulky, oversized, rose-colored sweater draped down over her jeans. She wore fuzzy blue slippers and rocked quietly as she stared out into the encroaching night.

Jed noticed the bandages were gone from her wrists. Thankfully, the cuts from the cord didn't appear as bad as they had under the bright glow of the emergency room lights. She had wrapped her hair in a towel, and she looked absolutely beautiful.

"Do you want to go back inside?" he asked. "Mamma always said cool air and wet hair don't mix. You're liable to catch a cold."

Jessie grinned. "Mammas say things like that, don't they?" She reached to the table, picked up her glass of wine, and took a sip. "I'm fine. Besides, my hair is mostly dry. I just didn't want to comb it out."

"If you want, I'll put new bandages on your wrists."

Jessie grinned again. "You're a regular mother hen. What I want is for you to get your wine and sit next to me."

That was a request Jed could handle. He grabbed his glass of Zinfandel and settled into the rocker next to Jessie.

"Tell me what happened to turn my world upside down," she said. "I know the connection about the Granvilles, and I know from the letter that they killed Carol Ann's father and conspired to wrongfully convict the two men for killing Bobby and Abby. What I don't understand is why Kristin had to die."

Jed detected a hint of perfume drift past his nose. He savored the scent of his first and only true love. "Being idealistic like most young people, I imagine she became furious at the idea a prominent family could get away with murder. She believed everybody should be held accountable, no matter who you are or how much money you have."

"I believe that," Jessie said.

Jed nodded. "So do I, but it doesn't always work out that way." He drank from his glass and thought back to the days right after Bobby's death. "Take Psalm 37 for instance. I happen to be real familiar with it and Psalm 11, too, because Daddy constantly read them to us after Bobby died. Looking back, I think he read those passages more to convince himself than to convince us. At any rate, the gist of it is that we can't dwell on those who commit evil and get away with it. We need to trust in God to handle those matters, and if we do, the evildoers will get their due."

"So, you're saying Kristin died because she wasn't patient or trusting in a bigger plan?" She shook her head. "I'm sorry, I can't accept that."

"No, I'm not saying that at all. I think Kristin stewed on the secret her grandmamma told her, and when Nell died in that car wreck, she felt it her duty to expose the truth. What she did then is what likely got her killed."

"Which was?" Jessie dropped her legs and turned in her chair.

"I think she called the sheriff to tell him what she knew, and as luck would have it in a small town, the deputy who talked to her happened to be Roland."

"Do you think Nell had the same bad luck and ended up talking to Roland too?"

"No, Parker confessed at the hospital," Jed said. "He thought he was about to die. I guess he wanted to set things straight before he did. Facing one's own mortality often loosens tongues."

"What did he say?"

"That Nell had come to him, accusing him and Bain of killing her husband. She confronted him, told him about the letter."

"That would explain the house being ransacked," Jessie said. "But I can't imagine Parker possessing the gumption to kill Nell."

"Nor can I," Jed said. "From what I understand, he confessed that he called his cousin with the dilemma. Bain was the one who made sure Nell wouldn't be a problem."

"Okay, help me here. If Roland wanted the Granvilles exposed for what they did to his grandfather, why didn't he just take Kristin's information and arrest them?"

"He didn't want them locked up. He wanted them wracked with terror. He wanted them to know someone was coming to kill them, and he wanted them to know it would be soon."

"Incredible."

"Actually," Jed said, "I believe even if Kristin hadn't called with what Nell had told her, Roland might still have killed her."

"Why?" Jessie's voice sounded weak.

"Her death was part of the notification to the Granvilles that an avenging spirit was coming for what they had done to Roy Nash. Since Sheriff Renfrow was already dead and couldn't be harmed, Nash's grandson decided to kill the sheriff's granddaughter."

"What about Sadie Dunlap?" Jessie asked. "Sims was alive. What not just kill him and spare her?"

"Here again, I think her death had to do with the psychological game Roland was playing. She may even have been told by her granddaddy what had really happened. Whatever the reason, Roland wanted Sims to know his time was coming. He may have even gotten the idea to kill the grandchildren when Kristin told him what she knew. Retribution against the grandchildren for the sins of the grandfather is almost Biblical—in a warped, perverted sense."

"Very warped," Jessie said. "Thank God he spared little Megan."

"Yes, and I don't really think he intended on killing Callie Hart. By then he was focusing on the principal targets. He might have been worried we were closing in on him and wanted to get on with what had to be done."

Jed stood and walked to the edge of the porch. He leaned against a support post. "According to what Stump told me, Callie and Megan were usually out on the night Roland struck. Megan was learning Braille, but she hadn't been feeling well that day, so they didn't go to her lesson."

Jessie rocked forward and stood to join Jed. She stared out into the water. "I have a confession," she said without looking in his direction.

"You do?"

"I wish I could have been the one who killed Bain Granville out there today. I'm glad he's dead. Roland too, but I wish I could have been the one."

"Can't blame you there," Jed said. "The highway to hell got a little more crowded when those two died. Besides, I wanted him dead myself."

Jessie asked, "Because of Bobby?"

"In part, but Stump told me about another confession Parker made—a full accounting, as they say. Guess he needed to scour his soul instead of just cleansing it."

Jessie's eyebrows arched.

"Years ago, Daddy participated in a prison ministry. He drove up to Columbia once a month to witness to the inmates. I think he made a personal effort to talk to Willie Sims, to forgive him for what he had done to Bobby. Of course, Nash was already dead by this time.

"Apparently, Willie took to being forgiven, so much so that he confessed to what really went on with the payoff for his testimony, and how he took the fall for Parker."

"Oh, my. Your father knew."

"Yes, and he didn't take it particularly well, if Parker's story is to be believed. Daddy must have pushed real hard, because the next thing anybody knew, the church burned to the ground, with him inside, presumably an accident after he had fallen asleep in his study."

"Oh, Jedediah, you mean—"

"Bain Granville hired a local thug wannabe by the name of Dewitt Roberts for the chore. Stump will be taking out a warrant for his arrest before day's end. My biggest regret is that I let a bigoted sheriff get away with doing nothing."

"Surely an autopsy would have shown he died before the fire started."

Jed shook his head. "Think about it, Jes. You had a black church, a black victim whose only surviving son lived three hours away. You had a powerful state senator pulling strings behind the scenes. I left the arrangements to a cousin I hardly knew. There was no autopsy—I didn't learn that until I came home for the funeral. That's when I tried to get the sheriff to conduct an investigation. He refused."

Jessie sidled close and nuzzled Jed's cheek. "You can't blame yourself."

"Yes I can, and I do. I'd been in homicide long enough to conduct my own investigation, ask the right questions, but I was too self-absorbed and didn't do what a dutiful son should have done. Now I have to live with the consequences."

Jessie kissed him. "You're not a bad son and definitely not a bad person—just the opposite in fact. Here in Tara, we always say, 'tomorrow is another day.'"

Jed laughed at the use of the famous line from *Gone With the Wind*. "You've been to too many movies."

Jessie wrapped her arms around his neck and kissed him again. "Maybe, but while we're on the subject, what are your plans for tomorrow and the day after?"

Before Jed could answer, she stepped back. She hooked her finger under the cord around his neck and pulled out the red pouch Etta Turpin had created.

"What's this?"

Jed cradled the pouch in the palm of his hand. "Do you believe in the power of the root?" he asked.

"I . . . I'm not sure," she said in a cautious tone. "Why?"

"Let's just say this is a hundred dollars worth of mojo." He pointed toward the creek behind her house. "In a couple of days I'm going to toss this bag into that water. If what I was told is true, I'll have all sorts of good luck."

Jessie looked across her backyard to the dock and boathouse and the creek beyond. She ran her hands up under his shirt and smiled. "You don't need a conjurer's potion. You're already getting lucky."

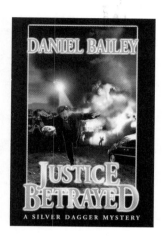

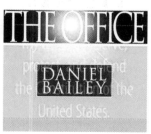

"Dan                                         a law enforce-
ment officer to his debut novel. The experience shows in the authen-
tic notes sounded in *Justice Betrayed.*"
—*Amarillo Globe-News*

"Wrapped in Southern charm, this action-packed realistic view
inside law enforcement and crime is reminiscent of Michael Con-
nelly with a Southern drawl."
—*Foreword Magazine*

"Bailey knows the Lowcountry and he tells a good story while
probing the underbelly of drug investigations where sometimes it's
hard to tell the good guys from the bad guys.
—*Jekyll's Golden Islander* (Jekyll Island, Georgia)

"Bailey's knowledge of anarchist groups and the people who support them has provided him with a colorful cast of characters for his
second work of fiction, *Execute the Office.*"
—*South Charlotte Weekly*

"Daniel Bailey brings thirty years of law enforcement experience
to bear in this tale of militia madness and political shenanigans."
—*Mystery Scene Magazine*

"Chief Deputy 'Chipp' Bailey not only catches bad guys, he
writes about them. They get their comeuppance, as they always will
in a Bailey book."
—*Charlotte Magazine*

Told in triptych, *Execute the Office* is a thriller about the lengths
to which politicos will go to stay in office and the unholy militant
militia who will do anything for their leader. Blackmail and murder
are the cost of doing business as usual.
—Pam Kingsbury, *Southern Scribe Reviews*